CANDLELIGHT

Supreme

"WELL, WELL, LOOK WHO WE HAVE HERE," DRAWLED A DEEP, FAMILIAR VOICE.

The blood froze in Gayle's veins.

"Get your things together," Ben said, pushing her into the room and slamming the door behind him. "You're coming with me."

"I'm not going anywhere with you. Get out of my room!"

"I hate to contradict you, but . . ." Ben swung her over his shoulder.

"Put me down!" Gayle shrieked, beating on his back with her fists as he strode through the hotel lobby. "This is kidnapping! I'll have you thrown in jail!"

Ben said nothing as he bundled her into the backseat of the Datsun and veered wildly away from the curb.

THE PERFECT LOVE TEST

Jan Oliver

A CANDLELIGHT SUPREME

Published by
Dell Publishing Co., Inc.
1 Dag Hammarskjold Plaza
New York, New York 10017

ISBN: 0-440-16917-8

Printed in the United States of America

September 1987

10 9 8 7 6 5 4 3 2 1

WFH

To Hud, with love,
and with thanks to special friends:
Joyce K. for inspiration,
Linda N., Nita C., and Leah F. for dedication,
and Elaine C. for the final prod

To Our Readers:

As of September 1987, Candlelight Romances will cease publication of Candlelight Ecstasies and Supremes. The editors of Candlelight would like to thank our readers for 20 years of loyalty and support. Providing quality romances has been a wonderful experience for us and one we will cherish. Again, from everyone at Candlelight, thank you!

Sincerely,

The Editors

THE PERFECT
LOVE TEST

CHAPTER ONE

"Well, if that doesn't just rot your socks!"

Gayle Summers glowered at the taunting buzz of the phone in her hand, then slammed it down and whirled her chair to face the window of her fifth-floor office.

It was going to be a long, cold winter. Propping her chin in her hands, she watched Denver's first snowfall of the season cover the ground below. The day matched her mood. It had started out sunny, then rapidly disintegrated. The storm began just moments before she got the phone call that may have sealed the doom of her new management consulting firm.

Things had been easier when her husband Greg was alive. They'd been a great team. After years of struggle they had perfected the Summers Profile, a revolutionary new personality test unparalleled for use in personnel selection, seminars, and management training. It had taken more years of struggle to establish their consulting partnership in Los Angeles. Finally, their work was becoming well known and companies were clamoring for their services. Summers and Summers was only a half step away from easy street—then her whole life had fallen apart. Now she was ready to tackle the world again, but she'd been out of the consulting business for a couple of years. People forget quickly. And now she was in Denver, not Los Angeles.

She rubbed the frown on her forehead. Now what?

As if in answer to her question, the phone rang.

Gayle automatically sat erect, straightened her navy blazer, and took a deep breath. "Summers Consulting," she answered in her most professional voice.

"How's business?"

"Not so hot," Gayle said honestly to her best friend, Ariel McDonough.

"What's wrong? I thought you'd be up to your ears testing flyboys by now."

"So did I, but it seems that Alpha Airlines decided to go with a 'more conventional, established firm' to quote Edwin Garfield. The old reprobate!"

"What happened?" Ariel asked. "I thought you were supposed to sign the contract this week."

"That's what I was led to believe, but I've been beaten out by the good old boy network again. And after I'd geared up for their business by sinking every dime I had left on this fancy new computer system. That account could have established my reputation in Denver and given the Summers Profile national recognition. I'll break in yet, but in the meantime I'll be freeloading in your guest house a while longer."

"Gayle, you know you're welcome to stay as long as you want. And if you need—"

"No, my friend. We've had this conversation before, but thanks for offering. I'm not licked yet. I'll think of something," Gayle said, rubbing the frown that had crept back on her forehead. "When are you coming home?"

"That's what I wanted to talk to you about. I'm in a

pickle down here and I need some help. How good are you at what you do?"

"Damned good," Gayle answered.

"Can you actually research an ailing company and diagnose the problems?"

"Of course. That's what I'm trained to do."

"Does that test of yours really work?"

"I'd stake my life on it, Ariel. You know that. Why are you asking all these questions?"

"Just checking your confidence level. I want you to pack it up and hop the first flight in the morning to Houston. I'm retaining Summers Consulting to get to the bottom of this mess."

"What mess? Ariel, what's going on? I thought you were just in Houston for your granduncle Calvin's funeral."

"I was, but it seems that Uncle Cal left everything to me. The hitch is, according to his lawyer, the company is on the verge of bankruptcy. Some guy named Ben Lyons is hounding me to sell out to him, and there's a board of directors meeting in a couple of days. I don't understand enough about it to explain, but I don't believe for a minute that McDonough Bearings could be about to go under. Either Uncle Cal surrounded himself with incompetents or somebody is lying. I feel as if I'm being railroaded, and the whole thing sounds very peculiar. You know that I have no head for business, but even I can tell when something stinks to high heaven. Will you come?"

"You know I will."

"Great. That's a load off my mind. Let me know your arrival time and I'll pick you up at the airport. See you tomorrow."

Gayle laughed and shook her head as she replaced the receiver. She felt as if she had been hit by a whirlwind. Ariel was a brilliant metal sculptress, her pieces were in demand by the top contemporary museums all over the country, but sometimes her verbal communication left something to be desired.

She sighed and got up to pack her briefcase and portable computer unit. At least she'd have an opportunity to check out the new system. Starting a business alone in a new area was proving to be more difficult than she had imagined. After Greg's death two years ago she had closed their consulting firm in California swearing that she never wanted to see the Summers Profile again.

The old blue Cadillac turned off Memorial Drive, lined with gracious homes on large wooded lots, onto a side street. Gayle smiled, watching her friend's intense concentration as Ariel herded the cumbrous, aging sedan through a narrow arched gate. The drive wound through tall pines and other lush trees, still green even though it was late October. The carefully tended lawn of the rambling old brick and cedar house was blazing with beds of golden chrysanthemums. When they had parked by the garages on the side, the back grounds, visible through the breezeway, caught Gayle's eye and she bounded from the car.

"Oh, Ariel, it's beautiful!" she cried as she ran to the back patio to get a better view of the winding bayou that cut through the property.

Huge weeping willows dipped their branches into the water. More of the blazing chrysanthemums spilled over the stone terracing that led to the stream's edge, and at least three rock waterfalls bubbled in the midst of other

14

thick golden beds of flowers. Stone steps cut a meandering trail into the sloping bank and a family of ducks swam at its end.

For a moment she was so caught up in the breathtaking loveliness of the scene that she didn't notice the man sprawled on one of the lounges.

"It's like the Garden of Eden," she said, her voice husky with the awe of such beauty. With a dazzling smile and eyes bright and wide with wonder, she whirled around toward Ariel, wanting to share the moment with her friend. But Ariel was still by the car, unloading the luggage. That's when she saw him.

He was lying on his side, head propped on one hand, watching her with a predator's eye. He reminded her of a big-game hunter, dressed as he was in scuffed boots and a khaki safari suit. He needed only an elephant gun and a bush hat with a leopard band to make the illusion complete. His skin was tanned the deep golden bronze of someone who spent his life in the sun. His tawny mane of hair was the same color except for streaks bleached pale from exposure. And his eyes. Shards of topaz glinted, mesmerized, pierced her from his unblinking squint.

A shiver slithered up her spine. This man was dangerous.

If this is the Garden of Eden, you must be the snake, she thought. When she saw a corner of his mouth lift in a lazy grin, she realized she had spoken aloud. She should have been embarrassed, but she wasn't. She didn't even drop her gaze. Nor did he. It wasn't a snake he reminded her of. Or a great white hunter. It was a jungle cat—a lion maybe—lazing in the sun, watching its prey,

15

waiting for the right instant to spring and tear it to shreds.

"If you're Eve, I'd rather be Adam." His grin widened and his eyes locked with hers. "You're the most magnificent woman I've ever seen in my life."

Only when Gayle's chest began to hurt did she realize that she had been holding her breath. She forced herself to take a couple of gulps of air and glance away for a few seconds to look at the flowers, the bayou, anything but the man on the lounge. She felt totally at his mercy, and it was frightening, but at the same time it was wildly exciting.

His eyes lightened a shade and the furrows at their corners deepened. Her gaze was released and she relaxed for a moment, weak from the intense encounter. She heard a rumbling laughter.

"Now I know exactly how ol' Adam must have felt. Angel, do you have any idea what just looking at you is doing to me?"

Shocked, she turned her face away. She cleared her throat. "Are you always so candid?"

"Always."

Struggling to shore up the breach in her defenses, Gayle lifted her chin a fraction and assumed her most professional tone. "While I admire honesty, some situations are more appropriately handled with a bit of discretion."

It grated her that he only seemed amused by her haughty rejoinder.

His lazy grin was back, accompanied this time with a little quirk of an eyebrow. "I prefer the direct approach myself. It cuts through a lot of crap." He glanced at her left hand. "You're not married?"

"No."

"Engaged?"

"No," she replied, becoming irritated with his line of questioning. Why was she standing here like an idiot answering him?

"Do you have a lover?"

Fury flashed over her, but she refused to let him gain the advantage by goading her into a childish tantrum. She managed to keep her voice measured with icy control. "I can't imagine what business it is of yours."

His eyes flicked over her with an almost possessive gleam. "I like to size up the competition. I'm just wondering who I'm going to have to fight for you."

Gayle felt as if every bit of blood had drained from her face. She wanted to lash out with some brilliant cutting remark that would put this cretin in his place, but her brain seemed to have turned into a rock.

All she could think of to say was, "Sir, I perceive you're no gentleman." Had she really said that? Surely she hadn't said that. She sounded like her maiden aunt Minerva.

He threw back his head and laughed. "You've got that right."

Before she said something else equally inane, Gayle whirled and walked swiftly toward Ariel. Grabbing a bag from her friend's hand, she hurried toward the house. The whole exchange couldn't have taken more than a few minutes, but Gayle felt as if a whole lifetime had come unraveled. She didn't react like that to men—at least she never had before. This was crazy.

With narrowed eyes, he watched her escape. He didn't miss the sway of her gently rounded hips under the soft folds of a dress the same electric-blue color of her eyes. Nor did he ignore the shapely long legs as her high heels clattered up the steps. The lush, thick waves that bounced around her shoulders reminded him of dark chocolate. He wanted to grab handfuls of it and kiss that sexy mouth until . . .

"Holy hell," he muttered, letting out a soundless whistle and sinking back into the lounge cushion. She was some kind of woman. He couldn't remember feeling this randy since his early adolescent fumblings with Mary Lou Oppenheimer behind the gym. No. What he felt was more than that. It was closer to when he caught his first touchdown pass or went up for his first solo flight.

Who was she? Probably some friend of Ariel's. What an unlikely pair. He grinned. While Ariel looked like a bull with freckles, this one could pose for a centerfold.

Before his mind wandered off again into thoughts of soft honeyed skin and sensuous lips, he forced himself to stand. There would be time for that later. He had to get back to work on the things he had taken from Cal's study.

Trying to make her question casual, Gayle asked Ariel as she followed her upstairs to her room, "Who was that man on the patio?"

"That was Ben Lyons. The one who's hounding me about selling out to him. It seems he was sort of Uncle Cal's partner for the last few years."

Gayle's heart landed somewhere around her ankles and she clutched the banister with a white-knuckled grip. She knew as well as she knew that the sun would rise in the morning that this project was going to test her skill to the limit.

"What is he doing here?"

18

Ariel set the bags inside a bedroom overlooking the bayou, the patio, and a small cottage she hadn't noticed before.

"Uncle Cal leased the guest house to him. He stays there when he's in the country."

Gayle fought the urge to look down at the patio below. Instead she busied herself unpacking her bags while Ariel helped her put things away.

"How was Ben Lyons 'sort of' your Uncle Cal's partner? Who owns the company? I thought your uncle was the sole owner."

"No. As I understand, Uncle Cal retained fifty-five percent. Ben has thirty-five percent, Winston Dasher, the company attorney, has a small amount, and the rest is owned by various other executives of McDonough Bearings. Ben wants to buy either all my interest or enough to give him control."

Gayle thought again of the bronzed hunter downstairs. Of course he would want control. Like his namesake, he had been lying in wait, ready to move in for the kill. He probably thought he could get away with offering Ariel, who was naïve in business matters, a pittance for her uncle's holdings. A thought struck her. She didn't know what kind of money was involved here. She had assumed that she was dealing with a small family-owned business.

"Ariel, how big is McDonough Bearings?"

"Lord, I don't know. I haven't been there in years. The plant is down by the ship channel."

Gayle chuckled. "That's not what I mean. How much is it worth?"

"To hear Winston tell it, it's not worth anything. But I seem to remember his saying that a couple of years ago

19

it was worth several million dollars. I forget the exact figure, but it was a lot less than I got for my father's business."

Gayle sank to the bed and ran her hand over the apricot velvet comforter. Ariel knew little and cared less about money. All she thought about was welding copper tubing to old bicycle frames and rusty tractor seats. It took a battery of lawyers and accountants to keep track of the millions Ariel had inherited from her parents.

"I may be out of my league. Why don't you check with your own attorneys about this?"

Ariel ran her hands through the wild brush of hair the way she did when she was nervous. "I did."

"What did they tell you?"

"They advised me to sell. I think they were overjoyed. Something about taxes and losses. But that was before I talked to Hector."

"Who in the world is Hector?"

"Hector Luna. He was Uncle Cal's gardener, chauffeur, and general handyman. He's worked here for as long as I can remember."

"Am I going to have to drag it out of you? What did Hector say to make you change your mind?"

Ariel walked to the window, propped her elbows on the edge, and stared out toward the bayou and the wooded area beyond. "I guess I need to start at the beginning. There," she pointed to the end of the steps where the ducks were still quacking as they swam and bobbed, "is where they found Uncle Cal's body. They surmised that he must have gone to feed the ducks, and some way slipped, hit his head, and fell in the water. He was seventy-six, you know. Not a young man anymore.

20

However it happened, he drowned and nobody was here."

Tears ran down her freckled cheeks and she wiped them away with her thick fingers. Gayle, feeling the pain of her loss, went to her friend and gathered the stocky body against her slender one.

"He was all I had left," she sobbed. "All my family is gone."

Gayle held her until the weeping ceased. "Are you okay now?"

Ariel nodded and blew her nose on a tissue she had fished out of her jeans pocket.

"What did Hector say?" Gayle asked.

Sighing deeply, Ariel sat down on the bed and began shredding the tissue. "The day he died was the housekeeper's regular day off. It was the day that Uncle Cal and Hector usually spent puttering around in the yard. Uncle Cal was semi-retired, you know. He only went to the plant two or three days a week. Anyway, that morning there was a call from the airport to pick up a package. Hector went to get it and while he was gone, Uncle Cal died."

Ariel burst into tears once again. Gayle knelt at her feet and patted her hand until she composed herself, then said as patiently as if she were speaking with a child, "What does this have to do with selling the company?"

"There wasn't a package at the airport."

Gayle looked blank. "So?"

"Don't you see? Uncle Cal never had a sick day in his life. He jogged every day. Jogged, for godsake. At seventy-six. He was as sure-footed as a mountain goat. He

21

didn't stumble. Somebody lured Hector away. And while he was gone my uncle was murdered!''

"Murdered?" Gayle was stunned. "Have you talked to the police about this?"

Ariel nodded. "At least Winston did after I told him what Hector said. I figured he'd know best how to handle it, being a lawyer and all."

"And . . . ?"

"They said there was no evidence of foul play. I don't know if the final report on the exact cause of death has been filed yet. They did a routine autopsy. Winston's supposed to check and let me know." The usual softness of Ariel's mouth was a grim, determined line. "I don't care if there were no signs of a struggle. I refuse to believe that it was an accident. Call me crazy, but I know it here," she said, slapping her ample bosom. "Uncle Cal was murdered. And it had something to do with the company. I can feel it."

Gayle didn't know what to say. Ariel seemed to have a sixth sense about some things. While the idea seemed unlikely, spawned more from grief than reality, she couldn't dismiss the possibility. She had learned from their many years of friendship that Ariel's hunches were very often right.

Then another thought struck her. If Calvin McDonough's death was not an accident, somewhere out there a murderer was loose. And they could be walking into a perilous situation by getting involved. A chill gripped her shoulders and she shuddered.

Slowly she stood and walked to the window. Her gaze was drawn to the winding pathway and its end. The tranquil beauty of the scene seemed incongruous with an act of deliberate violence. Mottled ducks still paddled calmly in the bayou; a breeze ruffled the willow trees, causing their branches to dip like lines cast to tease and lure lazy fish from the murky water. Somewhere in the distance she could hear the drone of a lawnmower. No. Nothing there spoke of malicious activity or danger. Her eyes wandered to the patio lounge below. It was empty.

"Gayle, will you help me?"

Good sense told her not to become involved, to let the proper authorities do their job. But good sense had little to do with it. Nothing could ever repay the support and unconditional love that Ariel had ladled out in heaping measures over the years. She had always been there. A port in the storm, a rock-solid source of unfailing faith, encouragement, and good humor. After the devastation of Greg's death, Ariel had flown to California and stayed with Gayle while she closed the Los Angeles firm, then insisted that Gayle come home to Denver with her.

The healing had taken a long time. For months Gayle was sure that she could never look at another Summers Profile report without reliving the trauma connected with it, but with her friend's love and patience, Gayle had overcome her fears. With Ariel's prodding, she had spent the past year gathering more data, refining the test, learning to trust her instincts again. Gayle owed her friend.

Turning from the window, Gayle saw the pleading in her friend's warm eyes. For perhaps the first time in her life, Ariel, the epitome of the giving earth mother, had asked something for herself. There was only one answer. She smiled. "What do you want me to do?"

Ariel's face brightened and her shoulders slumped as

if relieved of a burden. "As I told you on the phone, I'm hiring you as a consultant. You're the only one I can trust. First I want you to check out the company. Do whatever you need to and find out what's wrong. Dig into the books or whatever," she said with a wave of her hand, "and come up with some answers as to how Uncle Cal's business can be on the verge of bankruptcy. Second, I want you to evaluate every single person involved with McDonough Bearings with that miracle test of yours. Somebody in the company is a murderer and I want you to find him."

Gayle gasped. "I can't find a murderer with the Summers Profile. It's only a personality test, not a crystal ball. The whole idea's ludicrous!"

Ariel cocked her head and shook her stubby finger. "Don't tell me that. I saw the data from your prison studies. You could take a printout from one of those inmates you tested and describe him better than his police dossier. You could tell everything from what kind of crimes he committed to what he had for breakfast. Now, isn't that right?"

Gayle smiled. "I think you're exaggerating just a bit."

"Not much. I've been in your workshops, remember? I've seen the work you've done with companies. You're never wrong in your evaluations of people. You always hit them right on the button."

"A lot of that was Greg's work," Gayle said.

"Monkey feathers! You were always better at it than Greg was. Anyway, the test has been refined and your data base has quadrupled since then." Her eyes narrowed. "I thought you said that the Summers Profile was so good you'd stake your life on it."

"Sure it's good, but I can't accuse someone of murder based on a personality test."

"You can narrow down the suspects. In any case you'll need to test the employees for evaluation of job placement and all that stuff. I'll make it worth your while."

"Money isn't the issue. I can't charge you. You've practically supported me for two years."

"Don't worry about that. I've told you a million times, I've got more money than sense. I want this all official, with a legal document and everything. Winston Dasher is drawing up a contract and bringing it over this afternoon. I knew you'd want to talk to him anyway. Deal?" She stuck out her hand.

Gayle sighed and clasped her friend's hand. "Deal," she agreed reluctantly, knowing that they were stirring up a hornets' nest and dreading it. For all Ariel's bravado, she was basically naïve about human nature. But then, she hadn't lived with the horror and the guilt of Greg's death. Ariel hadn't spent the sleepless nights, the endless empty days longing to reclaim the past, savoring tender memories, damning herself, and weeping futile tears. Greg . . . her mentor, her partner, her lover, her husband. He had been working at his desk that afternoon two years ago when an enraged executive stormed into his office and shot him. The man had exploded and gone berserk when, based on the Summers Profile recommendation, his firm chose someone else for a promotion.

It had been Gayle who evaluated the executive's profile. Too volatile and unstable for the position, her report had said.

Her old fears rose like a monster threatening to devour her. Despite her disclaimer to Ariel, Gayle knew it was possible to identify the darker sides of personalities, to use the Profile to strip away the masks and shadows concealing the capacity for deceit, violence, even murder. If Ariel's hunch was right, using the test might put them in peril. People with villainous secrets were dangerous when they were threatened with exposure. Greg's death was testimony to that. What if it happened again?

The thought made her blood run cold.

CHAPTER TWO

The friends sat at a glass-topped table in the enclosed back porch overlooking the bayou and the wooded area beyond. The room was almost like a conservatory, filled as it was with lush plants hanging from the heavy beams and scattered about the rough tile floor. An abstract metal sculpture, obviously one of Ariel's, claimed a place of honor among a nest of potted ferns. Clear lucite louvers, which made up the three outside walls, were opened to admit the balmy fall breeze and screens kept out the insects, still a problem in Houston even so late in the year. Informal rattan furniture with plump colorful cushions added to the relaxed atmosphere. Gayle much preferred it to the heavier, more traditional furnishings of the rest of the big house.

Gayle waited until Mrs. Jenkins served their lunch—huge bowls of steaming gumbo—and disappeared back into the kitchen before she said, "For gosh sakes don't say anything to *anyone* about what we're doing or what you suspect. Let's keep it low key until we have more information."

Pursing her lips and looking incensed, Ariel shot back, "I'm not a complete idiot. I'll keep quiet and you do your Scarlett O'Hara bit." She giggled. "They'll never know what hit them."

Fighting a grin, Gayle asked, "Is my 'poor little ol' me' act that obvious?"

"Only to someone who knows that you have an M.B.A. from Harvard. You've come a long way from Jackson, Mississippi, honey child."

The Scarlett O'Hara act Ariel referred to was a tactic Gayle had perfected long ago. Perhaps it was devious, but the business world was a tough one. More than once her looks had cost her a contract from firms who couldn't see beyond the surface, but just as often she was able to turn her appearance into a business asset. Those times came when, dismissing her as no more than a pretty, empty-headed piece of fluff, executives and employees allowed her free access to gather information about their companies.

With men who treated her as the competent professional that she was, Gayle reciprocated. But with the self-styled Lotharios, the blatant male chauvinists, she had learned to use her dazzling smile instead of a smirk, to charm with a calculated flutter of long black lashes. Her soft Mississippi drawl would thicken until it dripped and oozed like a honeycomb on a warm summer day. Invariably they underestimated her. Invariably they spilled it all. She didn't think of it as deceit but simply using available resources to even the odds in a male-dominated arena. She was equally comfortable in ruffled chiffon or gray flannel. It depended on the situation. From what Ariel had told her, Gayle knew the kind of old-fashioned men she would be dealing with here.

Mrs. Jenkins bustled in with a basket of crusty buttered French bread and was about to leave the room again when Gayle glanced at the third place setting at the table. "Aren't you joining us for lunch, Mrs. Jenkins?"

"Oh, my, no, dear. That's for Mr. Ben. He said he'd be over in a few minutes and to start without him."

Gayle almost knocked over the glass of iced tea she was reaching for when her heart lurched. Could she handle this? A part of her was excited by the prospect of another encounter with Ben Lyons, but a bigger part of her wanted to run and hide under the bed until he was gone.

Taking a sip of the cool drink, she tried to keep her voice even as she asked, "Does he take all his meals here?"

"Just about. I gather that he and Uncle Cal were pretty close for the past three or four years. He acts like one of the family," Ariel said, digging into the steaming bowl. "Mmm, delicious. Nobody makes gumbo like Mrs. Jenkins. Taste it."

Sampling a spoonful, Gayle agreed that it was delicious, although the spicy dish barely registered on her palate. Her mind was still on Ben. "Hadn't you met him before?"

Ariel shook her head. "I haven't visited too much in the last few years. I feel kind of guilty about it. I loved the old curmudgeon, but you know how busy I've been with my work. The times I was here Ben and I must have missed each other. Now that I think about it, it seems that Uncle Cal did mention him once or twice. I don't think he took an active part in running the company. Sort of a silent partner, I guess. Other than that, I don't know anything about him."

Gayle toyed with a slice of the crusty bread. "How can I find out more about Ben Lyons?"

"Why don't you ask him?" a deep voice suggested.

The bread in her fingers plopped into the bowl as Gayle jumped a foot off her chair. She glanced to the doorway, where Ben stood propped casually against the jamb, hands in the pockets of his khakis and a smug grin on his face.

"An excellent idea," she replied, smiling to mask the awkward moment. "Won't you join us?" When he had ambled to the table and sat down, Gayle continued, "I don't believe we've been formally introduced, Mr. Lyons. I'm Gayle Summers, a friend of Ariel's." She extended her hand across the corner of the small table.

Instead of the usual business handshake she had intended, he clasped her hand lightly in his big callused one and slowly teased the back with his thumb while his eyes captured hers and held them. "Ben. Call me Ben."

A warm current rippled up her arm and radiated over her. She tried to draw her hand away but he held it firmly in his.

"Summers. It suits you. Lush and sultry." His thumb continued its maddening circles and his eyes their predator's gleam.

Ariel was all but forgotten as the two of them mentally tested each other—circling, thrusting, parrying, circling again.

"My husband's name. Not mine. My maiden name was Stone," she said with a wry smile, tugging at his grip.

Instead of releasing her, he squeezed more tightly as his bemused expression dissolved into a scowl. "Husband? I thought you said . . ."

"Gayle's a widow," Ariel interjected.

His eyes never left Gayle's face. "How long?"

"Two years," Gayle replied, and watched the scowl disappear. "If you don't mind," she said, glancing toward their clasped hands and giving a little tug, "I'd like to finish my lunch."

Ben grinned and released his grip as the housekeeper entered with his food. "I'd like some of that gumbo myself. Mrs. Jenkins is a superb cook, maybe the best in the world. I come here just to have her feed me."

"Oh, go on with you, Mr. Ben," the gray-haired woman said, tucking her head but glowing with the compliment. There was a definite spring in her step when she walked back toward the kitchen.

One of those, Gayle thought, bringing her attention back to her food. He probably has a string of women a mile long. She struggled to swallow a couple of bites before Ben asked, "What would you like to know?"

Gayle looked up to find him gustily devouring his meal. "About what?"

"About me," he said, and grinned in that infuriating manner of his.

How crass of him to bring up what he had overheard eavesdropping. She was tempted to dump the rest of her bowl over his head. Instead she smiled sweetly and batted her eyelashes. "May I ask anything?"

"Anything your heart desires."

"Are you married?"

"No."

"Engaged?"

A smile played around his lips. "No."

"Do you have a lover?"

Gayle heard Ariel give a strangled snort and Ben's

smile widened so that his teeth flashed white against his deep tan. "Not yet."

"Why do you want to buy McDonough Bearings?"

"Because Cal intended for me to take over. Our transaction was to have been completed this trip."

"Why would you want a company that is on the verge of bankruptcy?"

He propped his elbows on the table and leaned toward her. "Angel, there's no need to worry your pretty little head about business."

Gayle was sure that her blood pressure shot up fifty points. Yet when Ariel guffawed and started, "But she's—" Gayle kicked her under the table.

She only gritted her teeth and smiled her magnolia blossom, molasses-dripping smile. Touching his muscled forearm, she drawled, "But I find a man's work so fascinating, don't you, Ariel, honey?" She glanced toward her friend, then gave Ben her full attention. "What business are you in besides your interest in McDonough Bearings?"

"Import-Export."

"Are you successful, Ben?"

He looked amused. "I do well enough to keep you in pretty baubles, sweetheart."

She could almost feel his macho swagger. She giggled, fluttered her eyelashes again, and fought the urge to spit in his eye. "And where do you engage in this wonderful business?"

"Florida, the Caribbean, Colombia mostly," he said, frowning slightly. "Why the interrogation?"

Gayle's indigo eyes widened and she drew her lips into an enticing pout. Her Mississippi drawl oozed like warm butter over a plate of grits as she said, "Ben, honey, you said I could ask anything my lil ol' heart desires. A girl can't be too careful who she gets mixed up with nowadays, you know." She patted his arm for emphasis.

The grin was back. "Fire away."

"What sorts of things do you import-export?"

He paused. For the first time a tiny crack appeared in his composure. "Oh, bananas and . . . and other things."

"Bananas!" Gayle cried, clapping her hands together. "Well, I declare. I eat bananas on my cereal lots of mornings. Do you reckon it's your bananas I'm eating, Ben?"

"Could be."

Ariel had her fist shoved against her lips and her shoulders were shaking. Gayle kicked her under the table again. "Isn't this fascinating? I just knew it would be. And what other . . . things besides bananas do you handle?"

"Oh, this and that," he said. "Do you live in Denver, too?"

"Why, yes I do. I live in Ariel's guest house." She reached over to pat a stubby, freckled hand. "She's been the dearest, sweetest friend. She practically took me in off the street and comforted me in my darkest hour of grief." Although Gayle was laying it on a bit thick, real tears shimmered in her eyes. She dabbed at them with her napkin. "Look at what a sentimental crybaby I am." Forcing a bright smile, she leaned toward Ben, laid her hand gently on his arm once again. "Let's not talk about sad things anymore. Tell us all about your bananas and . . . whatever."

While Mrs. Jenkins cleared the table and brought dessert—thankfully it was pecan pie and not banana pudding, or the two women would have cracked up for sure —Ben launched into a discussion of banana plantations in South America and the Caribbean islands as well as the intricacies of transporting the crop. Gayle hung on to every word, interjecting an occasional, "How absolutely fascinating," to prompt more information about his business.

Gayle turned toward Ariel, who had a glazed look in her eye. "Can you believe it? Ben has a plantation in Colombia, a house in Florida, a condo in the Caymans, and a whole fleet of airplanes and ships. Why it's just like one of those Greek tycoons you always read about."

Ben laughed indulgently. "I hardly think a couple of cargo planes and a few banana boats put me in the same league."

"You're just being modest," she cooed. "Land sakes, you couldn't pay all those millions for Ariel's company if you weren't rich."

"Let's just say I've got good credit. I can scrape together enough if I can convince your friend to sell." He turned toward Ariel and asked, "Have you decided to accept my offer?"

Ariel kept a straight face as she answered seriously, "I've contracted with a consultant to evaluate the situation. I can't do anything until I receive a report and recommendation from the firm I've hired."

"A consultant? I'd like to meet with him as soon as possible."

"Her," Gayle said, fighting a smug smirk.

Ben looked blank.

"Her," Gayle repeated, flashing a broad smile and

giving an exaggerated wink as she stood to leave the table. "Angel, I'm the consultant."

Ben threw back his head and roared with laughter. She could still hear him as the two friends went into Uncle Cal's study and firmly closed the door behind them.

Pushing her irritation with Ben Lyons into the back of her mind, Gayle sank into the leather chair behind the dark walnut executive desk. Her quick survey of the study took in the filing cabinets in the corner, the pair of forest-green velvet wing chairs and ottomans flanking the fireplace, and a smaller metal sculpture, also Ariel's, on a pedestal in front of the bay window that over-looked the winding front drive. Bookcases and a bar stretched the length of one wall. A plush carpet in a muted pattern covered the floor and the paneled walls held two pleasant landscapes as well as several photo-graphs of the plant and company personnel spanning many years.

The polished desktop was cleared except for a tele-phone, an expensive pen and pencil set, and a folding frame with two pictures in it. One she recognized as the professional portrait Ariel used for her brochures. The second was an enlarged snapshot of Ben Lyons laughing into the camera from the deck of a sailboat. She cocked her eyebrow and tapped her fingernail against her teeth as she stared at it.

After trying the desk drawers and finding that they wouldn't budge, she asked Ariel, "Do you have a set of keys?"

"No," Ariel said, and sat down on a corner of the desk. "Maybe Mrs. Jenkins could help. Shall I ask her?"

Gayle shook her head.

35

A small stand beside the desk would be perfect for her computer and would provide easy access for telephone hookup to the Denver system. She'd bring the units down from her room later. Gayle was surprised that there wasn't a computer in the room already, but perhaps Calvin McDonough was one of the holdouts against the newer technologies.

The next thing Gayle did was to locate a locksmith in the yellow pages who promised to be there within the hour to install a new deadbolt on the door and secure the windows of the room. She also wanted to have the locks on the desk and file cabinets changed.

"Why in the world are you doing that? The house has an elaborate burglar alarm system."

"Yes, and no telling how many people know how to work it or have keys to the house. I'm sure your Uncle Cal kept important papers here and I don't want them 'walking off'—if they haven't already. I plan to use this as an office as well, and I don't want anyone to have access to my data."

Gayle got up and walked to one of the doors on either side of the brick fireplace. Behind one she found a half bath, the other was a storage closet containing shelves full of office supplies, photograph albums, and various boxes. She sighed. There was a lot of stuff to go through here, not to mention all that had to be done at the plant.

Glancing around the room again, Gayle had another thought. "Do you happen to know if your uncle had a safety deposit box or a safe somewhere here?"

"I know he had a wall safe," Ariel replied, walking to the closet and shifting a couple of boxes. "It's here."

She pointed to the small steel door that was revealed behind them.

"I suppose it's too much to hope that you know the combination."

Ariel grinned. "I do indeed. The first three numbers are my birthday and the last one is fourteen, the age I was when I came to live with Uncle Cal. He knew how awful I am with figures and said surely I could remember that. Do you want me to open it?"

"Not yet. I'll start on all this later."

Ariel replaced the boxes, wandered back to the desk, and picked up the gold double frame. "The banana king." She laughed as she studied the picture. "I thought I would die listening to you put him on." She set the frame back in its place and asked, "Do you think I should accept his offer? I'd like to if that's what Uncle Cal wanted."

"It's too soon to make a decision, but be careful of Ben Lyons. The man is dangerous." Gayle's job depended on her keen powers of observation, and she was good at it. She hadn't missed the almost imperceptible hesitation and slight discomfort when his business goods had been mentioned. "With his fleet of cargo planes and boats and the cover of a legitimate crop, I can just imagine what he deals in besides bananas."

"What are you talking about?" Ariel looked puzzled.

"He said he handled bananas and 'other things.' Don't you know what Colombia's big money crop is?"

Ariel shook her head.

"Drugs. Including marijuana—Colombian gold."

Gayle glanced at her watch and frowned. She had hoped to get to the bank before Winston Dasher came by at five thirty, but it was almost five o'clock now. The lock-smith had been competent but very, very slow changing all the locks in the study. Ariel had absolutely refused to keep the second set of keys to the new locks. "You know how forgetful I am," she had said. "I can't even keep up with my own car keys." So the best alternative was to put them in a safety deposit box. Even the nearest bank would be closed by now. Oh, well, she would tend to it the first thing in the morning. She had a set in each pocket. The bulk of the metal rings in the softness of the delicate challis skirt thumped against her thighs as she walked toward the garages in search of Hector Luna.

She found him in the driveway washing the aging blue Cadillac Ariel had driven to pick her up at the airport. Parked in the stalls of the four-car garage behind him were a small station wagon, a black pick-up that she imagined belonged to Hector, and a red Corvette. She didn't have to guess who that belonged to. It had Ben Lyons written all over it.

Hector looked up from his chore when he heard Gayle's approach. He was a short, wiry man with a liberal sprinkling of gray through his once-black hair, and knotted fingers showed the years of hard work. Though there was a melancholy droop to his dark eyes, his smile, brightened by the considerable gold in his mouth, was warm and welcoming.

"Hello," Gayle said. "You must be Hector."

"*Sí*, and you are Miss Ariel's friend from Denver."

She nodded. "I'm Gayle Summers." She stood silent for a few moments and watched him carefully polish the car. "It looks as if you take good care of things around here."

"*Sí*, I've taken care of Mr. Calvin's things for thirty

years, ever since I came from Mexico. My Rosa, God rest her soul, did too before we lost her."

"Was Rosa your wife?"

He nodded.

"Oh, I'm sorry. My husband died. I know how you feel."

He shrugged and continued his polishing. "It's a long time now. Twenty-six years. Mr. Calvin sent her to the best doctors, saw she had everything. He was a fine man, Mr. Calvin."

"You weren't here when he died, were you?"

The rubbing stopped, and Hector clutched the cloth in his dark fingers. Anguish twisted his face when he looked at Gayle. He shook his head, dropped his gaze, and resumed his buffing with a vengeance.

Gayle stepped closer to him and laid her hand on his shoulder. "Why don't you tell me about it?"

He stopped his work and leaned back against the sedan. "That morning me and Mr. Calvin was planning to mulch the rosebushes, but the airport called and told him he had a big package that needed to be picked up. He told me, 'Hector, you take the pickup out to the Blue Line Express office at Hobby Airport and get the package, and I'll start on the rosebushes.' His exact words. 'The Blue Line Express office at Hobby Airport.' Only when I got there, they said Mr. Calvin didn't have a package and nobody had called. The lady there checked with everybody in the office. When I got back I found Mr. Calvin at the bottom of the steps, his head and shoulders in the water. I pulled him out, but he was gone." Tears rolled from his eyes and he wiped them on the sleeve of his chambray work shirt.

Gayle waited a few moments, then asked, "What did you do next?"

"I didn't know what to do. I was here by myself, so I called Mr. Brewer at the plant."

"Mr. Brewer? The president of Mr. McDonough's company?"

Hector nodded. "He told me to stay calm and he would send somebody. Mr. Dasher came and the police came, and finally an ambulance took Mr. Calvin away."

"Have you told anybody except Ariel about the call from the airport?"

"No, only Miss Ariel. So much was going on and I was so upset about Mr. Calvin, I forgot it until I got to thinking about it later." He hesitated a few minutes, then drew a deep breath. "I'm not sure, but I've got a feeling that somebody didn't want me around. They wanted Mr. Calvin by himself."

"Hector, do you know what that might mean?"

"Yes, ma'am, I do."

"The police say that it was an accident. That he probably went to feed the ducks and something caused him to fall in."

The wiry man pulled a bandanna from his back pocket and mopped his face. "I don't know about that. I do know Mr. Calvin fed the ducks earlier that morning, and the rosebushes are in the other direction."

"Hector, Ariel and I would appreciate it if you wouldn't repeat the story about the airport to anyone until we can check further. Can we count on you?"

He nodded solemnly. "I won't say anything."

As Gayle turned toward the house, she glanced into the shadows of the garage, and stopped dead in her tracks. Ben Lyons was leaning against the fiery red Corvette. He must have heard every word.

Anger flashed through her as he ambled over to where she was standing. "What are you doing skulking around in the shadows? Don't you have something better to do than eavesdropping on my private conversations?"

A lazy grin broke over his tanned face. "Skulking?" He hooted. "I wasn't skulking. I was waiting to talk to you about my offer for the company. Didn't Ariel say you were in charge?" His eyes raked over her and he shook his head. "Are you really a consultant?"

Gayle's hands tightened into fists and she clenched her teeth. It was times like this when she wished she could be a man for just a minute. How she would love to sock him right in his smart mouth. She took a deep breath and forced herself to relax. "Yes," she ground out. "I really am a consultant. And a damned good one."

"I believe you," Ben said as he threw up his hands in mock surrender. "Let's talk."

Gayle glanced at her watch. The lawyer would be here any minute. "I don't have time right now. I have another appointment."

"Why don't we go out for dinner? We can discuss it then."

"I don't think so. I'm having dinner here with Ariel."

"All right, then. How about after dinner?"

"I have a lot of work to do tonight."

"In the morning?" he persisted.

"That wouldn't be convenient either. I have an errand to run and then I want to spend the day at the plant."

41

He sighed. "We're going to have to discuss it soon."

Gayle knew she was being unreasonable, but everything about him unnerved her. She masked her disquiet with a professional mantle. "There's no real hurry for us to talk. While I understand that Ariel is the sole heir of the estate and the transfer of property is a mere formality, it will probably take several months for the will to be probated. Until that time nothing can be sold. Why don't you submit your proposal to me in writing, Mr. Lyons? I'll study it carefully, and when I am better apprized of the situation, I'll get back to you."

"Several months! By that time McDonough Bearings will be bankrupt. Are you sure about this?"

"Quite sure." Her reply was cool. And it wasn't exactly accurate. Ariel also had been named executrix in Uncle Cal's will and had the power to administer the estate, but Gayle didn't like Ben's pushy attitude. She'd let him stew for a while until she knew more about the company's problems.

"I'll drive you in the morning. You can run your errand and we can talk on the way to the plant," he said in a tone that clearly indicated that the leash he had been allowing her to run on had been jerked sharply.

Gayle glared up at him and raised her eyebrow. "In writing, I said, Mr. Lyons." Before he could respond, she wheeled and stalked toward the house. She hadn't taken half a dozen steps when a powerful hand grabbed her arm and halted her in mid-stride.

"In the morning. I'll drive you." His eyes were narrow slits of cold determination. "And, angel, about what Hector told you . . ."

He *had* been listening. A feeling of grim foreboding rippled through her as she waited for him to continue.

". . . Stay out of it."

CHAPTER THREE

Gayle smiled as she accepted the glass of white wine from Winston Dasher. Ariel had slipped out to answer a phone call from an anxious gallery owner, and the two of them were alone in the formal living room, furnished with heavy traditional woods, cut velvets, and brocade. She sat down on beige plush couch while he took a place on its twin across the coffee table.

He's as different from Ben Lyons as day and night, she thought as she studied the lawyer sipping his Scotch and water. He was immaculately dressed in a charcoal three-piece suit, obviously custom tailored. His shirt was fine white cotton, his tie a correct, subdued stripe. His black shoes shone with the look of an expensive Italian manufacturer. She doubted if he would ever wear the scruffy boots that Ben did. Instead of the unruly bleached mane Ben sported, Winston's hair was a warm brown, sprinkled with fine webs of gray, that had a tendency to curl despite its stylish cut. He was a handsome man, lean and fit, with the quiet charm and polished manners of a typical southern gentleman rather than the raw dynamism of a work-muscled body and callused hands.

"Ariel tells me that you have a management consulting firm in Denver."

Still smarting from her earlier confrontations with Ben, Gayle answered a bit too sharply. "I have many years of experience and excellent references. Before I opened my own firm in Denver a few months ago, I was a partner in a well-known consulting group in California for several years."

The lawyer smiled and said, "I'm sure that you're eminently qualified to advise Ariel. I didn't mean to insinuate otherwise." His eyes shone with warm concern as he added, "I know this is a difficult situation, and I'd like to do anything I can to make things easier. Cal and Ariel have always been like a part of my family. How may I assist you in your work?"

Gayle couldn't help but like him. Something about him reminded her a bit of Greg. Perhaps it was his open boyish grin, or the hint of a disarming twinkle in his blue eyes, or the way he cocked his head and raised his eyebrows. She was immediately sorry that she'd snapped at him. "I didn't mean to be short with you, Mr. Dasher. It's been a trying day." She took a sip of wine and then added, "There are a number of questions I'd like to ask you."

"No need to apologize. And please call me Winston." He smiled, unbuttoned his coat, leaned back against the plump cushions, and said, "I'll be glad to tell you anything that might help. I've been around McDonough Bearings a long time. My father and Uncle Cal, as I've always called him, were close friends. They started the company together during World War Two. My father acted as attorney and originally held forty percent interest."

Gayle looked puzzled. "But he no longer has a share?"

Winston shook his head. "My father's been dead for over four years. Except for about five percent that he retained, he sold out to Uncle Cal over twenty years ago. He wanted to devote more time to his private practice, but he remained as the company attorney and served on the board of directors until his death. At that time I took over his duties and inherited his interest."

"Since you've been so closely associated, perhaps you could explain to me why a company that has obviously prospered for nearly forty-five years could suddenly be almost bankrupt."

Winston watched the ice cubes he swirled in his glass, then looked up. "It's a combination of things. The economic slump in general; the loss of several large government contracts that have in the past gone, almost routinely, to McDonough; some bad investments. Plus Uncle Cal was getting along in years. His vigorous leadership was missing."

"I see. Has his cause of death been established yet?"

"Yes, the autopsy report said accidental drowning." He downed the last of his Scotch and water, stood, and motioned toward her glass. "May I get you another glass of wine?" When she shook her head, he fixed himself another drink and returned to his seat on the couch. Kneading his forehead with the tips of his fingers, he said, "Uncle Cal's death has been a blow to me, too. I'll miss him. I always thought of him as invincible. He was like a second father to me, especially after Dad died. And Ariel. Well, I suppose she's the closest thing to a little sister I have, although I was already away at col-

45

lege when she came to live here. I'd like to do anything I can to make things easier for her."

"She's very concerned about the circumstances of Mr. McDonough's death. Especially after what Hector told her. I understand that you passed the information on to the police."

Winston nodded. "I talked to the officers in charge of the case and to the coroner's office. They didn't find anything to indicate foul play. As far as they're concerned, and I think I have to concur, it was a tragic accident."

By the time Ariel returned, they had agreed that Winston would meet Gayle at McDonough Bearings the next morning to introduce her to key personnel and assist her in locating any necessary data. He produced a contract for Gayle to sign as well as a power of attorney giving her full authority to act in Ariel's behalf. Gayle balked at the latter, but Ariel insisted, whispering that she would explain later.

Gayle stood and offered her hand to Winston. "Thank you for stopping by. I'm afraid we've kept you from your family too long."

"Not at all," he said, giving her fingers a gentle squeeze. "I'm afraid I'm a lonely bachelor these days. Perhaps you'll share an evening or two with me while you're here." He put his arm around Ariel, hugged her to him, and gave her a broad wink. "I'd be honored to escort both of you lovely ladies for a night out."

"Perhaps," Gayle said, hard-pressed not to respond to his easy charm.

Ariel walked Winston to the door and said a few words to him. When she returned, she giggled. "I think we'll be seeing a lot of Winston."

46

"What do you mean?"

"He seems *very* interested in you. Winston's a nice guy. He deserves some happiness after the mess he went through with his wife a couple of years ago. He adored her, though personally I never understood why. She threw him over for a Dallas millionaire. Good riddance, I said, but he was devastated. I wouldn't mind seeing the two of you get together."

"I'm not interested in participating in his love life. My interest is strictly business."

"I'm sure that's not what he's hoping for. I saw the way he was looking you over. It was almost as bad as Ben Lyons. Both of them are like chocolate freaks eyeing a box of Godivas."

The two friends laughed as they went upstairs to freshen up for dinner. Gayle was aware of the weight of the keys still bumping in her pockets. As soon as she was in her room she looked around for a safe place to stash them. Under her lingerie would be safe enough for now.

Gayle was almost disappointed when she found only two places set in the dining room, but she was determined not to mention Ben Lyons's absence. Instead she focused her attention on Mrs. Jenkins's fried chicken and the accompanying mashed potatoes, gravy, and vegetables.

"Ariel, why did you give me power of attorney? That's not necessary."

"Well," Ariel said, not looking up from the drumstick she was attacking, "I have a bit of a problem."

Gayle wiped her fingers and waited for her friend to

47

continue. When she didn't, Gayle said, "Okay. Out with it."

"That was Max Rodeiger on the phone earlier, and he's about to have a coronary. I'm scheduled for an opening at his gallery in two weeks, and I still have a couple of pieces that aren't finished. I can stay here until after the board meeting day after tomorrow, but then I have to get back to my studio and complete the work for the show." Ariel reached for another drumstick and looked toward Gayle, flinching slightly as if waiting for her to explode.

"And you want me to stay here and run things?"

"You're not angry?"

"Of course I'm not angry, but I'm not sure I want the responsibility. I don't think you have any idea of the scope of the problems involved."

"Sure I do. But I trust you implicitly. Do whatever you have to do; call in any experts you need. Just remember, I won't allow Uncle Cal's company to go bankrupt. He was a brilliant businessman and a proud old bird, and," she added using the chicken leg to emphasize each word, "I won't have his memory tainted."

Gayle propped her elbows on the table and dropped her forehead into her palms. "Ariel," she groaned. "Do you have any idea how much money might have to be poured into McDonough Bearings to keep it afloat? Millions!"

"Hell, I've *got* millions," she said, waving the drumstick. "I'll have my attorneys in Denver fix it up with a local bank so you can have all the money you need."

Gayle snorted with laughter. "I'll bet they will *love* that move."

"I don't care if they have apoplexy. It's my money

and I'll do with it what I damned well please. Besides, a real estate developer called me yesterday. Do you have any idea what the twenty acres of prime property this house is sitting on is worth?'' When Gayle shook her head, she added with a smug tilt of her nose, ''Almost as much as the company.''

Gayle grinned. ''I thought you didn't understand business.''

''I'm not a complete idiot. I'm simply interested in other things.''

''Perhaps the simplest way out would be to sell the company to Ben Lyons. He says that was your uncle's intention.''

''I may end up doing that, but not yet. You're forgetting the most important thing—Uncle Cal's murder.''

''Ariel,'' she said softly. ''Winston said that the coroner's office has ruled accidental drowning.''

''We've been over that ground before. I still don't buy it.''

Gayle gave up trying to argue with her stubborn friend. When Ariel had her mind set on something she was as tenacious as a snapping turtle.

After they finished their dinner, Gayle said, ''I'm going to change into something more comfortable and tackle the study. Want to help?''

''I wouldn't know what to look for. If you don't really need me, I think I'll watch an old movie on TV instead.''

Back in her room, Gayle shed her clothes, pinned up her hair, and drew a warm bubble bath. As she soaked in the scented water, she leaned her head against the cool tile, closed her eyes, tried to clear her mind and allow the tension to seep out of her body. She conjured up scenes of sunlit sandy beaches and palm trees swaying in the gentle ocean breeze. Waves washed the shore in a rhythmic ebb and flow. Sea gulls circled and called as they soared on the tropical currents overhead. The image was so real she could taste the salt in the air and feel the spray against her face. From the endless blue ocean a muscular, bronzed body emerged, like Neptune rising from the depths. Droplets clung to his sun-streaked mane. His golden cat-eyes narrowed with a predator's gleam, and one side of his mouth lifted in a lazy grin as he reached out his rough hand and slid it up her bare leg until it rested on her thigh, warm and wet from the ocean . . . the bath . . .

Gayle's eyes flew open. Water and bubbles threatened to slosh over the sides of the tub as she sat up. Good Lord! Where did he come from? How dare he invade her fantasies! Splashing water and trailing bubbles, she scrambled out of the tub and grabbed a towel.

"Stay out of my head, Ben Lyons! Stay out!" She couldn't understand it. Her relaxation techniques always worked before. Rubbing herself dry with a punishing briskness, she caught her flushed reflection in the bathroom mirror. "Traitor," she mumbled, giving herself a disgusted look and throwing the soggy towel against the glass.

If a man had to intrude into her daydreams, it should have been Winston Dasher. At least he was more her type. More polished. More handsome. More charming. Certainly not an impudent, scruffy savage with an overdose of male hormones.

Gayle muttered the whole time it took her to dress in her favorite jeans, butter soft and faded from washings over the years, and a baggy velour top in watermelon pink. She pulled on a pair of beaded moccasins, stuffed one set of study keys in her pocket, and hefted the computer units to take downstairs.

It only took a few moments to get set up in the study and begin her search. The desk seemed like a good place to start.

Later, when she glanced at her watch, Gayle was shocked to find that it was after one o'clock in the morning. And she hadn't made much headway. Although she had examined most of the personal papers in the big desk drawers, they were only a fraction of the things she had yet to go through. The file cabinets, the safe, everything else, would have to wait until tomorrow night. She was tired.

Arching her back, Gayle rotated her shoulders and rolled her head to ease the kinks. She had found one interesting bit of information. Four years ago, Calvin McDonough had co-signed a very large loan for Benjamin M. Lyons. In December of that same year, and twice yearly since then, Uncle Cal had assigned a five percent interest in McDonough Bearings to Ben. October and December of every year. A pattern. She stared at the photograph of Ben in one side of the gold double frame.

"What does it mean? Who are you?" she asked the laughing sailor. "Are you a business partner? A friend? A blackmailer perhaps?" She cupped her chin in her hands as she studied the candid shot. "What do you deal in besides bananas . . . and baloney?"

The picture seemed to mock her. She closed the frame and slipped it into a desk drawer. It didn't keep her from thinking about him, wondering about him. Her basic sense of order needed to be able to put him in a slot. The only thing she could be sure of was that he wasn't a murderer. Ariel had told her that Ben hadn't arrived at the house until the morning after Cal's death, and a bit of discreet checking with Mrs. Jenkins had confirmed that fact.

Why was she still thinking in terms of murder? Although Ariel was not convinced, Gayle was almost sure that the possibility could be ruled out after talking to Winston. The police would have investigated it thoroughly—especially after Winston reported the suspicious call that drew Hector away. There was probably some kind of mixup at the express office. It happened all the time. Every company seemed to have its share of employees who were either incompetent, careless, or simply didn't give a damn. After all, that sad fact was part of what kept her in business. She wouldn't be surprised to discover a package intended for Calvin McDonough shoved into some remote corner of the Blue Line Express office and forgotten. She would inquire into that tomorrow too.

Making sure that all the drawers were locked, she checked the windows and the file cabinets as well before she left the room. Gayle turned the deadbolt on the study door and trudged upstairs, anxious for sleep.

In her bedroom, she kicked off her moccasins and was reaching for the button on her jeans when she heard a phone ring down the hall. Who would be calling at this hour? Calls in the middle of the night always made her jumpy. They were usually bad news or heavy breathers. She'd better check with Ariel.

She hadn't made it to the door when Ariel started banging on it, yelling for Gayle, shouting, "Fire! The plant's on fire!"

Gayle yanked open the door. "How bad is it?"

"I don't know. Mr. Brewer just called me after the night watchman reported it to him. He was pretty upset," Ariel said, her face so pale that every freckle stood in bold relief. "What should we do? Do you think it's arson?"

"Don't jump to conclusions before we find out the facts." Gayle frowned. Knowing that neither of them would sleep until they found out what was happening, Gayle said, "Get your clothes on and let's get out there."

In a very few minutes they were running toward the garage.

"Let's take the Corvette," Ariel said as she yanked open the door of the red sports car. "We'll make better time."

Gayle jumped into the passenger seat and while they were buckling their seat belts she said, "I thought this was Ben Lyons's car."

"No. Uncle Cal's." Ariel started the powerful engine, backed out, and swung around to head out when another car rounded the curve of the drive, blocking their path. "Damnation!" Ariel said, blowing the horn. She leaned out the window and yelled, "Get out of the way, fool!"

Gayle watched Ben get out of the station wagon barring their way and saunter toward them. He was grinning as he stopped beside Gayle's window and stooped to look inside the car.

"And where are you ladies going in such a hurry at this time of night? Is there some emergency?"

The arrogant idiot! Gayle wanted to sock him again. Instead, she spoke between clenched teeth. "There certainly is. The plant's on fire. Would you please move so we can get out there?"

Ben sobered and yanked open Gayle's door. "Come on. I'll drive you."

Before Gayle could protest, he had deposited her in the front seat of his station wagon and was helping Ariel into the back. As soon as he was behind the wheel, Ben spun around and headed down the drive.

"How bad is it?" he asked.

"We don't know," Ariel said. "Martin Brewer called just a few minutes ago. The night watchman telephoned him."

Ben's full attention was on maneuvering the speeding car through the streets and onto the interstate. In the dim light Gayle thought she could see a muscle jump in his stone-carved jaw as he sped along the freeway. Thankfully the traffic was not a problem at this hour. She sniffed. "Is that gasoline I smell? Is something wrong with the car?"

"What?" Ben asked, as if distracted from thought.

"I smell gas. I asked if something was wrong with the car."

"I smell it too," Ariel said.

Ben reached under his seat and pulled out a crumpled white cloth. He rolled down his window and tossed it out. "That better?" He glanced at Gayle.

She nodded. "What was that?"

"It was my handkerchief. I'd forgotten I wiped my hands on it and stuck it under the seat." He chuckled. "I hate to admit it, but I ran out of gas tonight on my way home. I had the devil of a time finding a station open." One eye, gleaming gold in the soft reflections from the lighted highway, winked as he reached over and flicked a finger across her thigh. "It's a shame you didn't come to dinner with me. You could have kept me company on that dark, lonely road."

Gayle opened her mouth to say something like "fat chance," but the words wouldn't come out. She could only stare at his profile as his gaze returned to the concrete lane ahead.

The shiver that shook her had nothing to do with an evening chill or the rush to a fire. Indeed, all thoughts of the fire and their destination fled as she stared at the man beside her. The shiver had more to do with broad shoulders filling the soft dress shirt and muscular arms straining against sleeves rolled up tight around rigid biceps. Or with strong hands gripping the wheel and the memory of her fantasy as one of those hands had stroked its way up her bare leg . . .

As if he shared a memory of the fantasy, Ben's attention left the road. His gaze met Gayle's and a jolt of electricity arced between them. The air was fairly alive with hisses and crackles. He sucked in a quick breath and Gayle felt as if he had sucked it from her lungs. Her hand flew to her contracted chest.

Ariel giggled from the back. "Don't mind me. I'm just going to a fire. Or is one about to ignite the front seat?"

Gayle shot Ariel a quelling glance. But Ben simply chuckled with a deep, resonant, knowing sound that curled Gayle's toes and made her wiggle uncomfortably. Damn that man! What was he doing to her? He must have learned island voodoo along with the banana business. She was sure that she could feel primitive drumbeats pounding inside her and the frenzied rattle of gourds echoing in her head. A rhythmic, elemental surge made her want to shake her shoulders and rotate her pelvis to the beat. Instead, she wiggled again in the soft vinyl seat and glanced toward Ben. His eyes were locked on her. She felt hypnotized as she watched his tongue flick out and slowly circle his lips, leaving a wet, inviting trail . . .

Ben forced his attention back to the road. He could almost taste her. It was all he could do to keep from pulling over and pouncing on that sweet body. His fingers ached to feel the lush, unrestrained breasts outlined by the soft fabric of her blouse. He envied the jeans that touched her in all the hidden places his hands itched to explore. He wanted to rip off those damned jeans and feel her wiggle that sexy bottom under him and hear her moan . . .

Holy hell! If he kept this up he would wrap them around a light pole. Trying to ease the throbbing that was driving him crazy, he squirmed in his seat and gripped the wheel.

The trio rode in silence to the plant site.

They had to park a distance away and make their way through a dispersing crowd of curiosity seekers and television vans and cables to a policeman standing guard over the safety perimeter. No flames were visible but dark smoke still billowed in dying gray gusts above one wing of the office building, and the stench of wet ashes mixed with the acrid fumes of nearby chemical plants and the fetid, oily pollution of the ship channel. Red lights still flashed on the fire trucks, but the thick hoses lay limp along the wet asphalt.

"Officer," Ben said to the young cop, "we're the owners of this company. Could we speak to someone in charge?"

A tall, gray-haired man in a blue windbreaker stood talking with a group of men beside a fire engine. He caught sight of them and waved them over. Ariel introduced Gayle to Martin Brewer, president of McDonough Bearings, and a short, bald man with him who was the comptroller, George Schulze. It was obvious that both men had dressed in a hurry. Mr. Brewer was wearing house slippers and Schulze's striped pajama top was only partially tucked into his dark slacks.

"What happened, Martin?" Ben asked the tall, quiet man.

"We're waiting to get a report, but it looks like most of the damage was confined to the new wing in the office building."

"Which offices were there?" Gayle asked.

Mr. Brewer shoved his hands into his pockets and dropped his head. "Accounting, records, all the computer equipment."

"My department," Mr. Schulze said, rubbing his shiny head and shifting his weight from one foot to the other in jerky, agitated movements. "It's in ruins. It was faulty wiring. I know it. I tried to tell Calvin when he hired that contractor that he didn't know his ass from a hole in the ground, but he wouldn't listen. Now look at it. What are we going to do?"

"Now, George," the president said, "the wiring was not substandard. I checked those specs myself and helped supervise the job. We don't know what caused it yet. We'll have to wait until the chief takes a better look inside."

"There was probably a sprinkler system malfunction, too. I told you just last week it needed to be upgraded. But does anybody ever listen to me?" George Schulze scowled and walked off to watch the firemen roll the hoses and prepare to leave.

Martin Brewer shook his head and smiled. "Don't mind George. He acts like a child, but he's a fine accountant." He frowned. "I'm afraid this is going to cause some big problems. Some *big* problems. I hope it was something as simple as faulty wiring."

Ben walked toward the building and watched the lingering activity. Martin joined him.

"What is he talking about, Gayle?" Ariel asked. "What big problems?"

Gayle sighed. Before she could answer a black Porsche squealed to a stop in the now deserted parking lot behind them. Winston Dasher, dressed in a black tuxedo and ruffled evening shirt, jumped out and ran toward them. A busty blonde trailed behind him, hobbling as fast as she could in sausage-tight silvered sequins.

"Wait for me, Winnie," she whined after him.

"What happened?" Winston asked. "I was at a party in Galveston when my answering service contacted me about a fire."

"It's out now. It seems to have started in the accounting and records department. We're waiting to find out the extent of the damage." Gayle motioned toward the president. "The night watchman reported it about one o'clock. Mr. Brewer can tell you more about it," Gayle said.

The blonde caught up and snaked her arm around Winston's. "Oh, pooh. It's already out. We missed all the excitement."

Winston shook her off and looked annoyed. Ignoring the pouting woman whose heaving bosom glittered with every breath, he excused himself and walked toward the spot where Martin and Ben stood talking.

"Wait for me, Winnie," his companion squealed as she went hobbling after him.

Gayle and Ariel rolled their eyes at each other. "Somehow she doesn't seem his type," Gayle commented.

Ariel shrugged. "You were about to tell me about the problems the fire could cause."

"The loss of records and the complications caused by that are obvious. And if the fire wasn't accidental, that means it was deliberately set."

"You mean it really might be arson?"

Gayle nodded.

"But who would do such a thing?"

"It's often someone who has something to hide and wants records destroyed or, in the case of failing businesses, owners want to collect insurance."

Ariel's eyes grew wide. "Well, I certainly didn't set it."

"I know." Gayle looked up at the stars, bright tonight even through the polluted haze and city lights. Who would do such a thing? Why? She breathed deeply, then wrinkled her nose at the noxious fumes.

A sickening sense of dread twisted in the pit of her stomach. She remembered another noxious odor. The smell of gasoline on a white handkerchief.

CHAPTER FOUR

Don't jump to conclusions, Gayle admonished herself. It could be a coincidence. Still . . .

She startled when a finger stroked her cheek.

"You look exhausted," Ben said softly. "There's nothing we can do tonight. Why don't I take you and Ariel home?"

The sincere concern evident in his face and voice almost made Gayle ashamed of her censorious thoughts. Almost, but not quite. His behavior still seemed suspect, but at least she could reserve judgment until she had more information.

"Do they think arson is involved?" Gayle asked, searching his face for any hint of a guilty reaction.

"It's too early to tell. There'll be an investigation, of course. Thanks to the alert night watchman, the fire didn't destroy as much as it could have. It looks as if the worst of it may be smoke and water damage. Come on," he said, putting an arm around each of the women and steering them away from the building, "let's get you ladies in bed. We'll deal with this tomorrow—or rather later today, since it will be dawn in a few hours."

Ariel yawned. "Fine with me. I'm beat."

If Ben Lyons had set the fire, he was certainly playing

it cool, Gayle thought as they walked to the station wagon. She tried to get into the backseat for the return trip, but Ben deftly managed the arrangements so that Gayle was once again beside him.

"Wake me up when we get home," Ariel mumbled from the backseat.

As Ben pulled out of the parking lot and headed west, Gayle sat stiffly staring at the road ahead, her fingers clasped tightly in her lap. She was determined not to look at him, determined there would be no repeat of the wild behavior that had marked their earlier trip. What was it about this man who could ignite raw surges of excitement in her by merely looking at her? It was obvious that he was up to no good. There was every possibility he was involved in all sorts of unscrupulous activities, perhaps even arson.

Perhaps even murder.

No, she reminded herself, he hadn't been in Houston when Calvin McDonough died. And despite Ariel's hunch, the police had found no evidence that the death had been anything other than an accident. Still it was peculiar. The mysterious phone call from the airport, a "convenient" fire that might have destroyed a near bankrupt company—and certainly made a mess of its records. Too many coincidences. She tried to sort through the muddle of facts, but her thinking was fuzzy and her body buzzing with exhaustion.

"If you want to curl up for a nap, you can use my shoulder," Ben said, his voice a seductive murmur that slid across the space between them and coiled around her body.

"No, thanks. I'm fine," Gayle lied, blinking her gritty eyelids and clasping her hands so tightly they hurt. What was he doing to her? She'd read somewhere once that danger, excitement, and sexual arousal were closely aligned. Perhaps her elemental reaction to Ben was simply a by-product of an adrenaline rush. Goodness knows there had been enough excitement going on to keep her glands working overtime. It was certainly confusing. She didn't know whether to be angry with him, afraid of him, or to pounce on him.

Gayle frowned and shook her head. She was so tired she wasn't even making sense to herself. Sighing, she let her head drop back against the seat and closed her eyes. She'd sort all this out tomorrow.

Ben glanced toward Gayle and grinned as she began to slip sideways on the leather seat. Out like a light. Keeping an eye on the almost deserted freeway and his left hand on the wheel, he leaned over and, with his free arm, scooped her relaxed body next to him. She barely stirred except for a kittenish snuggling as she nestled her head against his chest and uttered a barely audible, but definitely contented, sigh.

God, but she felt good against him. Soft curves and sweet smell. He nuzzled his face in the silky strands of her chocolate-colored hair and reveled in the scent of her. Like wildflowers and sea air.

He stroked the velvety nap of her sleeve and fought the urge of his aching fingers to test the soft mound of her breast. What was this woman doing to him? He'd never met anyone quite like her. And he'd met his share of women in his thirty-five, nearly thirty-six, years. This one was different.

An odd feeling of ownership crept over him. He almost laughed aloud. He could just imagine her reaction to that. It hadn't taken him long to learn that the kitten had claws. Her fluttery southern belle act had fooled him for a while—he was glad it was only an act. He'd discovered over the years that he quickly grew tired of gushy, clinging women. Gram had always said he'd meet his match some day and the sparks would fly. Was Gayle his sparkler?

With all the complications caused by Cal's death and the mess with the company, maybe meeting Gayle now wasn't the best timing in the world, but he'd be damned if he'd walk away. He wanted her and he was going to have her. If she was determined to nose around places where he'd rather she didn't and stir up things before he was ready, he'd just have to watch her very carefully. Ben knew she was suspicious of him. The first thing he'd have to do would be to gain her trust.

Then when Gayle stirred slightly and her hand shifted to his upper thigh, Ben sucked in a whistle and gave a mocking grin. Well, maybe not the first thing.

A few minutes later, the station wagon pulled into the drive near the breezeway. Ariel roused when the engine stopped. "Are we home already?"

"Yes," Ben answered, and gave Gayle a gentle shake. She didn't respond. "Gayle, wake up." He shook her again. Still no response except the measured breathing of deep sleep.

Ariel leaned over the seat, rubbing her eyes with her fists and yawning. "If she went to sleep, you'll never be able to wake her."

"What are you talking about?"

"She's the soundest sleeper I've ever seen. We used to laugh about it in college. That's why we made such good roommates. I could hammer away all night and never bother her. Once she goes to sleep, an earthquake

63

wouldn't wake her. You may as well throw a blanket over her and leave her in the car."

"I'm not leaving her in the car."

"Suit yourself," Ariel said, staggering from the back-seat and slamming the door behind her. "But, trust me, she's out."

Ben carried Gayle, still snuggled against his chest, and followed behind Ariel as she stumbled into the house and climbed the stairs. At the door to Gayle's room, Ben said, "You look a little bleary-eyed yourself. Go to bed. I'll tuck her in." When Ariel hesitated, he grinned. "It's okay. Until she's conscious, she's safe."

With a little balancing and juggling, Ben managed to turn on a lamp and pull back the covers of Gayle's bed. "It's a good thing I spent most of my life toting bananas," he said to the sleeping bundle in his arms. "You're heavier than you look," he added as he deposited her on the smooth sheets. He brushed back a strand of dark hair that had fallen across her face and tangled in the thick sweep of long lashes. "But then you're a *lot* of woman."

He carefully slipped the moccasins from her feet, marveling at their slender softness, running his fingers over their graceful arches, touching the bright red polish her shoes had hidden. "You've even got sexy toes. Honey, it's a good thing I pride myself on self-control or Ariel would have reason to worry."

Standing with his hands on his hips, he looked down at her clothes and frowned. Should he or shouldn't he? "Pretend she's your sister," he muttered to himself as he reached for the snap of her jeans. He couldn't let her sleep in her clothes. He tried to keep one eye closed as he slid down the zipper and gently eased the jeans over her hips. It didn't help. He could see plenty with the other one.

"Holy hell, honey," he groaned as he stripped her long legs from their confinement and tossed the jeans in a corner. "It was bad enough to fantasize about what you were wearing underneath." His gaze was riveted to the tiny scrap of blue satin and lace that was more tantalizing than anything he'd conjured up in his imagination.

Desire rose hot and painful. "Where's your self-control now, Lyons?"

Of its own accord, his hand went to one slender ankle and slowly slipped up the silky skin to the curve of her calf. His thumb traced the delicate bones of her knee. His palm gently kneaded the soft swell of her outer thigh. When Gayle stirred slightly, rubbing closer, increasing the pressure against his callused hand, and made a tiny breathy sound in the back of her throat, heat ripped through him like a flashfire.

He tried to stop then. He really did. But his fingers had a mind of their own, and they eased upward to run themselves along the edge of lace stretched across the flat abdomen glowing golden in the lamplight. He could almost feel his pupils dilate as his eyes devoured the dark triangle shadowed beneath the thin blue sheen. Gayle had a body that was made for love, the kind that made men walk into walls.

Ben knew he was pressing the limits of his self-control, but he had to have one taste of that enticing skin. It beckoned him like a Lorelei, and he lowered his head and touched his lips to the tempting flesh above the lace barrier. The warm, sweet smell of her filled his lungs and bewitched his mind. His tongue wandered across her stomach and the moist tip dipped to taste her navel.

Gayle gave a little cry of pleasure, arched her back, and tangled her fingers in the tawny mane at her belly.

Ben stiffened and lifted his head. Her eyes were closed and her breath was still slow and deep, though maybe a bit more ragged than before. Cursing himself for seven kinds of a fool, he carefully disentangled himself and stood. Her lips were sleep swollen and slightly parted, almost begging to be kissed.

For several seconds he stared at those lips, licking his own and hurting with the ache in his groin. A childhood memory floated up of a fairy tale Gram had read of a prince and a sleeping beauty. He bent and kissed her gently, nibbling at the soft fullness. Then he straightened back up and waited.

Gayle only sighed and turned onto her side.

"Well, it worked for the prince."

He strode to the dresser, yanked open a drawer, and rummaged for a nightgown. When he heard the clink of keys, he smiled at Gayle's poor choice of a hiding place. Ben couldn't find a gown, but then he didn't look too hard. All the other little lacy scraps of red and beige and black slipping through his fingers were driving him crazy—reminding him of the blue ones riding low on the lush curves of the sleeping woman. Finally, he slammed the drawer and stomped back to the bed. He flipped the sheet over her body and beat down the urge to climb in beside her.

"Princess, that's the best I can do tonight. Hell, I haven't even got a sister."

66

Gayle's lashes fluttered and her eyes opened. Her arms were wound around a pillow in a lover's embrace, and for a moment she lay quietly savoring the elusive traces of a fading dream. When the full import of her dreams hit her, she almost blushed. They had been wildly erotic and all of them filled with Ben Lyons. They seemed so real she could almost feel his callused hands and soft lips on her body. So real that she could almost swear he'd been in her bed.

Her heart lurched and with a faint feeling of dread, her hand stole out to feel the mattress beside her. Empty. Thank God. Now she felt silly. It was only a dream after all. But what a dream. Her whole body still felt the effects of it, and she squirmed with discomfort. Damn that man!

Shoving away the sensual fantasies, Gayle yawned and stretched and sat up. She ran her hand over the velour top she still wore and frowned. Had she slept in her clothes? How had she gotten to bed? The last thing she remembered was riding home with Ben and Ariel after the fire.

She blinked her eyes and frowned at the clock. It was almost noon. Oh, no! She was supposed to be at the plant with Winston hours ago.

She bounded out of bed and ran to the door. "Ariel!" she yelled down the hall.

Mrs. Jenkins came out of Ariel's room with a dust cloth in her hand. "She's eating out on the patio. Said to tell you to come on down when you woke up."

"But I was supposed to go to the plant with Winston this morning."

"Mr. Dasher called earlier. With all the hullabaloo

going on, he said there wasn't much point going in until they got things cleaned up and sorted out. He said he'd come by later on this afternoon. Now you get dressed and go on down. I've fixed a nice brunch for you girls.'' She disappeared back into Ariel's room.

It hadn't dawned on Gayle until then that she had on nothing but bikini panties and a pink velour top. In her room she found her jeans neatly folded on a chair and the keys to Uncle Cal's study lying on top. She didn't even remember taking them off. Ariel must have helped her undress. It wouldn't be the first time. Even Greg used to tease her about how soundly she slept. She couldn't help it. Once she closed her eyes, she never remembered a thing. Nothing would rouse her.

Quickly she showered and dressed in a red jumpsuit and sandals. When Gayle found her friend on the patio, Ariel was reading the paper and sipping a cup of herb tea.

"Good morning." Ariel smiled and folded the newspaper. "There's nothing about the fire in the morning edition. I guess there wasn't time. Here," she said, picking up the teapot; "have some Red Zinger."

"I'd rather have coffee if there is any. I need the caffeine."

"There's some on the cart, I think." Ariel waved her hand toward a rattan trolley parked in an alcove near the patio table. "That stuff's going to rot your stomach."

"Maybe so." Gayle grinned as she poured a mug full of the steaming brew. They had a longstanding, but good-natured, disagreement about the merits of coffee versus herb teas. Ariel thought herb tea would cure anything. The two of them had drunk gallons of it after Greg died.

Ariel ladled a pink concoction into a bowl and set it at Gayle's place. "Mrs. Jenkins's special strawberry soup. It's fantastic. And there's quiche on the warming tray."

While Gayle ate, Ariel rattled on about the morning's events. "Did Mrs. Jenkins tell you that Winston called? He'll be over later. He said Mr. Brewer thinks it will take several days to clean up the damage and several more before they have things operational again. There was a lot about the fire on the morning news on radio and TV, but we slept through it. And, oh, yes, somebody named Glenn Sands called. He's from the fire department, and he's coming over at four thirty to talk to us. Arson investigation," she added in a conspiratorial undertone.

Gayle nodded absently. She felt guilty not being able to focus on all the concerns involved with Uncle Cal's death and the disasters connected with McDonough Bearings. After all, that's why she was here. She was committed to helping Ariel, but at the moment something else preyed on her mind. She had to ask. "Ariel," she said finally, "how did I get to bed last night?"

"Ben carried you in. You zonked out in the car coming home. He offered to tuck you in and I said okay. Are you mad at me?"

Gayle ground her teeth and she was sure smoke was coming out her ears. "Not at you, no," she ground out. "You didn't undress me?"

Ariel looked stricken. Her freckles stood out like polka dots as her eyes widened and she slowly shook her head.

"Damn!"

Ariel jumped up. "Listen, I've got to go to the drugstore and get some shampoo. Do you need anything?"

"Just a sharp surgical knife and somebody to help hold him."

Fighting back a giggle, Ariel beat a hasty retreat.

Gayle poured another cup of coffee and plotted ways to do slow and agonizing bodily harm to Ben Lyons. How dare he take advantage of her while she was unconscious! And knowing him and his overactive libido, she was sure that he had. But exactly what had gone on? How much of what she dreamed was real? She groaned at the thought. Never mind that the dreams were delicious and she had thoroughly enjoyed every wanton moment of them. That was beside the point.

Strangle him with rusty barbed wire. No. The first thing she was going to do was stake him over an ant bed and . . .

She was staring out toward the murky water of the bayou, so lost in machinations of terrible torture and venomous pronouncements that she failed to notice she was no longer alone.

"Good morning," Ben said, and dropped a kiss on her pursed lips. When she opened her mouth to protest, he kissed her again.

This time it was more than a quick peck. For a moment the incredible softness of his mouth and the tantalizing play of his tongue teasing its way around the edge of her lips thrilled her into forgetting her fury with him. Then she remembered and shoved him away.

"What are you doing?" she sputtered.

"Kissing you good morning. Or is it afternoon already?" Dropping into the chair Ariel had vacated, he mopped his sweating face with the towel hanging around his neck.

"And just what do you think gives you the right to

kiss me, whatever the time of day?" Her voice was frigid but her eyes were blazing blue fire.

Cocking one eyebrow, he gave a lazy, cheeky grin. "Sorry, princess, I forgot that I'm farther along in this relationship than you are."

"I'm not aware that we *have* a relationship, Mr. Lyons." When Gayle's eyes raked the length of him with a haughty disdain, her gaze froze mid-rake. Her mouth went dry. He wasn't wearing a stitch except for a tiny pair of purple satin shorts and scruffy-looking jogging shoes. Sweat glistened on his muscular sun-baked shoulders and ran in rivulets through the golden curls on his chest. She forced her eyes away from a droplet that was trickling in a maddeningly slow trail down his tautly corded abdomen, swallowed, and tried to resume her effort at elegant contempt.

"Don't give me such a hard time, honey. I've just run five miles trying to salvage my sanity." He downed the remains of the now tepid Red Zinger in Ariel's cup and mopped his face again. He looked at her and his topaz gaze almost melted the zipper of her jumpsuit. One corner of his mouth lifted and he shook his head. "It didn't help. Self-control is vastly overrated." He licked his lips. "I think I need to kiss you again."

With a quick catlike move Ben was hovering over her, one hand on each arm of her chair, effectively trapping her in a wrought-iron cage.

"Don't . . . you . . . dare."

His mouth stopped its descent. He looked almost hurt. "Princess, what's wrong? I thought after last night . . ."

"Exactly what happened last night? After you carried me to my room."

71

"You know about that, huh?" That disarming grin was back. "Not as much as I would have liked. I put you in bed, and because I hated for you to have to sleep in your clothes, I pulled off your shoes and jeans and tucked the covers under your chin."

"That's all?"

"Essentially." The word hung between and his grin broadened.

"Why do I have the feeling there was more?"

"Wishful thinking?"

"Damn you, Ben Lyons! You deserve to be shot! Let me up," she said, pushing against his arms. "I have work to do."

Ben immediately let her up and watched her cute little bottom wave like a red flag as she stomped away. "You were right, Gram," he said under his breath. "It's like the Fourth of July."

Determined to get her mind on business and off Ben Lyons, Gayle unlocked the door to the study and stepped inside. She still had mountains of material to go through. Taking a seat behind the big desk, she swiveled back and forth absently. She didn't even know what she was looking for, but something told her that this room held secrets. Maybe it was her imagination or maybe it was something in the quiet loneliness of the room. There was a kind of void, an emptiness without its vibrant owner.

Rooms, like people, had personalities and this one was no exception. Calvin McDonough's study was a reflection of the man. Gayle realized that she needed to understand the man before she could begin to understand the mysteries surrounding him. Using bits of information she had gathered from Ariel and things she could surmise from these private surroundings, she began to piece together a sketch of the old man.

She could tell from his desk and papers that he was well organized and meticulous, from the furnishings that he valued fine things. Despite the fact that he was a bachelor, he had made a lovely home. He was a hard worker with an iron will, yet he grew roses and displayed Ariel's artwork with pride. He was loyal and inspired loyalty in others. His home was conservative, yet at seventy-six he jogged every day and drove a red Corvette.

As young men, Cal and his older brother Andrew, Ariel's grandfather, had come to the United States from Scotland determined to make their fortunes. Unfortunately, the time they picked to arrive was the summer of 1929. That fall the great economic crash made it a time for losing fortunes, not making them. For the next five or six years, the two traveled the country picking up jobs where they could. One summer in Colorado, Andrew met and fell in love with Virginia Conn, Ariel's grandmother and the only daughter of the owner of a small brewery near Denver. Andrew stayed on to become partners (and make his fortune) with his father-in-law and Cal headed toward the Texas coast.

While working in a machine shop in Houston, Cal got the idea for a special kind of bearing and began to save his money. The chronicle of pictures on the walls told the story of his pride in the founding and growth of McDonough Bearings.

Gayle walked to the neat display of photographs covering one paneled wall and studied each one carefully. Some of the earlier pictures were a bit fuzzy, but she could identify a young, confident Calvin McDonough with his arm around a shorter, curly-haired young man who, despite his 1940s attire, looked remarkably like Winston Dasher.

She searched among the early collection and found Martin Brewer, no more than eighteen with his dark hair and faint mustache, grinning into the camera. Later George Schulze was there with bow tie and full, wavy locks. She studied the company's citations for the war effort, followed the growth of the plant from a small tin building to a large modern structure. But the person who drew her attention was always the tall, broad-shouldered Calvin McDonough. Gayle couldn't imagine why he'd never married. He'd been a handsome man in his youth with a thick mane of hair and an angular face. The mane had turned to white in his later years when he had posed for the corporate studio portrait, but she could still see the energy and determination in his lined face. Not much would escape those piercing eyes.

And at that moment Gayle knew that as long as Calvin McDonough lived, he would have never allowed his business to go bankrupt. Never. And she couldn't comprehend a reason for this vibrant man's relinquishing the reins of his corporation to putter among the roses. It didn't fit with her perception of his character. McDonough Bearings was his life. She *knew* it. Something was very wrong in that company and she vowed to discover the source.

"Help me, Cal," Gayle said aloud to the man in the picture. "Tell me your secrets."

She stood there for a moment as if she were expecting him to speak.

The safe. That's where secrets are kept.

CHAPTER FIVE

Kneeling inside the supply closet, Gayle moved a box of printer ribbons and shoved aside a heavy carton of continuous paper to reveal the wall safe hidden behind them. She dialed the numbers of Ariel's birthday and added fourteen. The handle turned easily and the door swung open a fraction.

Gayle paused for a deep breath and closed her eyes for a moment. She was an intruder into private, personal, hidden things. A sensation of thinly veiled uncertainty crept over her.

It was so quiet she could hear the tick of the mantel clock and her pulse thudding in her throat.

She could almost feel the piercing eyes of Calvin McDonough watching her, and the hair on the back of her neck prickled. Her hand trembled and her palm was damp as she gripped the cold metal handle. She chided herself for her incongruous behavior. Why was she so nervous about such a simple thing as looking in a safe? This was ridiculous.

Silly, a part of her affirmed.

But another corner of her awareness urged her to slam the door, pack her bags, and head back to Denver.

Retreat to safety. Flee from the threat of violence. Run like crazy.

"You gutless wonder," the strong part of her muttered. "Are you expecting the boogeyman to jump out of there?"

No. But she knew she would find another piece of the puzzle and would come another step closer to a commitment that reeked of danger. Someone, maybe even Ben, a tiny voice reminded, was involved in something to do with McDonough Bearings that was causing desperate, iniquitous acts of arson and even . . . murder.

Yes, murder. She shivered. For despite all evidence to the contrary, Gayle's hunch was growing as strong as Ariel's. And she knew that her reticence to open the safe, and thus become more deeply entangled in the situation, had its roots in her old fears.

Once and for all she had to decide. Was she going to perpetuate the anxiety caused by Greg's traumatic death? Was she going to allow fear to encumber her forever?

How *stupid.*

What had happened to her backbone, her confidence, her ideals? Neither she nor the Summers Profile was responsible for what happened to Greg. She *must* accept that. It was the twisted personality the Profile had so accurately described who had killed him. And if that same instrument could ferret out the perpetrator here, she would test everybody in Houston if necessary. Certainly she would be cautious, but she could not allow fear to rule her life and actions.

Gayle reached down into herself, pulled out a double handful of courage, dusted it off, and set her jaw with a fierce determination. She was going to get to the bottom of this insidious mess, and she was going to start with this safe.

Taking a deep, fortifying breath, she yanked the door open and peered inside the small steel hiding place. Gayle gave a short self-mocking laugh when she saw the sparse contents. After the savage diatribe she had subjected herself to, seeing such ordinary things seemed anticlimactic. There was cash, about three thousand dollars she estimated as she fanned the packets of bills, a small collection of gold coins, a maroon velvet jewelry case, and a common plastic folding pouch labeled "Important Papers."

She glanced over the coins. Because Gayle's father was an avid coin collector, she had absorbed enough of his expertise to tell that while Uncle Cal's were valuable, they were not remarkable. Next she picked up the velvet box and opened it. It held an old-fashioned gold pocket watch and chain. The delicate scrollwork on the front of the case was worn almost smooth, and Gayle squinted to read the faint engraving on its back.

For all time, the inscription read. Then the initials, *C. M.* and the date, *1929.*

Smiling, she ran her thumb across the letters in a gesture she knew Calvin McDonough had repeated thousands of times. Gayle could feel that it was a treasured possession. Inside the hands were permanently pointed to a quarter of three and opposite the watch face, a tiny lock of tawny gold hair rested atop a small photograph. Gayle pushed aside the strand that was tied with a bit of thread and studied the young woman's picture. It was a face filled with laughter and love and framed with a jaunty scarf and light hair cut in a curly bob reminiscent of the twenties. The likeness was crazed with the spidery lines of age, and here and there spots were worn smooth as if the thumb had often touched there as well.

Who was she? Gayle wondered. A sweetheart of his youth? Obviously Cal had loved her once. What had become of her? Gayle's imagination began to weave all sorts of romantic scenarios around the tall, broad-shouldered man and the laughing girl in the picture. Finally she forced herself to cease her musings and close the case.

Almost reverently, Gayle returned the watch to its maroon velvet box and placed it back in the safe. Next she picked up the plastic document pouch and unfolded it. Most pockets were identified according to content. Will, deeds, insurance policies, stocks and bonds. These she didn't disturb. Ariel would need to check them later. Two pockets of papers weren't identified. The first, she discovered when she examined the contents, held the legal documents pertaining to Ariel's guardianship as a teenager.

The second paper caused a puzzled frown. It was a photocopied birth record of a baby girl, Margaret, born in 1930 to Catherine McKeen Cameron and Michael Edward Cameron.

Strange. Why would . . .

"Gayle?"

She was so startled she almost banged her head on the shelf above. Her hand flew to her pounding heart as she looked up to find Winston Dasher standing not three feet away.

She gave a short burst of nervous laughter. "You almost scared the life out of me."

"Sorry. Ariel told me you were in here. I knocked and called, but you must not have heard me," he said, a smile crinkling his eyes. "What in the world are you doing sitting on the floor in the closet?"

"Just going through Mr. McDonough's papers for Ariel." Gayle hurriedly folded the paper she was holding and slipped it back into its pocket.

"Is there anything I can help you with?"

"No, no. Not a thing." Gayle fumbled with the pouch, then crammed it into the safe and stood. Stepping out of the closet, she closed the door behind her, anxious to keep Cal's private treasures from other eyes. It was enough that she had violated his intimate cache without flaunting his secrets before other people.

"I wouldn't mind at all, you know," he said quietly. "Although I wasn't Uncle Cal's personal attorney, I know quite a bit about his business. Things would go more quickly if I worked with you."

"I appreciate the offer, Winston, but I'm almost finished here." The lie slipped out before Gayle had time to examine her motive.

"Did you find anything you have questions about?"

"No, there was just the usual accumulation of personal papers," she lied again. There were scores of questions, but none she was going to ask yet. It was not that she didn't trust Winston, rather that she hesitated to confide her findings to anyone until she had more information. "I'm sorry I missed your call this morning. I'm quite anxious to begin interviewing company personnel and examining the records, but I'm afraid after all the excitement last night, Ariel and I both slept late."

"Nothing could have been done today. I was at the plant earlier and things were still in chaos. Everyone was pitching in trying to estimate the extent of the damage and to salvage as much as possible. Perhaps it will be more settled in a few days and you can begin."

Gayle frowned. "With the company's precarious financial situation, I hate to delay too long."

"I understand," Winston said. "But my advice is to forget any ideas about trying to save the business. It's too far gone and now the fire has complicated things even further. I think it would be best for everyone concerned if you could convince Ariel to declare bankruptcy."

"Or better yet, sell McDonough Bearings to me," a gruff voice said.

Gayle glanced toward the doorway of the study. Ben Lyons was casually leaning against the jamb. He'd probably been eavesdropping again. As he pushed himself away from his post and sauntered toward them, Gayle found herself staring at the disreputable-looking jeans hanging low on his hips. The screaming-yellow T-shirt stretched across his chest was embellished with the caricature of a busty female banana, winking one big eye and teasing down her peel. Bold black script shamelessly invited: "Take it off and try me."

"Dasher," Ben said, giving the impeccably dressed Winston a curt nod.

"Lyons," Winston replied with a similar degree of coolness.

"So, what are you two up to?" Ben asked, rocking back on the heels of his scruffy jogging shoes and sticking his fingers in the waistband of his jeans.

"Gayle was going through some things in Cal's safe," Winston answered.

Ben lifted his eyebrows. "Find anything interesting?"

"I haven't had time to check everything yet, but it seems to be just the usual stuff."

"I see." Ben sauntered over to the wall of photographs.

"Did you want something in particular?" Gayle asked Ben, who was bent over squinting at one of the early snapshots.

"No, it can wait. Don't let me interrupt you two. Go right ahead with your conversation. Pretend I'm not here."

Gayle shrugged and turned to Winston, who looked amused. "I was about to ask you to dinner tonight," he said.

"She can't go," Ben said, not looking up from the picture he was studying.

"I beg your pardon! I believe I'm competent to make my own decisions," Gayle said, her back stiffening.

Ben walked back to them and put his arm around Gayle. "Honey, don't get in such an uproar. I knew you were anxious to talk to Martin Brewer, so I invited him over to dinner tonight. Ariel said she was sure that you wouldn't mind."

Gayle shrugged his arm away. "I see." Her tone was frosty. However, good sense told her that she did indeed need to speak with Mr. Brewer before the board meeting tomorrow. She turned a warm smile on Winston. "Why don't you join us here for dinner?"

"I'd like that. Thanks for inviting me."

"Sure your girlfriend won't mind?" Ben asked.

Winston looked blank. "Girlfriend?"

"The blonde from last night."

"Oh, her," Winston said sheepishly. "I barely know

the woman. I was invited to a party in Galveston by one of my clients, and he asked me to give her a ride."

Rocking back on his heels again, Ben smirked as if he didn't believe a word of it. "Must have been some ride."

After an awkward silence, Winston cleared his throat. "If you'll excuse me, I need to get back to my office. What time shall I be here this evening?"

"Why don't you come about six thirty for drinks?" Gayle walked the attorney to the study door and said her good-byes. When he had gone she turned and stomped back to Ben. Her hands were on her hips and her eyes blazed with familiar blue fire. "You are, without a doubt, the most infuriating man I've ever known."

Ben grinned. Grinned!

"And you," he said, flicking the end of her nose, "are the most gorgeous woman I've ever known. Wanna smooch?"

Gayle tried to stay angry. Tried to keep a straight face. It was impossible when he was standing there with his disarming lopsided grin and that ridiculously suggestive T-shirt. "Smooch?" she said, fighting a chuckle. *"Smooch?"*

"Yeah, you know, make out—smooch," he said, reaching for her. "Here, I'll show you."

Gayle lithely sidestepped his embrace. "No, thanks. I understand the term. I just couldn't believe you said it. What are you doing in here?"

"You mean besides trying to save you from the Brooks Brothers Romeo?" He whipped a crumpled envelope out of his back pocket and handed it to her. "I wanted to give you this."

"Because Winston has charming manners and doesn't

look as if he selected his clothes from a rummage sale, doesn't mean he's a Romeo. He's simply being polite. Perhaps you could take a few lessons." She looked at the envelope in her hand. "What's this?"

"My proposal to buy McDonough Bearings. You said you wanted it in writing. I'd appreciate it if you would talk it over with Ariel and convince her to sell her shares to me. I'd like to take over as soon as possible."

A sobering, ego-deflating realization backhanded her. Was this the reason he had been coming on to her with such a desperate urgency? Of course. She was the key to gaining control of the company. And the scoundrel had turned his sex appeal on high and aimed it at her like a laser gun. It was an effective weapon. And she fell for it. Dumb, dumb, dumb!

"We'll see," Gayle said, her voice slightly unsteady. "Now, if you'll excuse me . . ."

"I can take a hint." Ben threw up his hands in mock surrender. "I was just leaving." He grasped Gayle's shoulders and looked at her solemnly. "Please consider my offer carefully. It's very important and the best thing for Ariel . . . and you. I don't want either of you to get hurt."

Gayle felt a shiver go up her spine and she broke out in goose bumps as she stared up at him.

"And, princess," he added, giving her a quick peck, "I don't want you going out with other men."

He turned and left. Gayle stood as if bolted to the floor, her emotions chaotic, conflicting, and incomprehensible.

"Gayle?" Ariel called from the doorway. "Glenn Sands is here."

Gayle frowned and tried to rouse an association. "Glenn Sands?"

"You know. The man from arson investigations. Will you come with me to talk to him?"

Gayle locked the study door and followed Ariel into the living room, where a thick-set man in a brown suit sat waiting for them. When they entered, he rose and adjusted his glasses. Ariel introduced Gayle and when they were seated, the investigator pulled out a small notebook and pen.

"Ms. McDonough, would you tell me in your own words what you know about this fire at the plant?"

Ariel ran one hand through her thick brush of hair. "Not much really. I was asleep when Mr. Brewer called and told me about it. It was around one thirty this morning. Mr. Brewer said the night watchman had spotted the fire, phoned in the alarm, then called him. Gayle and I, and Ben Lyons, drove out there, but it was almost out by then. It must have been a little after two when we arrived."

Mr. Sands nodded and scribbled in his notebook. "Ben Lyons?"

After Ariel explained his connection, the investigator scribbled some more. "I understand that McDonough Bearings is in financial trouble." When Ariel confirmed this, he said, "How much insurance does the company carry?"

"I have no idea. Mr. Brewer or Mr. Schulze would know that better than I." Her eyes were wide as she stared from Sands to Gayle. "Surely you don't think that *I* set the place on fire for the insurance."

"Then you believe it was arson and not an accident?"

"Of course it was arson," Ariel said with a stubborn set to her square jaw. "Wasn't it?"

The man pulled off his glasses and rubbed his eyes. "Let's just say that it's a highly suspicious fire." Replacing his glasses, Mr. Sands continued his questioning. "Do you have any knowledge that the sprinkler and alarms systems were on and working?"

"I don't know a thing about the plant, the insurance, or the sprinkler. I only inherited it from Uncle Calvin this week. I hadn't even seen the place in years until we went there this morning. And," Ariel huffed with righteous indignation, "I certainly wouldn't set fire to McDonough Bearings. I don't need the money. Why, I'm doing everything I can to save the business from declaring bankruptcy." Leaning forward, she waggled her finger as she added, "But let me tell you, there are some mighty peculiar things going on around here."

Gayle spoke for the first time. "Could you tell us how it happened?" What she wanted to ask was if gasoline had been used, but she didn't. She didn't want to hear damning evidence. She didn't want to suspect Ben.

"We're still investigating the circumstances."

This man wasn't giving away any information. Gayle tried another tactic. "What time did the fire start?"

"The alarm was called in at one thirteen." He turned to a fresh page in his notebook and looked up. "Does either of you have any idea who might want to burn the plant?"

"Yes, I do," Ariel announced. "Find who killed my uncle Calvin and you'll find who set the fire."

Leaning back in the bathtub, Gayle closed her eyes and tried to relax, but her mind was a whirlpool. She was emotionally exhausted. After Ariel dropped the bomb-shell about her theory of Uncle Cal's murder, Glenn Sands spent another hour questioning them. When he finally finished his interview, it was almost six. Their dinner guests would be arriving shortly.

Neither she nor Ariel had mentioned to Investigator Sands the gasoline on Ben Lyons's handkerchief or that he was just returning home when the two of them were leaving for the fire. Ariel probably hadn't thought of it or considered the possibility of Ben's implication, but it plagued Gayle. Gnawed away at her. She didn't have to be reminded that it was usually the owners of a failing business who were responsible for arson. Collecting in-surance to recoup huge losses was a powerful incentive. As the major shareholders, Ariel and Ben were the logi-cal suspects. She knew Ariel hadn't done it.

It had been one thirty-five when Ariel backed the Corvette out of the garage. Gayle remembered looking at the clock on the dash. Could Ben have made it from the fire to the house in twenty-two minutes? It had taken them more than half an hour to drive the distance this morning, and Ben hadn't been poking along. He couldn't have made it in twenty-two minutes.

Or could he?

Of course not. Ben Lyons might be infuriating and obnoxious and disconcerting. He might have all the fi-nesse of a Neanderthal, but he was no firebug.

Ariel had declared that since they were having com-pany, they would dress for dinner. Of course "dress" to Ariel could mean anything from feather boas to clean socks. After rummaging through her things, Gayle fi-nally decided on a long black crepe skirt, full and comfortable, and a green silk shirt. She added a colorful scarf sash and gold jewelry.

When Gayle came downstairs she found Ariel in the living room with Winston and Martin Brewer. Ariel looked lovely in a handpainted silk caftan in an Indian design of rust, turquoise, and white. Both men, in conservative business suits, were having cocktails and Ariel was drinking what looked like her latest passion, a Fuzzy Navel.

Winston saw Gayle first and rose to greet her. His smile was open and warm as he took her hand and held it. "How beautiful you look this evening."

"Thank you." Gayle returned his smile and nodded to Martin Brewer, who stood to acknowledge her entrance. "Please be seated, Mr. Brewer. I know you've had an exhausting day with all the turmoil at the plant. We appreciate your joining us tonight and we'll try not to keep you late."

"It has been busy," the courtly gray-haired gentleman said, "but the company of two such lovely ladies is relaxing to these old bones."

"May I get you a drink?" Winston asked, heading for the bar. "Wine or something else?"

"I made a whole pitcher of Fuzzy Navels," Ariel piped up.

"Great," a deep voice said behind her. "I love Fuzzy Navels."

Gayle turned toward the familiar voice and her eyes widened. Ben Lyons was magnificent, overwhelming, and stunningly, heart-stoppingly handsome. His pearl gray suit was exquisitely cut and skillfully mated with a white silk shirt, contrasting sharply with his deep tan and a paisley tie in shades of dusky rose and soft gray. A casual puff of rose silk spilled from his breast pocket. His hair was tamed into a full shock of golden lights, and his topaz eyes gleamed with amusement.

Her mouth must have been agape with astonishment as she looked him up and down, because he chuckled and said, "Are you surprised that I clean up so good?"

She was indeed. But how gauche of him to mention it. Of course Ben Lyons never adhered to social niceties, and tact was not in his vocabulary. What was even more grating was how often he read her mind, blurted it out, then dared her to deny it.

Then she laughed—at herself mostly, for her priggish attitude. His blunt comments always had the irritating effect of bringing out her pompously Victorian streak. A holdover from her genteel Mississippi upbringing, she supposed. She was really quite weary of acting the offended maiden to his audacious comments. Sometimes she thought he pushed her deliberately. This time Ben's typically open and direct manner demanded a like response.

She cocked one eyebrow. "A little. You look damned good."

Ben roared with laughter. "Princess, you never cease to amaze me." He greeted the others and turned back to Gayle. Throwing one arm around her and pulling her close, he said in a low, suggestive tone, "You look damned good yourself. Want to live dangerously and try a Fuzzy Navel?"

"I think I'll have wine. I'm never quite sure what Ariel puts in those concoctions she discovers."

"It's only vodka, orange juice, and peach schnapps. It's almost as delicious as you are," he murmured as he nuzzled and nipped her ear.

Gayle's eyes closed as warmth flashed through her and her knees went weak. A heady scent of musk and spice engulfed her. She almost forgot the others in the room. Almost. Suddenly stiffening, her eyes flew open and she stepped away. Thank goodness the others were talking about Ariel's upcoming show and hadn't noticed the exchange.

"I believe I'll pass. After living through a few of her exotic drink phases, I've learned the hard way to avoid B52s, Kamikazes, and Orphan Annies."

"I've heard of the first two, but what in the world is an Orphan Annie?"

"The ingredients escape me, but it's guaranteed to curl your hair and make your eyes bug out."

When Ben laughed and walked to the bar to get their drinks from Winston, Gayle approached Ariel and Martin Brewer, who were sitting together on one of the couches in deep conversation.

"Tell him, Gayle," Ariel said with a wave of her hand, "that I am determined to keep McDonough Bearings from bankruptcy whatever the cost."

Mr. Brewer sighed and looked at Gayle, who shrugged and said, "She's determined and I'm committed to help." Gayle sank into the soft cushions beside the pleasant-faced executive.

"She's as stubborn as Calvin. He had been keeping the company afloat from his personal funds for several months. He wouldn't listen to anybody. Just like a mule when he had his head set on something." Worry lines creased his brow and his eyes took on a haunted look. "I told Calvin when he made me president two years ago that I wasn't the man for the job. I'm a plant superintendent, nothing more. I was due to retire this past June, but he persuaded me to stay on until fall. He said we'd have some young blood coming in to turn things around."

"Who was the young blood?" Gayle asked.

"Me," Ben said, handing Gayle a glass of white wine.

Maybe, maybe not, Gayle thought as she accepted the drink without comment. Why would Cal hand his beloved company over to an outsider? "Mr. Brewer, you knew Ariel's uncle for a long time. Perhaps you can explain something which has been puzzling me. Why did he decide to retire from the company? It doesn't fit the image I have of him."

"You know, I'm not sure," the older man answered. "Calvin was always pretty close-mouthed about his personal business. The Scot in him, I guess."

"I can explain it," Ben said. "Two years ago his doctor discovered a serious heart problem and strongly advised him to retire immediately. He was forbidden any strenuous activity and only allowed to go to the office for a few hours each week."

"That's strange," Ariel said. "I spoke with Dr. Phegley after the funeral. He's been Uncle Cal's physician and friend for years and was shocked over his death. He talked about how vital and robust my uncle was. They played tennis together every week. Dr. Phegley said Uncle Cal beat the pants off him just last Tuesday."

"I often saw him golfing with his cronies at the country club," Winston added. "Where did you ever hear a tale like that, Lyons?"

Ben was frowning. "From him," he said quietly.

Mrs. Jenkins announced dinner and the subject was dropped, but Gayle puzzled over this latest enigma as the group adjourned to the dining room.

The more she learned, the more muddled the situation became. Did Calvin McDonough tell Ben some story about his heart? Why? Or, she wondered, remembering the shares of the company signed over to Ben, was this a fabrication devised to explain Ben's takeover? What hold did Ben have over the old man to make him relinquish the business he held so dear? Was it blackmail? Gayle couldn't seem to picture Ben as a blackmailer. It went against his whole personality.

At the table, Ben skillfully arranged the seating so that Ariel and he were at the head and foot. Gayle sat on his right with Martin Brewer beside her. Winston was left as odd man out on the opposite side.

As they ate another of Mrs. Jenkins's delightful meals, Gayle explained her role in evaluating the company for Ariel. "While I understand that it's impossible to examine the records for a few days, I'd like to begin testing with the Summers Profile immediately."

"The Summers Profile?" Mr. Brewer asked.

"Yes, it's a rather simple questionnaire I helped devise. I've found it very useful when dealing with personnel and management matters. We'll start with the officers, upper level management, and staff tomorrow after the board meeting." She explained the procedure while they finished dinner.

"Martin," Ben said after the chocolate torte was served, "have they found out what caused the fire?"

"The arson boys have been nosing around and they're plenty tight with information, but I've heard a few rumors. I haven't got the whole picture yet, but a mighty peculiar thing happened. When the shift came on this morning, one of the foremen found Roosevelt Weems—he's the night watchman who reported the fire

91

—slumped over his desk sound asleep. Nobody could wake him. The foreman got scared and called an ambulance. From what we can figure out, somebody must have doctored his coffee. He usually has a cup or two with his supper at midnight, but his wife has been nagging him about too much caffeine with his high blood pressure so he didn't drink any until later."

Gayle felt an icy prickle. "Do you mean that if the watchman had followed his usual routine, he would have been asleep when the fire broke out?"

Mr. Brewer pursed his lips and nodded.

"I knew it!" Ariel said. "I told Glenn Sands—"

Gayle shot Ariel a sharp glance and cut her off. "What else can you tell us about the fire, Mr. Brewer? How did it start?"

Martin Brewer glanced at Winston, who frowned, then gave a brief assenting nod.

The older man cleared his throat nervously. "Well, we don't have all the facts, you understand, but as near as we can piece together, there were supposed to be two fires. Roosevelt surprised whoever did it before he could set the second one." He glanced toward Ben, then looked at Ariel, almost apologetically. "We didn't want to upset you any more after everything else."

"I appreciate your concern, Mr. Brewer," Ariel said, "but tell us everything."

Martin Brewer took a deep breath and blew it out. He looked like a man being led to the guillotine. "Someone turned off the sprinkler system and disconnected the smoke detectors. In both the plant and part of the offices, he doused several areas of combustible material with a flammable liquid and used some sort of simple ignition device—probably something like a book of matches wrapped around a lighted cigarette. If the night watchman hadn't seen a man running from the building and caught the fire just as it broke out, the whole plant would have burned to the ground."

"A flammable liquid?" Gayle asked quietly. "Like gasoline?"

He nodded.

Gayle felt an intolerable dread building in the pit of her stomach. She couldn't have swallowed another bite of chocolate torte if her life depended on it. Her lips felt frozen and her insides were a writhing mass. Her head swiveled toward Ben and she stared at him.

CHAPTER SIX

The stricken look on Gayle's face hit him like a poleax. Then he remembered the gasoline on his handkerchief. Damn! With so much on his mind, he'd forgotten about it.

He shoved his chair back and stood. "If you'll excuse us," he said, grabbing Gayle's arm, "Gayle looks a little pale. I think she needs some air."

Gayle wrested from his grip. "I do not need air, and I'm not going anywhere with you. I haven't even finished my dessert."

Snatching the fork from her hand, he polished off the torte in Gayle's plate with two huge bites and yanked her up. "You've finished now," he said, pulling her behind him as he stomped toward the patio door.

Once they were outside, Ben caught Gayle by the shoulders and stuck his face so close to hers that their noses almost touched. "What's going on in that pretty little head of yours?" he almost roared as he gave her a shake.

Gayle's teeth were chattering, her eyes wide and unblinking. "I . . . I don't know what you're talking about."

"I think you do. You believe I set the fire, don't you?" He gave her another shake. "Don't you?"

Gayle tried to speak, but she was so frightened she felt as if she were going to swallow her tongue. The dim lights around the patio reflected in the tears shimmering in her eyes. "Please," she whimpered, "you're hurting me."

Immediately Ben relaxed the grip on her shoulders and pulled her close against him. "Oh, honey, I'm sorry," he said, kissing her hair, nuzzling the side of her neck. "God, I wouldn't want to hurt you for the world." He cupped her chin and lifted it to look into her eyes. He gently kissed each lid. "Will you forgive me? Hell, I ought to be keelhauled."

Seeing the sincere concern etching his face, Gayle managed a weak smile. "I'll add keelhauling to my list. It has a certain appeal."

"Oh, princess," he said, and hugged her to him again. "It tore me up to see the look on your face. Have you been imagining I set the fire? I would *never* do something like that. McDonough Bearings is too important to me. I want to buy it, not burn it."

Gayle looked into his eyes, his face. Looked long and hard and deep. "I want to believe you," she whispered.

At that moment the very atmosphere was transformed. The tension charged vibrations sparking between them made a subtle shift and they both trembled with a new awareness, a sensual awareness of one another.

Gayle's nipples sprang into taut peaks and a hot flush suffused her lower belly. Ben pulled her closer against him. A deep groan ripped from him as he closed his

95

eyes and threw back his head. The flush spread lower still.

"Oh, my God," he ground out and his mouth sought hers with a fierce devouring hunger.

Her hunger matched his as moist lips melded, as searching tongues thrust and tasted, as moans were swallowed up in a kiss of such awesome power that Gayle thought she would dissolve in his arms.

Ben tore his mouth away and rained kisses over her face, licked the hollow of her neck. One strong arm scooped her hips closer; the other slipped along her back, fingers splayed and exploring the flesh under slippery green silk. Gayle was seething sensation, mindless abandon, invincible delight arching intimately toward the solid source of pleasure.

"I may die from wanting you," Ben said before he claimed her lips in a savage urgency.

They clung to one another, feeding and being fed, yet starving for more. Blended into a single shadow behind the darkened shrubs surrounding the flagstone patio, they were heedless of time and space.

"Gayle? Are you okay? Gayle?"

Gayle heard her name called from very far away.

"Gayle!" Ariel's voice was frantic.

Breaking the kiss, Gayle tried to speak but her brain was fogged and the words wouldn't come. She had never in her life experienced sensations and emotions of such potency, so blatant and raw. It was overwhelming, frightening. She tried again to speak and finally managed a feeble, "Yes, Ariel."

"Gayle, are you okay?" Ariel called from the back door.

"I'm fine." Her breathing was ragged and her heart was pounding.

"Fine," Ben murmured as he nipped her earlobe. "Woman, what you do to me ought to be against the law."

"Winston and Mr. Brewer have to leave and they wanted to say good night," Ariel called from beyond the flickering shadows.

"I'll be there in a moment, Ariel." She pushed against Ben's chest, but he held her locked to him. "We have to go in."

"My arms won't let go."

Gayle rested her head on his chest and chuckled. "Speak to them firmly. We have to go in."

Ben sighed and loosed his hold. "You go ahead. It's going to take me a while to recover."

"Think it was the Fuzzy Navels that did it?"

He groaned. "Honey, don't mention navels. It reminds me of a sexy little one peeking out above blue satin and lace."

"Ben Lyons!"

She could see the lopsided grin in the moonlight. "I couldn't help it. I haven't got a sister."

"A sister? What are you talking about?"

"Never mind. You'd better go in before I throw you over my shoulder and head for parts unknown." He gave her a quick peck on the nose. "Good night, princess. I'll see you in the morning."

"Good night." She started back to the house.

"Gayle?"

She stopped and turned around to face the man who had awakened a longing in her that was stunning in its intensity. Even now she wanted to run to his arms, wrap herself around him, and lose herself in delicious sensation. "Yes?"

"Have you had a chance to evaluate my proposal to buy the company?"

A freight train hit her. She was stunned. Stunned speechless. He'd been playing games with her. Romancing her to gain her support. She had plastered herself against him like an animal in heat, behaved like a wanton, and he'd been playing games. Gayle wanted to die from the humiliation of it.

"Damn you, Ben Lyons! Damn you! No!" She stomped to the house and slammed the back door so hard it could be heard on the next block.

"God, woman, you're making me crazy!" he shouted at the stars.

His first impulse was to go after her, demand to know what in the hell was going on. He even made a few determined strides toward the house, then thought better of it. By morning she'd be cooled off and they could talk rationally.

Rationally, ha. He, who'd always prided himself on his cool control, never had a rational thought in his head when Gayle Summers was around. In any case, she'd probably start insisting on explanations. Explanations he couldn't give her. The way her sharp little mind worked, he was surprised she hadn't confronted him already. It wouldn't do for her to know that all she had to do was rub against him a couple of times and he would spill anything he knew.

He yanked off his tie and strode to the guest house, muttering all the way.

"Calvin McDonough, you old coot. You've certainly manipulated me into a hell of a mess."

It was long after midnight. Gayle punched her pillow and turned over for what seemed like the two hundred and fourteenth time. Her mind and her body were having a mighty struggle and Ben Lyons was the cause of the conflict. Why did she melt into a puddle when that conniving predator so much as looked at her? Not even Greg had ever made her . . .

No, she thought, punching her pillow and flipping over again. She wouldn't allow herself to think about Ben anymore. Not his libidinous tactics, his outrageous comments, or his sexy lopsided grin. Not his broad shoulders, narrowed gold eyes, or the deep rumble of his voice that made her warm just to hear it.

Nor would she allow herself to remember the smell of him or sweat trickling down a tanned, muscled torso or the feel of his tongue, his lips, his hands.

Through the night, Gayle wrestled and battled and slept and dreamed. Yet it was not thoughts of Ben that riveted her awake at eight the next morning. The moment her eyes fluttered open, it struck her and she sat straight up in the tangled covers.

"Dear Lord, I forgot to lock the safe!"

Relax, she reminded herself. The study was locked. Still, something told her to check it, nagged at her until she got out of bed and grabbed her robe. When she looked in her purse for the study keys, they were missing. They couldn't be; she distinctly remembered putting them there before dinner last night. Dumping the contents of her bag on the dresser, she felt along the lining and searched through the articles again. Gone.

She yanked open the lingerie drawer and clawed around her underwear. The extra set was there.

As Gayle flew downstairs, she passed Ariel coming up. "What's the matter? I was just coming to wake you," Ariel said, following behind Gayle as she charged toward the study.

The door was open and a vacuum cleaner droned inside. Grace Jenkins was humming "Rock of Ages" as she pushed the sweeper back and forth across the floor. When she looked up and saw the women at the door, she smiled and turned off the machine. "Good morning. Are you ready for breakfast? I've made some fresh blueberry muffins."

"What are you doing in here?" Gayle asked sharply.

The housekeeper's face fell. "Why I'm cleaning the carpet just like I always do every Monday and Thursday."

"How did you get in?"

Mrs. Jenkins cast a bewildered look at Ariel, who said, "I let her in with your keys. Isn't that okay? She needed to clean."

Before Gayle could respond, Hector Luna came in whistling and carrying a plumber's snake. *"Buenos días,"* he said tipping his cap. "I'll have the drain fixed in five minutes."

Gayle rolled her eyes heavenward. "So much for the illusion of security. This place is like Grand Central Station. What's wrong with the drain?"

"She's running slow," Hector answered.

"I had him put some liquid down it yesterday," Mrs. Jenkins said. "It didn't seem to do much except make fumes. But I left the bathroom window cracked so it wouldn't smell up the room and disturb your work."

"Yesterday?" You both were in here yesterday? And the window has been open ever since?" Gayle glared at

Ariel, who had the good grace to look contrite when she dangled the keys in front of her face. Gayle snatched them from her hand. "How did they get in yesterday?"

"Uh," she said, wincing. "I let them in. You were dead to the world and I didn't want to disturb you."

Gayle bit her tongue and counted slowly to ten.

"You want me to fix the drain now?" Hector asked, shifting back and forth from one foot to the other and looking uncomfortable.

"Yes, of course. I'm sorry. Mr. Luna, Mrs. Jenkins, I should have explained. I'll be doing some important work in the study, and the doors and windows must be locked at all times. If you need to come in, please check with me directly. Okay?"

"Sí," Hector said and hurried away with his tools.

Mrs. Jenkins nodded and said, "I understand. Mr. Calvin often kept private things in here. Right picky he was about them, too. I'm all finished in here for today. I'll see to your breakfast."

When the housekeeper had gone, Gayle fought the urge to shake Ariel. Of all the lame-brained stunts. What if something—

The safe!

Gayle ran to the closet door and jerked it open. The safe was still ajar, just as she had left it. She breathed a sigh of relief when she dropped to her knees and saw the packets of money, the coin case, the maroon velvet box, and the pouch still there.

"Ariel," she said to her friend, who had knelt beside her and was peering over her shoulder at the contents, "there are some things here you need to check." She reached for the plastic folder. "And something I'm curious about," she added, thinking of the birth record.

When she unfolded the pouch, she gasped.

"It's gone!"

"What's gone?" Ariel asked.

"The copy of a document I found yesterday." Gayle searched through the other pockets, thinking that in her haste when Winston had interrupted her, she might have stuffed it among the other papers. It was nowhere to be found. Another thought struck her and she checked the contents again. "The copy of your uncle Cal's will is missing as well. I didn't examine it, but I'm almost positive it was in this pocket yesterday afternoon. You didn't take anything out of here, did you?"

Ariel shook her head. "What could have happened to them?"

"It's obvious that someone took them. But the question is who and why? It could have been anybody. Thanks to you this place practically has a swinging door."

"Should we call the police?"

Gayle thought a minute. "And tell them what? Your uncle's will is already in the probate process. His lawyer had a copy. It's hardly a major burglary with several thousand dollars worth of cash, coins, and negotiable bonds left behind. And the other paper couldn't have had any real value. I think I remember most of the information on it. Ariel, have you ever heard of someone named Margaret Cameron?"

"No, I don't think so. Why?"

"Good morning, ladies." Ben Lyons was peering around the study door. "Mrs. Jenkins has breakfast ready."

"We'll talk about this later," Gayle whispered, quickly stuffing the pouch back in the safe and turning the dial as Ben approached them. She stood and looked at the man who created such turmoil inside her, and her breath caught. Why did he have this effect on her? Dressed in a navy suit with a red patterned tie and white shirt, he was even more handsome than he was last night. Did he look good in everything? She could feel the tingles start and she clenched her teeth.

No more, Casanova. I've got your number. She would not be seduced into agreeing with his scheme to buy McDonough Bearings.

"She's working now," Hector said, tipping his cap on his way out.

Ben looked Gayle up and down, then grinned. "We're going to have to hurry if we don't want to be late for the board meeting. We need to leave in half an hour."

"The board meeting!" Gayle's hand flew to her disheveled hair. She hadn't even taken time to comb it. With no makeup and in her bathrobe and bare feet, she was suddenly painfully aware of her appearance. "I'd forgotten all about it. I've got to get dressed."

She tried to hurry past Ben, but he caught her arm. "Gayle, we need to talk."

"Not now. I have to dress. Later."

"Count on it," Ben stated firmly.

Gayle ran up the stairs. Hearing the keys jingle in her pockets reminded her that she had left the study unlocked. Damnation. Ben Lyons kept her so rattled she could hardly remember her own name.

She waited on the landing until their receding voices indicated Ariel and Ben had gone to breakfast and crept back to the study. Making a quick search of the closet, she reassured herself that the missing documents hadn't accidentally fallen on the floor. Next she checked the locks on the desk and file cabinets and inspected her computer equipment. Everything looked in order. After she made sure Hector had secured the bathroom window, Gayle locked the study door and raced to her room.

There was only time for a quick shower. She hurriedly donned her undergarments, wishing desperately for at least a cup of coffee. She had just pulled on a tailored white crepe blouse and a charcoal pinstripe skirt when there was a knock on the door.

"It's me," Ariel called.

"Come in only if you have a cup of coffee with you."

"I do indeed. Open the door. I've got my hands full."

Gayle admitted Ariel bearing a breakfast tray adorned with a yellow chrysanthemum. "That looks like manna."

"Compliments of Mrs. Jenkins. The mum was Ben's idea. Stop and eat something. They can't start the meeting till we get there." Ariel placed the tray on a small table by the window and flopped down on the bed. "I'm really sorry about the keys, Gayle. I simply didn't think."

"It's okay. I'm sorry I made such an issue of it, but you can see now why I did." Gayle sipped her coffee and ate a warm, buttered muffin.

"Who do you think took the stuff?"

"Since the window was open, it could be anybody. What I don't understand is why they only took those two things."

"Are you sure we shouldn't call the police? Maybe it was Uncle Cal's murderer. Maybe it has something to do with the fire."

"Ariel, face it. If the police didn't believe your uncle

104

was murdered, they aren't going to get excited about two insignificant documents missing from a safe full of cash. Believe me, if we call them we'll be tied up all day for nothing. Right now the board meeting takes precedence."

Ariel followed Gayle into the bathroom while she applied her makeup and wound her hair into a business-like coil. "Couldn't they check for fingerprints or something?"

"Sure," Gayle said. "And they'd find mine. You forget that I handled everything after our thief did. If we called in the police it would accomplish nothing except to tip off whoever took the things to be more cautious. Let's keep this to ourselves for the time being. Okay?"

"Okay. I'll trust your judgment. Meet you downstairs," she said as she went out the door.

Gayle selected a red patterned silk tie, slipped it under her collar, and made a soft bow. She kept her jewelry simple: delicate gold earrings, a watch, and a small gold pin on her lapel. After she put on the jacket to her suit and medium-heeled black pumps, she took a final survey in the full-length mirror to be sure she fit the professional image she aimed for. Satisfied, she collected her purse and briefcase and went downstairs.

Ben was waiting for her in the breezeway. He whistled and lifted his eyebrows. "Very nice, Ms. Executive."

"Thank you." Gayle tried to be cool, but muffed it by smiling. No matter how many lectures she gave herself, she wanted to be attractive to Ben. "Where's Ariel?"

"I told her to go ahead and we'd meet her there. I need to talk to you."

How dare Ariel go off and leave her alone with Ben!

She'd strangle her. "I don't believe we have anything to talk about." With as much disdain as she could muster, Gayle said, "I'll take one of the other cars. I plan to work at the plant after the meeting today and I'll need transportation home."

"Ariel can leave the Corvette for you and I'll bring her home, then take her to the airport."

Gayle could see she'd been outmaneuvered again. She decided to give in gracefully. After they were on their way, Ben said, "Did you read my proposal?"

"I did." Gayle stared straight ahead, her back stiff and her hands clenched in her lap. There would be no repeat of their last trip along this route. If she didn't look at him she could handle being close to him without her hormones running rampant.

"And?"

"It was very clear."

Ben sighed. "Babe, you know what I'm asking."

"I'm afraid the answer is still the same. Ariel is not ready to make a decision at this time. Not until I've completed an evaluation of the company."

"But I thought maybe, after everything that's happened . . ."

Keeping her eyes on the rotating mixer of a cement truck in the lane ahead of them, Gayle could feel a lump the size of a grapefruit forming in her throat. *I know what you thought,* she lashed out mentally. *You thought you could stalk me, tempt me into your lair, and I'd agree to your terms.*

She swallowed twice, swallowed again, and forced herself to answer in a calm professional tone, "Ben, let me make this as plain as possible. I've agreed to represent Ariel's interests and carry out her wishes to the best of my ability. I am committed both legally and morally, and you cannot seduce me into breaking that trust."

Ben didn't say another word. He didn't have to, Gayle thought. His silence confirmed her suspicions. There was no feeling of triumph in being right about the reasons for his pursuit of her. Instead, she felt miserable. Her heart hurt. Insidious tentacles of pain snaked around her chest and squeezed the breath from her lungs. Why did it hurt so badly? Why didn't he deny her accusation?

Her eyes burned and she blinked, refusing to allow tears. She schooled her features into an emotionless mask and continued to stare at the cement mixer ahead as it went round and round like the bile in her throat.

The silent trip seemed to take forever, but finally they pulled into the parking lot of the factory. A crew of workmen were scrubbing soot, the last of the external signs of yesterday's fire, from the brick on the side of the office building. Still refusing to look at Ben, Gayle reached for the door handle to make her exit.

Ben's hand shot out and grabbed her arm. He was not rough, but his grip was firm. "Gayle," he said quietly. "It tears me up that you question my integrity. My feelings for you as a woman and my desire to take over McDonough Bearings are two separate issues. You have to understand that. I can see we need to clarify some things between us, but since the meeting starts in five minutes, this doesn't seem to be the time. Will you have dinner with me tonight so we can talk?"

The tentacles of pain withered as she felt a rush of relief. She closed her eyes and took a deep breath. She wanted to believe him. She *did* believe him. But it was foolish to become any more involved with this potent man than necessary. She would be inviting grief. She was too vulnerable to his raw appeal. While there was no question that he was wildly exciting, she was correct in her initial assessment of him. He was dangerous. He stirred feelings in her of such unknown and powerfully primitive emotion, it terrified her.

"No, I don't think so." Gayle didn't dare look at him, afraid that she would be like Lot's wife—doomed. "Ben, I don't understand this thing, whatever it is, between us. But quite honestly it frightens me."

"If I promise to behave like a perfect gentleman, will you go? We won't discuss McDonough Bearings, and I'll bridle my tongue and sit on my hands if necessary. I'd like for us to spend time together, to become friends."

"It wouldn't be wise." Despite her own warnings, Gayle defied caution and committed a ruinous transgression. She looked at him. His rough-planed features had softened and his eyes were tender and pleading.

"Please, princess," he implored gently. "It's my birthday."

CHAPTER SEVEN

Could any woman alive resist Ben Lyons? Gayle couldn't. Her resolve melted, her shoulders slumped, and she breathed a resigned sigh. Just when she thought herself armored against him, he would come up on her blind side. How could he have guessed that she had a special fondness for birthdays?

"Okay," she said. "But only because it's your birthday."

"I knew you'd take pity on a lonely man." Ben grinned. "Now let's get to the meeting."

Knowing she'd been suckered in by a master of manipulation, Gayle wasn't sure whether she should laugh, cry, or give him a swift kick in the posterior.

They crossed the parking lot to the two-story building which served as the offices for McDonough Bearings. According to the pictorial history Gayle had seen on the study wall, the present sand-colored brick structure had been built about twenty years ago. Additional wings had been added through the years. It sat in front of several large metal buildings resounding with the usual noise and activity of a manufacturing plant. The grounds surrounding the office were neatly landscaped, and beds of yellow chrysanthemums and red begonias lent warmth and color to the area.

Inside the double glass doors, the lingering odors of smoke and wet ashes hung as grim reminders of the fire. Even though the reception area was well lighted and attractively decorated with plants and plush chairs, with colorful prints brightening the paneled walls, there was a pall in the air. Something in the atmosphere reminded Gayle of a funeral home and she shuddered. It was as if nothing were left of the company but the shell, and they were all gathering to view the neatly painted and dressed remains.

The receptionist, a gamin-faced blonde in her early twenties, glanced up as they entered. "Good morning," the young woman said, smiling broadly at Ben and sitting a little straighter. "I'm Angie. You must be Mr. Lyons and Ms. Summers." When they nodded, she rose and added, "Mr. Brewer asked me to show you to the conference room. Ms. McDonough is already there." As they followed her down the hall carpeted in plush bright green, Angie said, "Isn't the smell just awful? You kind of get used to it after a while, but everything's been crazy around here since yesterday."

At the door to the meeting room Angie turned another blinding smile on Ben, and with a flutter of her lashes said, "If there's anything I can do for you, let me know."

"Thanks," Ben said.

Gayle had to bite her lip to keep from chuckling, but nothing in his facial expression indicated that Ben had paid particular attention to the young woman's flirtation.

They greeted Winston Dasher and then Martin

Brewer, who introduced his secretary, Sylvia Norman, a svelte middle-aged redhead in designer glasses. Gayle nodded to a harried-looking George Schulze, who nervously ran his hand over his bald head and fussed about what a mess his department was in.

"I don't know how anybody can expect me to get anything done," the comptroller said. "We're trying to sort through the debris and salvage what we can, but the computer system is completely destroyed. What the fire didn't get, the water ruined. We don't even have an adding machine that works. The insurance company won't cover our losses until there is a complete investigation, and nobody will issue us credit for new equipment."

"Now, George, calm down," Martin Brewer said as Gayle took a seat next to Ariel.

Ariel leaned over to Gayle and whispered, "Buy the old fussbudget a computer and an adding machine and whatever else he needs."

"I'll check it out this afternoon."

When Ben, George Schulze, Winston, and Sylvia were seated at the table, Martin Brewer took his place at the head and called the meeting to order. When the staggering facts were presented, it was even worse than Gayle had imagined. No wonder Winston was urging Ariel to file for bankruptcy. The company was flat broke and in mountainous debt. Creditors were demanding payment. Although many workers had been laid off in recent weeks, there was not enough to make the payroll of those remaining, even if they could reconstruct the records. It seemed hopeless.

One of the biggest setbacks to business had been the major loss of government contracts which McDonough

Bearings had always been awarded in the past. Over the last four years, the contracts had slowly dwindled until they had received only a fraction of their former orders. The other serious source of loss was the sales and warehousing project in Singapore. The company had gone into the Far East market two years ago with high expectations, but the venture had cost millions in inventory and building expenses with little return in revenue.

"It pains me to admit defeat," Mr. Brewer said. The tall, gray-haired man's face was drawn and his shoulders bowed with the weight of the failing company. "But I see no other alternative but to concur with our attorney's advice and declare bankruptcy." His brow was furrowed and his eyes were misty as he turned to the owners. "Ariel, Ben, I'm sorry. I've done all I can. As long as Calvin was alive, he tried to fight this thing, but we've come to the end of the road."

"We are *not* declaring bankruptcy," Ariel stated firmly. "There will be no more discussion of it."

"It's the one thing Ariel and I agree on," Ben said. "Though we need to file a Chapter Eleven to give us time to turn things around."

Ariel stuck out her chin and glared at the men around the table. "We're not filing a *Chapter* anything. I won't have the stigma attached to Uncle Cal's name or to his company."

"But, Ariel," Mr. Brewer said, "we have no operating capital, no credit, and not enough business to offset even the interest on our loans. Where's the money to come from?"

"From me," she said.

"Ariel," Winston interjected gently, "it will take a tremendous amount of money to keep the company op-

112

erational. You can't be serious about this. I thought once you'd had time to consider—"

"I've considered! Tell them, Gayle."

Gayle had to admit that McDonough Bearings seemed beyond saving. If bankruptcy was not to be an option, at least Ben's idea seemed more sensible. But she knew Ariel's mind was made up and nothing would budge her. Gayle doubted if anyone present was aware of the extent of Ariel's fortune. Keeping this business afloat for a year would be no great burden, but it did seem a foolish waste of money. She drew a deep breath and stood.

"She's considered all the options," Gayle affirmed. "I have been empowered to investigate the company's situation and keep McDonough Bearings operational for the time being."

When there was general grumbling among the men present, she added, "While I realize that you all have some share in the business, Ariel holds the majority and the decision is hers. I would appreciate it if all of you would remain in your present positions and assist me in my work for at least a month to six weeks. At the end of that time, we can reevaluate the alternatives."

Ben shook his head in disgust as the others discussed her proposal. Things were not going as he'd planned. By now he should have been president of the company. Ariel and Gayle were two of the most hardheaded females he'd ever run across. Singly each was bad enough; together they were murder. If his hunch was right, there would be hell to pay before this thing was resolved. Of course he still had his ace in the hole, but it wasn't time to play it yet. He didn't want to play it at all unless there was no other way.

He watched Gayle as she sat quietly studying the reports handed out earlier, and he felt the familiar urge rise hot and heavy. Damn, but she was one hell of a woman. It was a shame she was mixed up in this mess. He was going to have to tread carefully and quietly. He'd try to wait her out for a while, try to convince her to sell to him, but he knew he couldn't hang back a month to make his move. Too much was at stake.

Gayle sat at the large desk in Calvin McDonough's old office nibbling on a soggy tuna fish sandwich Angie had brought her two hours ago. The soft drink beside the foil wrapper sat in a wet puddle on the glass top. It had long since lost its fizz. Since the meeting she had been in a constant whirl. Ariel had hugged her good-bye, handed over the car and house keys, and left with Ben to pack and catch a flight back to Denver.

Ben, she thought, looking at him smiling from the deck of a sailboat. She couldn't even escape his presence here. A duplicate of Ben and Ariel's photographs from the study sat on the corner of this desk as well.

She was irritated with Ben's behavior at the board meeting. When the members had finally acquiesced in the matter of her proposal, not that they ever had any real choice, he alone refused to cooperate. He declared Ariel's decision, "A stupid move to pour money down a hole. Chapter Eleven is the only sensible solution."

Later when she brought up the testing with the Summers Profile—admittedly Gayle hadn't explained the full ramifications of the process—Ben refused to participate. Refused! "I'm not taking some damned personality test or placement test or whatever the hell it is. I know my personality and I know my *place*," Gayle mimicked in a gruff voice, hands on hips and shoulders wiggling in a arrogant swivel.

His intimation was clear. It was Gayle who didn't know her place. Thank goodness for Winston's coming to her rescue. At least he had understood when she had explained the importance of the officers taking the test and setting an example for the other employees. Winston had been the first to volunteer; however, not even Winston's action had shamed Ben into agreeing to fill out a questionnaire.

Gayle dumped the remnants of the inedible sandwich in the trash and mopped up the wet ring left by the drink. With so much else to do of an immediate concern, the testing would have to wait until next week. After the conference with Martin Brewer, her list was already two pages long, and a visit to George Schulze's department was next.

There was a knock on the door and Winston stuck his head in. "Need any help?"

His open, boyish smile was a balm to her waning spirits. She returned the cheerful expression with one of her own. "A little. Do you happen to have an army with you?"

He laughed. "Only me. It's time for a break," he said entering with a box and a sack. From the sack he extracted two Styrofoam containers of coffee and handed one to Gayle.

She took a sip, closed her eyes, and said, "Umm, that's wonderful."

"Wait till you taste one of these bits of heaven." He opened the baker's box and took out two paper plates. On each of them he laid a chocolate eclair resting on a doily, then handed her a fork and a napkin with an exaggerated flourish. "For milady."

"Oh, Winston, those are the most sinfully delightful-looking confections I've ever seen." When she had eaten a bite, Gayle added, "And they taste even better than they look, if that's possible. Eclairs are one of my favorite things. How did you know?"

He laughed. "A lucky guess. There's a wonderful French bakery in the Village near my office, and I thought of you when I passed it."

"How sweet of you, but it was a long trip back here to bring this."

"It was my pleasure. I wanted to offer my help if you need it. And I wanted to ask you to have dinner with me tonight. We can have drinks at the Remington and dinner there or at Tony's."

"Winston, I'm sorry. I already have plans for this evening." He looked so crestfallen, she patted his hand and said, "But I'd love to go another time."

Frowning, he said, "I was hoping to see you tonight. Tomorrow I'm going out of town on business for several days. I should be back by the end of next week. Are you free next Friday?"

His expression was so open and hopeful, his behavior so thoughtful, Gayle was touched. She smiled. "It's a date."

He brightened. "I'll call you when I get back in town. We'll have an elegant evening."

When the attorney had gone, Gayle sat staring at the photograph on the desk. It was a shame that Winston Dasher didn't cause the same heart flutters that Ben Lyons did. She and Winston could never be more than friends and she hated to lead him to believe otherwise.

From what Ariel had told her, his divorce had wounded him badly. Oh, well, she reminded herself, she'd only promised dinner. It's not as though he offered a proposal of marriage.

A few minutes later, Gayle paused at the receptionist's desk on her way to see the comptroller. "Angie, I'll be with Mr. Schulze in case anyone needs me."

The young woman nodded as she licked a dab of chocolate and whipped cream from her fingers. "I'll make a note of it, Ms. Summers. Oh," she said as Gayle started to turn away, "since you're going there anyway, would you mind taking this envelope to Mr. Schulze? Win—Mr. Dasher said it was very important and, since everyone is on break, I can't leave the switchboard right now."

"Of course," Gayle said, tucking the envelope inside the pocket of her leather portfolio.

When Gayle stepped inside the suite housing the accounting and records department, she understood George Schulze's distress. Even though much of the damaged material had already been removed, the odor was overpowering and the charred destruction tragic. Expensive, once efficient computer terminals were now blobs of curled, blackened plastic and crazed glass heaped into a pile of trash. Microfilm and copying machines were beyond salvage. The carpet had been ripped up and the walls were sooty, soggy, and sagging.

George and five other people were rummaging through cans of computer tape and drawers of files. The comptroller looked up when Gayle entered. He waved his hand over the debris. "Now do you understand what a mess we're in?"

"I do. Is anything intact?"

Mr. Schulze gave a short sarcastic snort. "We found a pencil sharpener that still works."

"Didn't you keep copies of records stored off-site?"

The short bald man drew himself up in a huff. "Of course. But as you can see, we have no equipment and the offices are unusable."

Knowing that new facilities and equipment were the first priority, Gayle told the comptroller that she would get back with him when she had made arrangements.

By five o'clock Gayle had located and leased a large, climate-controlled trailer to be delivered the next day. Bank business and equipment would have to wait until tomorrow, Gayle thought, slipping off her shoes and wiggling her toes. It had been a tiring day, and there was the matter of Ben's birthday yet to consider.

Still annoyed with Ben's uncooperative stance in the board meeting, Gayle considered canceling their date. No, birthdays should not be spent alone. They were days for special concessions, for sharing laughter and gifts. *Gifts!* She'd forgotten about a gift. Birthdays just weren't birthdays without presents. Scrambling into her shoes, she grabbed her purse and briefcase.

On her way home, Gayle swung by an exclusive men's store. Luckily she found the perfect thing: a soft cable-knit fisherman's sweater. A clerk wrapped it in colorful plaid paper with a yarn bow and stowed the package in a sack for smuggling it into the house. She loved surprises and special occasions. Shopping for Ben had taken the edge off her pique with him; now she bubbled with expectation.

Of course she was still a little ticked off at him, but that was business, she reminded herself. This was personal. For ethical reasons as well as her own peace of

118

mine, she was determined to try her darnedest to keep the two separate.

It seemed to take forever for Gayle to make her way home through Houston's infamous traffic. When she finally wheeled the red Corvette into the driveway at dusk, she spotted Ben and Hector leaning against the old blue Cadillac, talking and drinking beer. Ben was waiting when she came out of the garage.

He looked at her face and frowned. "You look tired. Do you feel like going out?"

"Sure I do. A long soak in the tub will do wonders."

"Need somebody to wash your back?"

"I can manage, thank you." She cocked an eyebrow at him. "I thought you were going to bridle your tongue."

"I did," he said, a slow grin breaking over his face. "It wasn't your back I was thinking of."

"Ben Lyons!"

"Sorry, princess. You go soak and put on your prettiest party dress. We'll go someplace fancy and have something I can't pronounce."

"Wouldn't you rather go somewhere more casual? After all, it's your birthday we're celebrating. I don't need candlelight and French wine."

"You're sure?"

"Positive. Pick your favorite place."

Ben thought for a minute. "I know just what my mouth's watering for. Put on something comfortable, and I'll be back for you in forty-five minutes."

Ben was waiting when Gayle came downstairs at seven thirty. Approval shone in his eyes as they traveled from the tips of her soft black flats over the trim black slacks

119

and loose blue sweater to the fluff of dark hair and back down again.

"Very nice," he said when she stopped on a riser that put her face even with his. His fingers cupped the nape of her neck and his thumb stroked her cheek. Eyes closing as he breathed in deeply, he said, "I love your smell. It seeps into my dreams. It's like ocean breezes through a tropical garden." Bending forward, he lightly touched her mouth with his lips and tongue. "And the way you taste . . . has been on my mind all day."

Gayle began to melt like butter in the sun as tiny nibbles gently teased, his lips soft and warm and full of promises. Spicy aftershave mixed with mint and soap and male to surround her, tantalize her. One of her hands squeezed the box she carried and the other gripped the bannister for dear life as she stood unmoving, suffused in sensation.

He drew back enough to scan her face while his thumb continued its stroking across her cheek, then moved with a gossamer tracing along the curve of her lips.

"You promised," Gayle whispered, her blue eyes locked with his darkening ones.

"What did I promise, angel?" His voice was husky, quiet.

"That you'd keep hands off."

"I must have been out of my head." His thumb made one last lingering pass across her parted lips and reluctantly withdrew. He moved back to allow her final descent.

When she left the support of the bannister, her knees were shaky. Glancing down at the package clutched in her fingers, it took a moment to register its purpose.

"Here," she finally said, holding the gift out to him. "This is for you. Happy birthday."

His eyes widened, then narrowed as a slow grin spread over his face. "You bought me a present?"

Gayle nodded. "Open it."

Like an impatient child on Christmas morning, Ben ripped off the paper and tore open the box. "It's a sweater," he said, holding it up, his eyes shining and a grin still lighting his face. "You bought me a sweater."

Gayle fought her laughter at his excitement. "I know."

"Here," he said, thrusting it at her and jerking his plaid shirt from his jeans.

"What are you doing?" Gayle squealed as he bared his tanned, muscular torso.

"I'm going to wear my new sweater."

Gayle could only shake her head in wonder at the change in his behavior. Mr. Macho was acting like a kid over a simple gift. She could have almost sworn he had tears in his eyes. He pulled the knitted garment over his head, gave his hair a couple of rakes with his fingers, and peered into the hall mirror. The off-white fabric accentuated his golden good looks, molded his broad-shouldered build as if it had been made with him in mind.

Obviously pleased with what he saw, Ben put his hands on his hips and turned to Gayle. "It's a perfect fit. How did you manage that?"

"I have two brothers about your size. Do you like it?"

"Like it? Of course I like it." Forgetting his earlier pact, Ben impulsively pulled Gayle into his arms and swung her around. He planted a hard, smacking kiss on her laughing lips. "It's the nicest present I've had in years. Maybe ever. Thank you."

His spirits still high, he smacked her again and said, "Let's go eat. I could eat a bear and I know you must be hungry."

Gayle nodded. "Starved."

"Can you hold out until we get to Tomball?"

"To where?"

"Tomball. It's a little town on the outskirts. I hope you like chicken-fried steak." With one arm under her elbow, Ben hustled her out the door and to the station wagon.

Outside, the evening was pleasantly cool with the beginnings of a fall nip in the damp night air. Someone in the neighborhood, in overoptimistic anticipation of chilly weather, was enjoying a fireplace, and the pungent smell of woodsmoke wafted through the trees and stirred nostalgic memories of football games and hayrides and carefree days. Gayle felt almost giddy with delight from the night and the warm, electric presence of the man by her side. She was determined, just for tonight, to put aside all thoughts of McDonough Bearings and the perplexing knot of problems facing her.

Tonight was for Ben. Tonight was for fun.

Feeling the weight of her responsibilities fall away, Gayle breathed in the crisp air and smiled up at the stars beginning to wink through the scattered clouds. "Isn't it a glorious night?"

"It is," Ben said, giving her shoulders a hug and grinning down at her.

Gayle laughed for no reason other than pure delight with the man, the mood, and the night.

"I want to hear some more about your brothers," he

said as they drove away. "And your sisters, and your parents, and your grandparents, and your aunts and uncles and cousins."

"Are you checking my pedigree?"

"No, princess. It just occurred to me that, other than the fact you make my blood boil if I come within fifty feet of you, I don't know anything about you. Tell me about your family."

With occasional prompting from Ben, Gayle told him about her family, explaining that she had no sisters, only twin brothers six years younger than she. "Don's beginning the first year of his surgical residency, and Mike plays first base with the Mavericks."

"Mike . . . Mike Stone's your brother?"

"Yep. My baby brother. Ever see him play?"

"Only on television. He led the league in home runs for the year. It's a shame the Mavericks didn't make the playoffs this season. What about your parents? Are they still living?"

Gayle laughed. "Are they ever. Dad's a high school principal and my mother is a CPA. I have the usual assortment of grandparents, aunts, uncles, and cousins. Most of them live in Jackson. Christmas is wild at the Stones' house. What about you? Do you have a big family?"

Ben was quiet for a moment, then said, "No, there's only me."

Something in his tone clutched at Gayle's heart and she laid her hand on his shoulder. "I'm so sorry."

"Hey, it's okay," Ben said, laying his hand on hers and giving a squeeze. "My mother died when I was born, and since my dad knew more about boats than babies, my maternal grandmother came to live with us and raised me."

"What happened to your father?"

"The summer after I graduated from college, a bunch of drug dealers highjacked his boat off the coast of Florida and killed him."

"Oh, Ben, no."

"It was a long time ago, but as you might imagine, I don't have much patience with drug trafficking."

"And your grandmother?"

Ben smiled. "Gram was a special lady. We were very close. But she was very ill for a long time. She died about five years ago." He glanced over at Gayle. "Hey, don't look so glum. How did we get off onto sad subjects? This is supposed to be a celebration. Tell me, did you have any pets when you were a kid?"

Their conversation turned to laughter and reminiscences of everything from pet goats to goldfish until they pulled into the parking lot of a roadside café.

Gayle stared at the neon sign and giggled. "Ma Goodson's? We're having dinner at *Ma Goodson's?*"

"Now don't get uppity on me," Ben said as they got out. "You should have seen the old place before they moved to these fancy new quarters. Trust me, the food's delicious."

The smell of frying steaks teased Gayle's empty stomach as they walked toward the door. Inside they walked on plank floors past the gumball machines and potted plants to the dining area.

"Want to have a drink in the bar first?" Ben asked.

Gayle shook her head. "That noise you hear is my stomach growling."

Ben grinned and held up two fingers to the harried waitress coming their way.

"Have you a table in just a minute," the woman called, sticking a pencil in a bedraggled topknot of dish-water-blond hair.

There were about twenty or thirty wooden tables of various sizes scattered around the room, each outfitted with mismatched wooden chairs which looked as if they'd been collected at a hundred different garage sales. Most of them were full of casually dressed folks of every size, age, and description. A George Strait song competed with the din of conversation, laughter, and clink of hardy diners relishing a no-frills meal. Lining the walls were all sorts of old-fashioned pictures, advertisements, and implements of a bygone era.

"Over here," the waitress said, mopping a table in the corner with a rag she'd pulled from her back pocket. "Something to drink?" she asked when they were seated.

Gayle ordered iced tea and Ben a beer. When Gayle picked up the plastic-covered menu, Ben took it from her hands. "The best thing to order is chicken-fried steak. The only question is, Do you want the regular or the large?"

"Oh, I want the large."

Ben looked amused. "You're sure?"

"I told you I was hungry. I haven't had chicken-fried steak since Ariel and I were in college at U.T. I love it."

"We'll have two large ones with French fries and salad," Ben said to the woman.

"It'll be out in a shake," she said, dashing off toward the kitchen.

A middle-aged waitress passed their table with a tray

of drinks and stopped. "Is that you, Ben? It's good to see you."

"It's good to see you, Irma."

"Happy birthday. It is your birthday, isn't it?" When Ben nodded, she said, "I wasn't sure you'd be here this year, what with Mr. Calvin dying and all. Read about it in the paper. Sure was sorry to hear about it." Turning to Gayle, she said, "Mr. McDonough always used to bring Ben for chicken-fried steak every year on his birthday. Them two was a sight, always laughin' and cuttin' up like a couple of kids."

When the waitress moved on, Gayle felt her resolve to forget about McDonough Bearings fall around her ears. Just what was Ben's connection with the old man and the company? He had never explained, and now, she decided, was the perfect time to ask.

CHAPTER EIGHT

Gayle waited until their drinks and salads were served, then looked directly at Ben and said, "You and Calvin McDonough seem an unlikely pair, but obviously you had a close relationship. How and when did you meet?"

Here it comes, Ben thought. He had known it was just a matter of time until Gayle confronted him. Not wanting to tell the complete truth, yet finding lies abhorrent to his nature, he was between the proverbial rock and a hard place. Evasion would only make her more suspicious, and he could tell from the glint in those gorgeous blue eyes that she was ready for some answers. Stalling for time to organize his thoughts, he took a swallow of beer. It was best to stick to the facts as much as possible. Not all the facts, of course, but maybe enough to satisfy her for now.

Ben shrugged his shoulders and cupped both hands around his glass. "I first met him a little over four years ago. We seemed to hit it off right away. You know, that instant attraction you have for some people," he said, reaching for Gayle's hand and brushing her knuckles with his thumb. The slow lazy grin and rakish quirk of an eyebrow was just short of licentiousness.

When his eyes narrowed into a sexy stare, she could

almost feel her sweater dissolve under his gaze. A quick rush of excitement stirred and flashed over her. That suggestive look of his never ceased to curl her toes. Lord, she thought, if Ben turned it on high, the cook could fry a whole pot of steaks over the electricity generated between them. Gayle eased her hand away and took a cooling gulp of iced tea. The relief was minimal.

Was he deliberately trying to sidestep her question? Well, Mr. Lyons, she thought, quirking her eyebrow at the same angle as his, two can play your little game. Planting her elbows on the table and propping her chin against her fists, Gayle fluttered her eyelashes a couple of times and allowed a slow molasses-dripping smile to part her lips. Scooting onto the edge of her chair, she kicked off her shoe and reached out with her foot until she made contact with Ben's leg. Still smiling, she rubbed her toes along the inside of his calf, up to his knee and just a bit beyond.

Ben's eyes widened and he downed the rest of his beer in one swallow.

Managing to hold back her laughter, Gayle fluttered her lashes and said in a breathy drawl, "You were tellin' me all about meetin' Calvin McDonough."

Ben grabbed her foot as it slid higher up his thigh. "Holy hell, honey. Cut that out or I'm liable to be arrested."

"Arrested?"

"Another five seconds of that and, promise or no promise, you'd better move the ketchup bottle because I'm crawling over this table after you."

Withdrawing her foot, Gayle laughed and slipped back into her shoe. "Then stop trying to distract me and answer my question."

"I wasn't trying to distract you, princess. When you're around, I can't think of much else but you." He gave a soundless whistle and a short, self-mocking laugh. "Right now I'd tell you the number of my Swiss bank account if I had one."

Ben held up the empty glass and signaled for another beer before he answered seriously, "A mutual acquaintance first suggested that I meet with Cal. I was having some financial problems at the time, and Cal loaned me some money. We had some other business dealings over the years and became friends as well." Ben had a far-away look as he toyed with his empty glass. "He was a lonely old man and I didn't have any family left. We shared a common need, I suppose. You might say that he came to think of me as a nephew or a grandson. And for me, he filled the void left when I lost Gram."

Ben encouraged Gayle to eat her salad and he took a few bites of his before he continued. "Cal's company was very important to him—his whole existence, really, except for the few years that Ariel lived with him. For most of his life, it took the place of a family, of children. He nurtured it and watched it grow into something he was proud of. He wanted it to continue after he was gone, but he knew that Ariel had neither the interest nor the inclination to run McDonough Bearings, nor did she need the money. He'd been hounding me for the past couple of years to take over the presidency, especially after business began to decline. Finally I agreed. Unfortunately, before we could complete the transition, he died."

They were both quiet for a moment, each lost in their separate thoughts. Then Gayle asked, "If what you say is true, why didn't Cal make his wishes known in his will?"

Ben shrugged.

The subject was dropped when their waitress returned with two large platters. Gayle's eyes grew wide as she stared at the amount of food before her. A tenderized round steak, battered and deep-fried, covered the entire dish and hung over the sides. "Good Lord!"

Ben hooted with laughter. "You said you were hungry, babe. That ought to hold you for a while."

While Gayle made a valiant effort to make a dent in the Paul Bunyan proportions, their conversation turned to gentle, teasing banter and discovery of shared interests. They found they each loved mystery and detective novels, especially those by Agatha Christie and John D. MacDonald. Both confessed a weakness for hot fudge sundaes, popcorn on rainy afternoons, and fishing.

"You like to fish?" Ben's surprise was evident.

Gayle nodded. "I haven't been in a long time, but I used to go with my father and brothers quite often. My mother hated fishing, but I never missed a trip. Why, I'll have you know I still hold the Stone family record for lake bass and river catfish. Unfortunately, Mike has the deep-sea record. But one of these days, I'll beat him."

"Somehow I can't picture you baiting a hook. You're not one of those women who squeal over worms, are you?"

"Are you kidding? With two brothers to tease me if I did? I learned to bait my own hooks and manage my own catches. And after I had to untangle a few of my own backlashes, I became quite expert at casting."

"I'll have to see it to believe it." Ben cocked his head in skeptical amusement. "Say, you want to go to Lake Conroe tomorrow?"

Gayle shook her head. "Sorry, but I have to put in a full day at the plant. There are a million things to do."

After Ben did a bit of skillful maneuvering, Gayle agreed to his helping her at the plant on Friday so that they could take a fishing trip to the lake on Saturday.

Later when they left, with Ben carrying half of her steak in a doggy bag, Gayle felt relaxed and content to walk snuggled in the crook of his arm.

"Do you like country music?" Ben asked as he drove away from Ma Goodson's.

"Some of it, sometimes. Why?"

"Virginia City is on our way. I thought you might like to go dancing for a while."

"You like to dance?" Greg never liked dancing and Gayle missed it after they were married. "I used to love country dancing, but I haven't been in years."

Ben grinned and said with a satisfied smirk, "I'm a two-stepping terror."

And indeed he was, Gayle discovered a few minutes after they entered the big hall. Decorated like an Old West town and saloon, the lights were low and the music so loud its vibration could be felt from the boards of the huge wooden floor. Neon signs sizzled from behind the bar and a thick haze of cigarette smoke hung like clouds over the brims of ten-gallon hats. For nearly an hour they danced everything from a polka to the Cotton-Eyed Joe. It hadn't taken long for Gayle to remember the steps she'd learned in college.

Laughing and exhausted from the foot-stomping number they'd just finished, Gayle fell into Ben's arms. "I'm afraid I'm out of shape. I've got to rest," she gasped.

"You can't rest now," Ben said as a slow ballad began. "This is the kind of song I've been waiting for.

131

Here," he said, pulling her close against him, "lean on me. We'll move slow and easy."

It was seduction to music as Janie Fricke sang of love and promises and feelings in the night. Bold strength turned to tenderness as Ben tucked her head under his chin, kissed the palm of her right hand and laid it on his chest. Both his arms wound around her as he swayed and moved slowly to the rhythm of the tune.

Being in his arms felt so right. At that moment Gayle realized that not only was she enormously sexually attracted to Ben, but also that she liked him. Just plain liked him. A bit of a rascal, of course, and sometimes too frank to turn loose in polite society, he was nevertheless endearing. It was impossible to stay angry with him, no matter how devilishly outrageous or downright annoying his behavior. His total honesty was refreshing after the insincerity, game-playing, and sometimes malicious deceit she often encountered among the people in business. Even though there were still many unanswered questions, she instinctively trusted him.

Oh, he was no weakling. Ben was tough. She pitied anyone who tried to jump him in a dark alley. He was a strong, formidable opponent, but at the same time he had a depth of character that appealed to her. While he sometimes had all the finesse of a buzz saw, he was also loyal and as steady as a rock. She was beginning to understand why Calvin McDonough would be willing to place his precious company into Ben's keeping. Ben Lyons was a white knight in the original sense of the term. With only the tiniest push she could fall for a man like Ben.

Under her hand, Gayle could feel the strong beat of his heart and it was thudding to the same tempo as hers.

His chin nuzzled the crown of her head and he feathered tiny kisses over her hair. Pulling her closer along the length of his body, he crouched slightly and captured Gayle's right leg in the juncture of his thighs. Pressing against her hips with strong, splayed fingers, he rubbed against her in time to the haunting wail of the singer.

It was wildly erotic, and Gayle's knees went weak as liquid fire spread over her. She grabbed a handful of his sweater and clung to the back waistband of his jeans to keep from collapsing into a puddle of mindless yearning.

"Oh, babe," Ben murmured into her ear. "I'm burning for you. Touch me," he said, capturing her right hand and sliding it down his torso.

From somewhere in the midst of her growing desire, reason fought its way to the surface. "Ben! We're in the middle of a dance floor."

He froze and sucked in a deep shuddering breath. "Holy hell," he growled, grabbing her hand. "Let's get out of here."

Their way was blocked by a big, good-looking bruiser in a black cowboy hat and a silver belt buckle half the size of Texas. He was swaying slightly as he looked Gayle up and down. "Say, little mama, you're one fine-lookin' woman." His words were slurred and his grin was more comic than seductive. "Want to rub bellies with me for a while?"

Ben shoved Gayle behind him and squared his shoulders. If the intruder hadn't been drunk, he would have recognized that narrowed golden glint as deadly. Ben's tone was as cold and harsh as a Colorado mountain peak in winter when he said, "Cowboy, you've just insulted my lady and me. If you don't get the hell out of our way right now, I'm going to make dog meat out of that pretty face of yours."

There was no mistaking the malice or intent of Ben's words. He *could* do it, and he *would* do it. If Gayle hadn't been so terrified that Ben was about to start a barroom brawl, the look on the cowboy's face might have been funny. It was as if he sobered instantly. And he might have stepped aside if one of his drinking partners hadn't snickered just then.

Male pride made the cowboy stand his ground. He tossed a cocky smirk at his friends and gave Gayle a suggestive leer. Then he thumped the brim of his black Stetson and drawled, "I'd like to see you try it, buddy."

The words were barely out of his mouth before Ben grabbed a handful of plaid shirt and slammed the man against a post. Pressing his left forearm across the cowboy's throat, Ben dug his knee a few inches below the silver belt buckle, pinning him against the rough cedar like a bug specimen. He drew back his fist. "Apologize to the lady," he said between clenched teeth, shoving his arm tighter against the man's Adam's apple. "Now."

Gayle watched in horror as the cowboy's eyes bulged wide and he clawed at the stranglehold. "Sorry." The word was a soft gurgle.

Ben increased the pressure of his knee. "She didn't hear you." His voice was cold venom.

"I'm sorry, ma'am," he gasped louder.

Ben flung the man aside and took Gayle's arm. By the time he had steered her out the door and gotten her into the car, Gayle was shaking like a leaf in a March wind. This was a side of Ben she hadn't seen before. Strong, yes; stubborn, yes. But this incident showed a capacity for raw violence, a deadly streak. God only knows what his Summers Profile would show. She shuddered and drew herself into a protective ball.

Before he started the car, Ben glanced over at Gayle sitting huddled against the door. "Honey, what's wrong?"

"What's wrong?" she almost screeched. "You scared me, that's what's wrong. You would've really decked that guy, wouldn't you?"

"I would. I protect what's mine."

"I'm not yours, Ben Lyons," she ground out, her blue eyes flashing fire in the dim light of the parking lot.

"Oh, but you are." His words were incredibly soft and tender as he reached and stroked her cheek with the pad of his thumb. "Accept it, princess. It's inevitable."

"Cretin! Neanderthal! Churlish savage!" Gayle snatched another pair of pantyhose from the dresser drawer and slammed it shut. Already this morning she had broken a fingernail and snagged a brand-new pair of stockings. And it was all Ben Lyons's fault. He was making her crazy, confused, clumsy. Her behavior was totally out of character. She had come to Houston to help Ariel, to investigate McDonough Bearings, to test company employees. There was arson and theft to contend with, a company on the brink of going down the tubes, and very possibly a murderer was running loose. But was she tending to business? No. She was sopping up Ben's honey-dripping words and acting like a porno queen on the dance floor with that—that barbaric banana king.

Not much had been said after they left the dance hall. She'd given him a tight-lipped kiss good night—but only because it was his birthday. She hadn't slept worth a flip after his macho display last night. Memories of the violence vibrating from Ben when he confronted the drunken cowboy still made her shudder.

And his possessive cave-man pronouncements. "I protect what's mine," Gayle mimicked in a gruff imitation of Ben's deep voice. "Me, Tarzan; you, Jane."

Refusing to acknowledge or examine the niggles of excitement bubbling in the corners of her awareness, Gayle continued her furious muttering while she finished dressing.

As of this moment, she declared to herself as she walked down the stairs with her briefcase, *I'm getting my priorities straight. I will not allow Ben Lyons to distract me from my purpose. From now on, my thoughts and energies will be focused on the business at hand.*

Her resolve lasted all of thirty seconds, for Ben stood waiting at the foot of the stairs. Over a pale blue shirt and paisley tie, he wore a camel jacket which echoed the honey-gold streaks of his hair and accented the tawny irises shining up at her. More handsome than she dared remember, his broad smile and flashing eyes would have melted the heart of a stone goddess—and Gayle, a mere mortal, never had a chance. Her foot faltered and her breath caught as she felt the power of his consuming gaze.

"My God, you're beautiful," he said, holding out his hand and guiding her down the last few steps. "My memory never does you justice." Tucking her hand firmly in the crook of his arm, he took charge of her briefcase and guided Gayle toward the breakfast room.

"I don't want any breakfast," Gayle protested, glancing at her watch. "Mrs. Jenkins brought me coffee earlier and I need to get to the plant."

"A few minutes won't make any difference," he said, ignoring her efforts to tug her hand away. "Everything is waiting for you."

Rather than waste more time arguing, Gayle sat in the chair Ben held for her and sipped her juice as the housekeeper bustled in with a plate of bacon and eggs, buttered biscuits, and honey.

"Aren't you eating?" Gayle asked Ben when she noticed only one portion of food was served.

"I had breakfast a couple of hours ago. I'll just have some coffee with you."

Gayle managed a few bites, but it was disconcerting trying to eat with Ben scrutinizing every movement with those narrowed cat eyes and a lazy half-grin. Every so often his tongue stole out to lick his lips as if he were savoring every morsel she ate.

"Stop staring at me," she said irritably. "You make me nervous. If you're hungry, ask Mrs. Jenkins for a plate."

"It's not food I want. I like to watch you," he said, his gaze still fixed on her. "I never realized how sexy eating could be until I met you. Nor did I ever imagine I could be jealous of a biscuit."

Gayle tried to swallow, but the bit of bread refused to go down as her throat closed around it. It took two more tries before it continued its journey.

"Here," he said, reaching across to touch her lower lip with the tip of a finger, "you missed a drop of honey."

Her tongue automatically darted out to the spot, but Ben's finger didn't move until it followed her tongue's retreat and stayed between her lips demanding that she lick the sweetness from it. The sensuality of the gesture flashed through her and she felt her insides tighten and her breasts swell.

When Ben gently withdrew his finger, his hand slipped to the nape of her neck. Pulling her toward him as he leaned forward, he murmured, "I think I see another drop."

His tongue circled her lips and Gayle gripped the arms of her chair. He nibbled and teased against the softness of her mouth and she felt her insides turn over. Returning the warmth of Ben's kiss and deepening it, her hand reached up to caress his cheek. When he groaned and moved to pull her closer, it took every ounce of self-control Gayle possessed to break away.

Taking a deep calming breath, Gayle grabbed her cup with a trembling hand and gulped the last of her coffee. "We have to go," she said, and pushed her chair back. "And if we're going to work together, it must be understood that I expect you to conduct yourself in a professional manner, as will I."

Ben snapped a brisk salute and said soberly, "Yes, ma'am. Professional. Of course." Then he ruined his serious pronouncement by adding with a wink, "During business hours."

This is ridiculous, she chided herself as they rode to the plant. A grown woman ought to be able to handle a sexual attraction without turning to a writhing mass of nerve endings. Clenching her teeth she gave herself a repeat of the lecture that was becoming too familiar. With new resolve nailed firmly in place, Gayle directed their conversation toward the activities of the day.

By the time they reached Calvin McDonough's office,

it was decided that while Gayle dealt with the banking arrangements, Ben would supervise the placement and other details of the temporary offices for George Schulze's department. This afternoon they would locate suitable equipment for purchase or lease with delivery by the first of the week, and by mid-week the off-site copies of data could be secured and the accounting and records department would be operational.

Gayle was relieved that their discussions had been congenial and completely businesslike, without any suggestive undercurrents. Ben acted as befitting any professional colleague—until he saw the roses.

Sitting in the middle of the desk was a large crystal vase filled with at least two dozen long-stemmed red roses. Ben scowled as he plucked the card from its holder and opened it.

"Hey!" Gayle said, reaching for it. "That's mine."

Ben scowled even more as he read the card. "The Brooks Brothers Romeo again. What does Dasher mean 'Until Friday night'?"

"We have a dinner date when he gets back in town."

"The hell you do! You're not going out with him."

Gayle planted her hands on her hips as her eyes shot blue fire. "I'll go where I please, when I please, and with whom I please, Ben Lyons. It's none of your business."

"It damned well is my business. You're not going out with another man. I've already told you once."

"Well," she said, sarcasm dripping from her voice, "and since Mr. Banana King decreed it, I must kowtow, of course." Her expression and tone turned to barely leashed fury. "My plans are made. I *am* going."

"You're not." His words were quiet, firm, definite.

"Watch my dust."

Gayle grabbed her briefcase and slammed the door as she stomped out. Still shaking with anger, Gayle fled to the ladies' room to collect herself before her meeting with Martin Brewer.

Ben could have kicked himself from here to Bogotá. Why had he behaved like such a jealous ass? He had accomplished nothing from his green-eyed fit except to set his relationship with Gayle back a hundred paces. And after last night things were already on shaky ground. He hadn't meant to upset her then either. But when that smart-mouthed cowboy had said what he did to her, Ben had wanted to ram that black Stetson down his throat, grind that fancy belt buckle into his backbone. Picking fights had never been his style. In fact, he'd always been a live-and-let-live kind of guy. Cool. Controlled. Reasonable. Until he met Gayle Summers.

What was wrong with him? He'd never been jealous of a woman before. But then no woman had ever affected him like Gayle. The very thought of that smooth-talking attorney taking her out to a fancy restaurant, watching her smile, smelling her perfume, maybe even putting his hands . . .

"Goddammit!" Ben ground out as he banged the side of his fist against the desk. "She's mine!"

He could almost hear Gram chuckling over his predicament. "One of these days," she used to say, "you're going to find a bonnie lass, and she'll turn your heart inside out. You're like me," she had said patting his callused, sun-baked hand with her fragile, blue-veined one. "You'll only love once, fiercely and forever."

As the words echoed through his memory, Ben startled and sobered. Love? Was he in love with Gayle? In love with a stubborn blue-eyed fire-eater he'd known for less than a week? In love with a chocolate-haired beauty who haunted his dreams until he ached with wanting her? In love with a princess who made him want to fight duels and slay dragons? A slow smile broke from his grim lips, widening until he was grinning like a blooming idiot.

"Well, I'll be damned." He threw back his head and laughed. "Well, I'll be damned." Once he had labeled his feelings and accepted them, Ben relaxed.

He leaned back in Calvin McDonough's big chair, laced his fingers across his stomach, and narrowed his eyes in thought. It was time to get this mess with the company cleared up and out of the way so that he could devote all his time to convincing Gayle Summers that her place was with him. Permanently. And he knew just how to go about it. Slow and easy. He would stop coming on to her like a rutting bull. He would be patient, gentle, gain her trust, her friendship. It might mean a lot of jogging and cold showers, but it would be worth it.

The first thing he did was to call and book a flight to Singapore for Sunday. The second thing he did was to dump the roses in the trash and make a call to order replacements. Roses didn't suit Gayle anyhow; she needed something unique and exotic.

Gayle kicked off her shoes and leaned back in Calvin McDonough's big chair. It had been a long, tiring day. Productive, but tiring. Financial matters were under control for the time being. The payroll had been met. George Schulze had spacious new quarters, and thanks to Ben's help, furniture and office equipment. The computer system would be in place by Tuesday afternoon. Gayle would give them a few days to get things back in order before the auditors were scheduled to descend. And Monday morning she would begin testing with the Summers Profile.

Swiveling back and forth, she smiled as she looked at the flowers on the sideboard: a dramatic arrangement of torch ginger and ti leaves in a copper and brass compote. "I'm sorry, princess," Ben's note had said.

Oh, she had been irritated to find the expensive red roses wilting in the wastebasket, but the truth was, she hadn't particularly cared for them. Greg had always sent her the traditional red roses as well, and she never had the heart to tell him she really preferred exotic flowers or even simple mixed bouquets to the unimaginative choice of the customary long-stemmed buds. But Ben had known. Somehow he had known.

As if her thoughts had conjured him up, Ben rapped on the open door of the office.

"Tired?" he asked.

Gayle sighed and nodded. "My feet always tell me when it's the end of a day."

Ben walked over and squatted beside the chair. His strong hands lifted her stockinged feet onto his thigh and massaged the slender toes. Broad thumbs kneaded along the aching arch and ball of first one, then the other.

"Mmm," Gayle sighed. "That feels wonderful. Where did you learn to do that?"

"I used to do it for Gram. It sometimes helped her sleep when she was in pain."

For several minutes Ben quietly worked his gentle

142

magic, and Gayle's tension and weariness evaporated under the skillful manipulation of his fingers.

"Better?" he asked.

Gayle wiggled her toes and rotated her ankles. "Perfect. You should give lessons."

Ben smiled and reached under the desk for her shoes. After slipping the pumps on her feet, he stood and pulled her up. "It's almost seven o'clock and everyone else, except the security guards, went home long ago. Let's go have a drink and some dinner. Do you like seafood?"

She nodded and stretched. "Is Mrs. Jenkins fixing another of her specialties?"

"Mrs. Jenkins has gone to visit her sister for the weekend. I thought I'd take you to Shanghai Red's. It's close and the food is good."

"Shanghai Red's? It sounds like something out of an old Humphrey Bogart movie."

Ben laughed. "Trust me. You'll enjoy it."

On their way out, Gayle touched the exotic magenta blossoms on the sideboard. "Thanks for the flowers. They're beautiful."

"Better than roses?"

"Much better. How did you know?"

"Just a hunch," Ben said. "You don't seem the typical rose type to me."

"I hate to leave them here over the weekend. Could we take them home?"

Feeling secretly smug that his choice had pleased her, Ben hefted the three-foot arrangement and followed Gayle from the empty building.

From the outside, Shanghai Red's seemed to be everything the name implied. But the ramshackle, unpainted wooden building which looked like a huge old warehouse alongside the ship channel was, in reality, a carefully constructed façade for a fine restaurant. Once inside, they were led to a private alcove on an upper level with flickering candlelight and an excellent view of the water. Under cover of darkness, the brackish unromantic channel was transformed into a shimmering surface of polished ebony and twinkling lights. Rusty tugs became dim silhouettes slipping silently through the shadows.

They enjoyed a fine wine and a leisurely dinner. Over coffee and dessert, Gayle stifled a yawn. "I'm sorry. It's not the company. I feel like I could sleep for a week."

Ben smiled. "It looks as if you didn't get much rest last night either." When Gayle dropped her eyes, he chuckled. "We'd better get you home to bed. Five o'clock comes early."

"Five o'clock?"

"Sure. Have you forgotten? Tomorrow's the day we're going fishing. We have to be on the lake by sunrise."

Later, when they arrived at the sprawling brick and cedar house off Memorial Drive, Ben carried the large flower arrangement inside.

"Are you sure you don't want me to take these upstairs to your bedroom?" Ben asked with a mischievous arch of his brow as he set the container down on the spot Gayle indicated.

"Positive." Gayle answered firmly. "The hall table will be fine. They're lovely there."

"I'm glad the ginger pleased you," Ben said, turning to gather her into his arms. "I want to do everything to please you."

144

He lowered his face to hers so slowly that Gayle could feel his breath play across her cheek and she leaned toward him. Their lips met, warm, moist, seeking. Ben molded her body against his and murmured again, "I want to do *everything* to please you."

CHAPTER NINE

A raucous buzz split the cozy fabric of sleep. Frowning, Gayle tried to ignore it and settle back into the delicious world of slumber, tried to recapture the wonderful dream teasing the edge of her memory and slipping away as the jarring racket persisted. She groped for the alarm and gave it a disgusted swat.

Raising her head, she peered at the clock and saw that its red digital numerals read five o'clock.

"Five o'clock," she mumbled. "Nobody gets up at five o'clock on Saturday morning."

There was a sharp rap on her door, then Ben strode in, flipped on the overhead light, and cheerfully announced, "Rise and shine."

Gayle scowled and pulled the covers over her head. "Go away," she groaned. "It's still the middle of the night."

The bed sagged as Ben sat down on the edge. "Wake up, sleepyhead. The fish are waiting for us."

"Mmmfftt," she said from under the blanket.

Ben laughed and folded the cover back from her head. "I've brought you a cup of coffee, and breakfast will be ready in fifteen minutes. Get a move on," he said, giving her backside a whack.

When Ben had gone, Gayle emerged from her cozy cocoon and stretched. She took a sip from the steaming mug Ben had left on the bedside table and forced herself toward the bathroom. This was the only part of fishing that she hated. It made absolutely no sense to have to get up before dawn. She'd always found that the fish bit just as well at midmorning. It was some sort of crazy secret ritual that men had. Her father had been the same way.

After a quick shower, Gayle dressed in jeans, T-top, and a white cotton shirt. She added thick socks and sneakers, then pulled on an old red sweatshirt and a worn navy windbreaker she had pilfered from Ariel's closet. Gathering her hair in two loose clusters beneath her ears, she secured them with rubber bands. After a quick dash of lipstick, she stuck the tube in her pocket and grabbed her wallet and the house keys from her purse.

Damn, she thought as she found both sets of the study keys still in her bag. She'd meant to leave one set at the bank yesterday. Glancing around the room for a suitable hiding place, she dismissed each choice as too obvious. Then she remembered another of Ariel's pieces at the end of the upstairs hall. It was made from an old pot-bellied stove, a bird cage, and assorted sizes of pipes, springs, and ball bearings.

After wrapping both sets of study keys in a black scarf, Gayle crammed her other belongings, including a red stocking cap of Ariel's, into the pockets of her windbreaker and stepped out into the hall. The smell of cinnamon and frying bacon drifted through the house and her stomach growled in response.

She quickly stowed the scarf-wrapped keys deep inside the dark recesses of the pot-bellied stove and went downstairs. In the kitchen she found Ben, dressed in jeans and a plaid flannel shirt, whistling and taking up a plate of bacon from the frying pan.

"Good morning," she said.

He set the crisp bacon beside a heaping platter of French toast on the breakfast table and cast an appreciative glance over Gayle. "Good morning. You look a little more cheerful than the last time I saw you." He grinned and gave one side of her hair a playful tug. "I like your pigtails. You look about sixteen years old. Where's the glamorous executive?"

"I left her upstairs," Gayle said as she sat down and speared a fat piece of toast. "Fishing is serious business. You can't worry about looking gorgeous and catch the big ones."

"Princess, you'd look gorgeous in curlers and a gunny sack."

Gayle felt suddenly shy, and she covered her discomfiture by saying, "This breakfast looks wonderful. I would never have dreamed that you could cook."

"I'm a man of many talents." His voice was husky, seductive, rife with hidden meaning.

Gayle saw that familiar gleam begin to flicker in his eyes as he watched her pour syrup over the cinnamon-dusted wedges in her plate. She managed to eat one piece to his four by keeping her attention totally focused on the food and not glancing at him once.

By a few minutes past five thirty, Ben had packed a cooler of food and drinks along with their gear, and by six o'clock they were on I-45 headed north toward Lake Conroe. The predawn morning was a little chilly, but if the past few days were an indication, it would warm up in a few hours.

"Are we going out in a boat?" Gayle asked.

Ben nodded. "You can't fish for bass without a boat."

"Will we rent one when we get there?"

"No, Cal's is at our place."

"Whose place?"

"Cal's and mine. We bought a lakehouse a couple of years ago so we could spend a few days fishing now and then when I was in town."

Gayle frowned. "I don't remember a lakehouse listed among Mr. McDonough's property."

"The deed's in my name," Ben said quietly.

"Oh."

"Before the wheels start turning in that sharp little brain of yours and coming up with all the wrong conclusions, perhaps I'd better explain."

"Perhaps you'd better."

"Cal always loved to fish, but before two years ago, he had an old clunker of a boat that he had to load and hitch and drag to the lake. It was hard to handle and temperamental and required a lot of hard work. After his doctor warned him about his health and suggested that he retire, I was concerned about his trying to wrestle with that old relic, so I bought the lakehouse and gave him a new boat for his birthday. The boat stays at the lake and can be lowered and raised by an electrical system in the boat house. The whole idea was to make things easier for him."

Gayle felt tenderness swell her heart over Ben's thoughtfulness of an old man. "That was very sweet of you." Then she remembered that Calvin McDonough was supposed to be in perfect health, and a whole new set of questions arose.

"Ben," she began tentatively.

"Yes, sweetheart?"

"Why did Calvin tell you he was ill if he wasn't?"

Ben sighed and shook his head. "God only knows. I suppose it was all part of his scheme to manipulate me into moving to Houston and taking over the business. And I fell for the old duffer's sad story. I would have stopped his clock if I'd known he was playing games with me."

A eerie frisson akin to alarm flashed through Gayle, but she pushed it aside. "Maybe somebody did."

Ben's eyes left the road and turned on her. He was frowning and his jaw was clenched. "What are you getting at?"

"That somebody killed Calvin McDonough."

"Forget it, Gayle. It was an accident, nothing more. An accident." He turned his attention back to the highway.

"And I suppose the fire at the plant was an accident as well?"

"No, I suspect it was deliberately set by a disgruntled employee. Maybe one who'd been laid off recently. For a while you thought I might have set the fire. Now do you think I killed Cal, too?" Although Ben's voice betrayed no sign of emotion, his knuckles were bloodless as he held the wheel in a death grip.

"Of course not," she said indignantly. "You didn't even arrive in town until the day after he died." She might have suspected Ben of a lot of things—and still have a tiny nagging doubt or two about a few of them—but she never seriously considered him a murderer.

There was a long moment of silence between them as the tires whined along the interstate in the gray pre-dawn morning. "How did you know that?"

"Both Ariel and Mrs. Jenkins told me."

"I see." His knuckles gripped the wheel even tighter and the muscle in his jaw quivered.

Gayle could feel the tension radiating across the seat from Ben. But it was not the sexual tension usually present between them, so powerful that it was almost palpable. This was different. It was bewildering and a little frightening. Once again she wished for his Summers Profile so that she could truly understand him. She was becoming so emotionally entangled with this man that she could no longer trust her judgment to be objective. But she did know, as surely as she knew her own name, that Ben Lyons had secrets. He wasn't telling her everything. And until she knew all the answers, she would do well to keep up some barriers, maintain some healthy degree of wariness. After all, although Ben might really be attracted to her as a woman—and God knows, he could push all her passion buttons—the bottom line was that he still wanted control of McDonough Bearings.

The moment of tension gradually faded so that by the time they reached the lakehouse, they were laughing and swapping fish stories which had long since passed any semblance of credibility.

"That one fish," Ben declared, "fed a whole town for three weeks."

Gayle laughed at his audacious tale. "I don't believe a word of it."

The small split-level house of unpainted cedar and glass blended so well with its surroundings that Gayle almost missed it in the dim light beginning to break

151

from the east. A boat shed extended over an inlet carved from the lake and shored by a bulwark of heavy cedar posts.

They got out of the car and while Ben went to unlock the door, Gayle walked toward a small bluff and stood on the bank of the lake watching the sky gradually lighten with pink and gold streaks of dawn. The air was crisp and clean with the scents of pine and damp fallen leaves slowly returning to the richness of earth. Closing her eyes, she breathed deeply, savoring the freshness of the day.

The waterfowl were beginning to awaken and flutter along the silvery surface of the water. Their cries echoed across the waiting stillness of the coves and inlets below, through the trees overhead.

Sunrise was coming; the world was stirring from its darkness.

As the great orange ball rose over the shimmering, watery horizon, it cast sparks of fire on the dew-moistened leaves of the surrounding foliage. The sweetgum and tallow trees stood in flaming relief from the green of the pines and cedar, and their red, orange, gold, and yellow seemed like a fiery wake as the sun crested and rose from the water.

Gayle was so caught up in the beauty of the sunrise, she didn't realize for a moment that Ben's arm was around her or that she snuggled instinctively against his warmth.

"Isn't it magnificent?" she asked, looking up at him. Her breath caught when she saw a fire to rival the sun blazing from his golden eyes.

"Magnificent."

When Ben lowered his mouth to hers, Gayle's lips

were waiting. Moist, parted, ready to taste the sun. His touch was warm, hot, scorching. He clutched her along the length of his taut body, increasing the force of the kiss, plunging his tongue between her teeth as if he sought to consume her with his own brand of fire. Her arms went around him and she pressed against his back with aching palms and curling fingers.

His searching hands slid inside the back of her sweat-shirt and yanked the blouse from the waistband of her jeans until he could feel soft skin beneath his kneading fingers. His left arm held her lower body crushed against his, while his right hand sought the smooth mounds of her breasts and his tongue continued its plunder in the moist heaven of her mouth.

He moaned as his fingers touched her nipples made hard by her desire for him. When Gayle whimpered, he broke the kiss and stared at her upturned face with heavy-lidded eyes gone black with wanting.

"I've got to see you," he said. He shoved the layers of fabric up until her breasts were bared to his eyes and cupped in his hands. "Oh, my princess." His face was contorted with passionate agony, and his voice a husky rasp.

He bent to taste; to circle with a wet, rough tongue; to suckle; to nip; to moan against the creamy flesh. Sure she was dying of pleasure—Gayle was mindless, lost in sensation as she arched her back against his supporting arm and offered the sensitive peaks of her breasts to his tongue.

She could barely breathe from the longing, from the inferno ignited within her. His mouth dipped lower and he dropped to his knees before her. With a savage moan, he jerked open the snap of her jeans, shoved the zipper down, and buried his face in the softness of her belly.

Barriers, barriers, she tried to remind herself. She couldn't allow this to happen. But only a strangled cry escaped Gayle's constricted throat and she grabbed handfuls of hair for support. "Damn you, Ben Lyons," she managed to gasp. "Don't do this to me."

Ben froze. With his arms wrapped around her buttocks and his face pressed against the warm, smooth skin of her lower abdomen, Ben stilled and drew a deep, shuddering breath. Then another.

Gayle could barely stand and her whole body was drawn tight and trembling with anticipation. Yet he didn't stir except for the ragged breaths of warm air that blew against the skin just below her navel.

"Babe, I'm sorry. I'm sorry." With fingers that were shaky, yet infinitely gentle, he tugged down the T-top, the white shirt, and tucked them into the band of her jeans. Still kneeling before her, he zipped her jeans and snapped them, pulled the sweatshirt back in place and gave it a little pat. Without looking up he clutched her to him and leaned his forehead against her soft form.

"Oh, my love, I'm sorry," he whispered. "You deserve better than to have your clothes ripped off in the woods and be thrown on the ground by a horny bastard like me."

Tears sprang to Gayle's eyes and she threaded her fingers through his hair and cradled his head to her. "Shh, it's all right."

Ben dropped his arms from around her. "Go inside and wait for me."

"But—"

"Give me a couple of minutes. I'll be right in."

When she had gone, Ben shook his head. "Cute, Lyons. Real cute." He stood and rearranged his jeans to accommodate the ache that plagued him constantly these days. Walking over to lean against a tall pine tree, he sucked in a deep breath and called himself every name in the book.

Was this any way to treat a woman like Gayle? A woman he knew he was in love with? Hell, no. Gram would have had his hide. Gayle wasn't just any woman with a case of the hots. God, yes, he wanted her—and he was sure he could have taken her just now. But he wanted more than just a quick roll in the leaves.

He wanted . . . well, if he couldn't have her love just yet, he at least wanted her trust. And he could see the wariness in her eyes; she didn't trust him as far as she could spit. With good reason, Ben had to admit.

Guilt. That's what he felt. A damned, giant-sized, son-ofabitching case of guilt. If he hadn't exactly lied to her, he'd certainly skirted the truth. Hell, he might as well admit it. He'd lied . . . and stolen. Maybe he should come clean with her. Tell her the whole story. Maybe she'd understand. Maybe . . . No, he couldn't tell her yet. If he did, he could just picture her turning on him with fire in those beautiful blue eyes. Or worse yet, she might get scared and . . .

The thought of her being in danger made his blood chill.

He wanted to keep Gram's name and memory untainted. He wanted to keep his promise to Cal. He didn't want Gayle hurt. He didn't want Ariel hurt. There were too damned many horses to ride. Somebody, and he had narrowed down the candidates, was playing hardball, and Ben was caught in the middle.

155

Maybe this trip to Singapore was the answer. Maybe when he got back . . .

One thing for sure, he vowed to himself, until he could look Gayle in the eye and know that she trusted him, he'd keep his pants zipped and his hands to himself.

He raked his fingers through his hair and slapped the side of the pine with a bellow of frustration. A squirrel sitting on a branch above his head started chattering down at him.

Disgusted, Ben looked up at the scolding creature. "So you want a piece of me, too? Well, buddy, you'll have to get in line."

"Get the net! Get the net!" Gayle yelled as she reeled in a beauty. When the black bass was hauled into the boat, she held it up proudly. "Would you look at that? It must be six or seven pounds at least."

"At least," Ben said with a good-natured grumble. "How many does that make?"

"Five keepers for me, two for you, but who's counting?" Gayle couldn't resist a smug little smile as she dropped her latest catch into the live-well. "Want me to give you a few pointers?"

Ben laughed and made a whirring cast, and the plum-colored plastic worm landed with a plunk just beyond a rotted stump protruding from the murky water. "Why don't you get me another beer instead?"

Gayle scratched through the ice chest and came up with a can, popped the top, and handed it to Ben. "Brr," she said with a shiver, putting her chilled hands between her legs for warmth. "I don't see how you can drink that cold stuff." She rubbed her palms together and blew on them. "I would have thought it would be warmer by now, but I think it's getting colder."

Pouring herself a cup of coffee from the thermos, Gayle held it to her mouth and let the steam from the hot liquid warm her nose. She sipped it slowly, savoring the warmth and watching Ben reel in and cast again. It was long past noon and they had been fishing for several hours. Earlier they had stayed in the shallows, casting with spinner or crank bait. Now they had moved to deeper water, away from the protection of trees along the shore.

After the promise of such a beautiful dawn, the day had turned gloomy about midmorning. Not much above sixty degrees, the damp chill crept into Gayle's bones. She was grateful for the extra insulation of the bulky life vest she wore. Gayle would have suggested they leave, but Ben seemed to be enjoying himself so much, she hated to be a spoilsport. Tugging the red stocking cap farther over her ears, she hunched down in the padded chair and took another swallow of coffee. It was definitely getting colder.

"Are you tired? Too cold?" Ben asked. "We can go in if you are."

"No, I'm fine," Gayle lied.

"Are you sure?"

"Positive. I'm just giving you a chance to catch up before I go after the next five."

Ben grinned and winked. "I understand the crappie are pretty good around here too. Want to drown a few minnows?"

"You just want to see if I'll bait my own hook, don't you?" She reached for another rod, added a bobber and a small hook. "Watch me," she said, grabbing a minnow from the bucket and deftly spearing it on the end of her line.

"Not bad."

"Not bad? I'll have you know, it's perfect. Bet I'll catch a crappie before you catch another bass."

Ben's husky laughter floated over the water as he reeled in and cast again. "You're on. What are the stakes?"

"The loser has to clean all the fish."

"I think I've been hustled," Ben said a few minutes later when Gayle displayed a small crappie dangling from the end of her line.

After adding her latest catch to the well, Gayle wiped her hands and rummaged through a paper sack to retrieve a box of raisins. She shook out a handful and sat down to nibble on them and watch a waterbug skimming the surface of the water.

Despite the less than ideal weather, they had been having fun. Except that Ben had been acting a bit peculiar. He was not his usual cheeky self. And he hadn't leered at her once. That alone made her want to take his temperature to see if he was coming down with something. Oh, she had caught him staring at her once or twice during the day, but his expression was different from the cat-eyed predator's glint she had grown familiar with. It was softer, with almost a wistful quality.

The change in him had come after their encounter this morning. As the water gently lapped at the side of the slim fiberglass boat, she closed her eyes and remembered the power of that kiss, the feel of his hands moving over her. Her breasts swelled again as she recalled the exquisite agony of his mouth and tongue on their sensitive peaks. Regardless of her protests, she hadn't wanted him to stop. She had desperately wanted him to make love to her then, there on the leaf-strewn ground. The fire between them, which had been building for days, had burst into full flame. Now it lay banked and smoldering, ready to flash again at the least provocation.

He knew it; she knew it. It was only a matter of time.

It was folly, madness, the height of absurdity to allow herself to become more deeply involved with Ben. They were on opposite sides. She didn't completely trust his motives. But, irrational or not, she wanted him, ached for him. And more than that, God help her, she was falling in love with him.

In love?

Her eyelids flew open. Ben was standing at the prow, rod and reel idle in his hand, staring at her with a hunger that matched her own. She stiffened and sucked in her breath as she felt the boat rock beneath her and the wind whip the collar of her windbreaker. Neither moved. They were locked in a shared vision of longing so potent that it was painful.

The boat rocked violently and Ben's head jerked up to search the sky. When Gayle looked up, she saw a bank of black boiling clouds rolling rapidly toward them. The wind was picking up and the trees on the distant banks were bending and swaying with the force. The lake, which had been calm all morning, had suddenly become a mass of choppy whitecaps.

Ben cursed, threw down his rod, and hauled in the anchor of the bass boat. A jagged streak of lightning pierced the darkening sky and a boom of thunder rumbled close behind. He yelled at Gayle to hang on as he slid into the captain's chair and started the motor.

159

"What's wrong?" Gayle yelled as the powerful outboard roared to life.

"Storm coming!"

Gayle felt the first fat drops of rain as Ben headed the flat boat toward the lakehouse. They were only a few miles away, but it seemed like forever as the boat bumped along the rough surface, jarring her teeth with every bounce.

A gust caught the paper sack of food and swirled it overhead before tossing it into the churning jaws of the lake. The bucket of minnows overturned and the silvery bait flopped on the carpeted floor of the craft as the Styrofoam pail rolled from side to side, then flew overboard.

The boat whined and thumped over the frenzied choppiness as they rode against the wind. The drops were coming faster and harder. The sky grew blacker. Another flash of lightning electrified the darkness, another deafening boom of thunder followed in its wake.

Gayle wanted to yell at Ben to hurry as the drops turned into a frigid downpour, but she gripped the armrests of her chair and clamped her mouth shut as they slammed over the rising waves.

Within seconds her cap, her hair, and her clothes were drenched and plastered to her skin like a wet, heavy shroud. So dark was the sky, so thick the pelting deluge, that she could barely see Ben, three feet in front of her, hunched over the steering wheel, fighting the growing swells that could capsize them at any moment.

Panic attacked her, invaded her mind, ripped away composure. Gayle wanted to scream but the sound froze in her throat. She was panic-stricken, numb with terror.

Just as a jagged streak of lightning lit the whole horizon, Gayle saw the grotesque skeleton of a rotting tree looming directly in their path. She shrieked as Ben swerved sharply.

It was a hopeless, heart-freezing nightmare. They were going to die.

The boat flipped as it was catapulted high into the air, and Gayle was flung into the frigid, frenzied waves.

The force of the blow drove the breath from her lungs. Walls of churning water swallowed her, sucked away cap and shoes, tugged at the zipper of her life jacket.

In the midst of the violent lashing, a feeling of calm resignation settled over Gayle. *Ben,* she thought with painful regret, *I never told you that I love you.*

CHAPTER TEN

Ben clung to the offending tree and alternately cursed and prayed as he yelled Gayle's name through the howling storm. How was he going to find her when he could barely see six inches in front of his face? He was only a few yards from shore, a few yards more from the shelter of the lakehouse, but it might as well have been a thousand miles.

Railing against his feelings of impotence, his fury matched the violence around him as he bellowed her name through the driving rain and whipping whitecaps. Secure in his life jacket, Ben had no fear for himself. He was a strong swimmer and was used to the caprices of bodies of water bigger than this lake. He'd battled the elements all his life. But Gayle . . .

"Goddammit, Gayle," he roared, "where are you? Answer me! Gayle!"

He was sick with fear for her. Bile rose in his throat and choked him. He cursed the raging storm; he cursed the churning lake; he cursed his own stupidity. If he hadn't been so damned carried away with a colossal case of the hots for her, he would have seen the signs, known that a sudden storm was brewing.

He'd failed her. He might even have killed her.

"Oh, God," he groaned, anguish twisting his features as tears mixed with the rivulets of rain pouring over his face. "God, help me find her, and I swear I'll take care of her. I'll love her and keep her from harm and treasure her all the days of my life." His words were a strangled sob mingled with the tearing wind. "Give her back to me."

His eyes searched the wet gray curtain as it pounded the dark, pitching surface. There was a brief slack in the deluge, and he saw a flicker of orange about thirty feet away. His heart was in his throat as he struck out toward it with frantic, powerful strokes.

It was Gayle! Her orange life vest bobbed her head above the angry water. Half-conscious, she choked and moaned, but she was alive. She was alive!

Towing her behind him, Ben cut through the waves like a maddened bull. When he reached the shallows, he scrambled to his feet, hoisted her sodden form over his shoulder, and broke into a run toward the car. All he could think of was getting her to a hospital.

She was still coughing and gagging as he put her in the passenger seat. He stripped off his life jacket and felt in his pocket for the keys. Thank God they were still there. He started the wagon and swung it around toward the small road. Not fifty feet ahead, a huge post oak lay uprooted across the only way out.

"Damn! Sonofabitch!" Ben pounded the steering wheel in frustration.

Shoving the gear in reverse, he backed the car to the door of the lakehouse and carried Gayle inside to the bathroom. The hum of the emergency generator told him that the power had been knocked out. Thankfully the water heater used propane, so there would be warmth from the shower to drive off the chill. She was almost blue with cold. He didn't think they had been in the water long enough for her to have severe hypothermia, but he didn't know.

He turned on the shower, adjusted it for warm, and began to strip away her sodden clothes. Gayle was still groggy and mumbling teeth-chattering, indistinguishable phrases between coughing spasms. Her flesh cold and pale, she shivered and trembled all over.

Ben, still fully dressed in his drenched clothes, lifted her into his arms and stepped into the shower.

The warm spray felt like heaven to Gayle.

"Ben, I thought I was dying," she managed to say.

"I know, sweetheart, but you're safe now."

Very gently he stood Gayle on her feet so that the spray could warm her. Holding her steady with one arm, he managed to struggle out of his clothes. When he had kicked them aside, he pulled her close so that the water cascaded over both of them.

"Are you getting warm, honey?"

Still feeling a bit groggy and disoriented, she nodded. "I need to wash my hair."

"Wash your hair?" Ben almost shouted. "Holy hell, Gayle—" He stopped short when he saw her screw up her face like a child about to cry. Possessively he drew her against him. "Shhh, princess. We'll wash your hair. Can you stand by yourself?"

With infinite care, Ben pulled the rubber bands from the tangles and tenderly lathered the shampoo through the dark strands. His fingers felt for any signs of hidden bumps or cuts but found none. By the time he had rinsed the last of the soap away, Gayle's exhaustion was taking its toll. Her legs almost gave way and she grabbed Ben for support. Scooping her into his arms, he stepped out onto the bathmat.

Gayle's arms circled his neck and her head lay against his shoulder. "Ben?" she whispered.

"Yes, sweetheart?"

"We're naked." Her words were drowsy and slurred.

He chuckled. "Yes, love, I know. Can you stand up for just a minute so I can dry you?"

When she sighed and nodded, he set her on her feet and grabbed a stack of towels. He dried her hair as best he could and, with Gayle holding on to his shoulders for support, briskly rubbed her body with the others, checking for any evidence of injury as he went.

Every square inch of her, down to those cute red-tipped toenails, was perfect. His task was sweet agony.

After wrapping a towel around her wet hair, Ben took a blanket from the linen closet and swaddled Gayle like a cocoon. He lingered only long enough to pull on a brown terry-cloth robe he found hanging on the back of the bathroom door before lifting her and carrying her to his king-sized bed.

"I was so scared," Gayle murmured. Her words were listless and weak. "And I was sorry I never . . . I never . . . I'm so tired."

"Shh. You need to rest," Ben said, slipping her between the covers and climbing in beside her. He held her close and watched her until her long, dark lashes fluttered and lay still against her pale cheeks.

Only then did he realize that he was trembling. For once it was not with wanting her, though God knows his desire clung to him like a constant shadow. He shook with the aftereffects of a fear so potent that just thinking about Gayle lost in the stormy water caused his heart to race and his muscles to tighten into a quivering mass. Forcing himself to breathe deeply and relax, Ben took comfort from the soft curves of her body lying securely in his arms. Thank God she was safe. He loved her more than he ever thought it was possible to love anyone.

Very gently he laid the back of his hand on her forehead, her cheeks. Her skin was soft and warm. His gaze went to the curve of her slightly parted mouth, and he fought the urge to kiss the sleeping lips. She was his princess. *His.* And his stupidity had almost snatched her from him. His muscles tightened once more and anxiety clutched at his guts with a steel hand. From now on he would protect her. Nothing would be allowed to harm her or worry her.

Once or twice today he'd started to tell her everything. Now he was glad he hadn't. It would only add to her concerns, complicate her job, perhaps place her in more danger. No. He'd get things straightened out alone. Soon.

Ben allowed himself only a feather-light stroke of her lips before he rose and dressed. He had to get that damned tree out of the way and get Gayle to a hospital as soon as possible. She'd had a hard jolt and there was no way for him to know if she had any internal injuries or was in danger of pneumonia or something worse. His guilt-laden mind conjured up all sorts of dire consequences from the bone-chilling episode in the lake.

In less than an hour, the storm had moved on and the late afternoon sun shone brightly on Ben as he wielded the power saw on the oak blocking the road.

* * *

Gayle awoke gasping for air and thrashing about in the constricting blanket. She was drowning! "Ben!"

When she became fully conscious, Gayle realized that she was safe in bed and relaxed. Her breathing slowed and she blinked her eyes, getting her bearings, trying to remember what had happened. She vaguely recalled Ben pulling her from the frigid water after the boat capsized, holding her under warm spray, putting her in a cozy bed. Details escaped her.

Struggling from the confines of the gold blanket wrapped around her, she got out of bed and discovered she was naked and her hair was still damp. Gathering the blanket sarong-style around her, she wandered through the small house looking for Ben. It took only a few moments to discover that she was alone. Where was he?

Hearing the whine of a motor outside, she parted the draperies in the step-down living area and spied him working with a chain saw on a large oak lying across the road. Dressed in only a pair of faded jeans, his bronzed torso glistened in the sun as muscles strained and rippled with his task. Even from this distance she could almost feel the strength of his broad back and shoulders. Her fingers ached to touch him and her heart swelled with love for him. Knowing him as she did now, how could she ever have suspected Ben of devious motives?

Ben had saved her from certain death, had tenderly cared for her. A bond had been forged between them that Gayle couldn't deny. Nor did she want to. She loved him. For all the complications it might cause, she loved him.

What did he feel for her? There was no question that

he desired her but was there more? He seemed jealous, possessive, but that wasn't love, it was only a male staking territorial rights. It was too early in their relationship to talk of love and commitment. Time would bring answers.

Anxious to talk to him, she set about finding something to wear. Her own clothes were in a soggy heap in a corner of the bathroom. In a second bedroom, she discovered a man's gray sweatsuit. It was a bit baggy, but the elasticized waist and ribbed bands at ankles and wrist made it a reasonable fit.

With a brush she found in the bathroom, Gayle worked the tangles from her damp hair and fluffed it into its naturally wavy style. She retrieved her lipstick from the zippered pocket of the sodden windbreaker and added a dash of color to her face. The best she could find for shoes was a pair of shower thongs at least four sizes too big, but she found if she scrunched up her toes and slid along carefully, she could manage.

Cautiously she picked her way between the puddles on her way to Ben. He looked up as she approached. Killing the motor on the chain saw, he laid it down and walked to meet her, a smile breaking across his sweating face. A kingdom's gold couldn't rival that smile.

Suddenly the smile faded and a frown took its place. "What's the matter? Are you okay?" He grabbed her shoulders and searched her face. "Are you sick? Are you in pain?"

Gayle laughed and reached up to caress his cheek. "I'm fine thanks to you." She looked toward the tree and said, "What are you doing, cutting firewood?"

Ben scowled at the half-sawn trunk. "I'm trying to get

the damned thing out of the way so I can get you to a hospital."

"A hospital? What in the world for? I'm fine."

"You need to see a doctor. You need to be checked over."

"I'm perfectly all right, believe me."

"You're sure?"

"I'm sure. Just a bit hungry and I think we lost our supper." She gave a teasing little grin and asked, "Are you sure you didn't stage the whole thing to keep from cleaning all those fish?"

Ben's scowl deepened and his eyes narrowed to amber slits. "That's not funny, Gayle."

"Well, you don't have to be such a bear."

Pulling her into his arms in a crushing hug, Ben said, "Princess, I'm sorry. Because of my stupidity, I almost lost you and it scared the hell out of me." He released her and stepped back to scan her features. "Can you forgive me?"

"Ben, there's nothing to forgive. It's not your fault that we were caught in a storm." His bleak expression told her that he still felt guilty about the accident, but she dropped the subject for the moment. "How do you like my outfit?" she asked, pulling out the sides of the baggy pants and doing a slow turn made awkward by the oversized thongs.

He was smiling again when she finished her rotation. "Ravishing. You may set a new trend. But the sandals don't look too great for walking." He scooped her into his arms and started toward the cottage with a determined stride. "Let's go feed you."

Gayle squealed and kicked her legs, sending the

thongs flying. "Put me down, Ben Lyons. I can walk, for heaven's sake."

"I don't want you to break your pretty neck in those things. Angel, I couldn't stand it if something else happened to you." His voice was low, gentle.

Winding her arms around Ben's neck, Gayle relaxed against him, nestled her cheek upon the bare bronzed skin that smelled like sunshine and damp virile male. She felt safe, secure, cherished. A contented sigh escaped her lips, and she slipped one hand from his neck and slid it slowly across the slope of his shoulder and down over his chest. Ben's pectorals, flexed with the weight of her in his arms, rippled under her touch. She could feel his heart thudding beneath her fingers and the tempo of her own heartbeat increased.

Ben radiated masculine power. It surrounded him like a vibrating aura, permeating her senses, spawning alarming urges deep inside her that made her tremble.

As he carried her up the steps and through the open door, Gayle could feel Ben's body trembling as well. She knew it wasn't the exertion of carrying her that caused the tremors, or his ragged breathing. He wanted her. She could feel his desire.

When he set her on her feet, Ben stiffened his arms to his sides and balled his hands into fists. Standing only inches away, Gayle watched as he closed his eyes, dropped his head back, and sucked in a deep shuddering breath.

She knew exactly how he felt. Her own body ached for his touch, throbbed with longing. The hunger she'd felt since she'd first laid eyes on Ben that day on the patio had been building, prowling through her like a stalking cat.

"Ben," Gayle whispered.

His head lifted and his eyes slowly opened. His heavy-lidded gaze scorched her soul.

Mesmerized, Gayle's hands reached out and splayed across the golden sheen of his taut abdomen. When he flinched at her touch, she smiled, feeling heady with her power to excite Ben as much as he excited her. Slowly she slipped her outspread hands up the front of his chest, pausing to circle his nipples with her palms, to weave her fingers through the fine tawny curls.

Ben's hands covered hers and squeezed. His features were drawn into a mask of exquisite agony. "Sweet heaven, love. Stop it. You're killing me."

Gayle was puzzled. And hurt. This was the second time he'd rejected her. "I thought you wanted me." There was a tiny quiver in her soft voice.

When he heard her words and saw the look on her face, it was as if a knife were slashing him open. As gently as if he were holding a butterfly, Ben cupped her chin in his palms and his shaking fingers feathered against her cheeks. "Princess, I'm afraid I might hurt you. We've got to get you to a doctor."

Relieved, Gayle chuckled. "Ben, I'm perfectly all right. I don't need a doctor."

"But—"

"Ben," she said firmly, "I'm fine." She trailed one finger across his collarbone and up his throat to his chin. "Why don't you shut up and kiss me?"

"Yes, *ma'am,*" he said, gathering her in his arms and lowering his mouth to hers.

He held her as if she were delicate porcelain, and his lips were incredibly soft and gentle as they touched hers. Gayle melted against him as his tongue slipped

171

into her mouth, tasting its sweetness, exploring its recesses. He pulled her closer to the heated need of his body, lighting a flame deep inside her.

Clutching the muscled strength of his back, Gayle strained toward him and Ben's hands slid down her spine, curving over the swell of her buttocks to cup and lift her closer to his hardened readiness.

Still concerned that Gayle might be injured, Ben slowly unleashed the hunger that was burning a hole in his insides. He meant to be gentle, meant to pleasure her softly. But when Gayle rubbed against him and a small sound vibrated in the back of her throat, Ben went wild. The tender kiss became savage, his tongue a lance of fire. He licked her lips and trailed a wet path to her ear. Nipping at the lobe with his teeth, he groaned, "I've got to have you, love. I'm hurting."

"Oh, yes," Gayle murmured. "Yes."

Ben scooped her up and strode into his bedroom. When he set her on her feet Gayle reached for the hem of the baggy sweatsuit she wore, but Ben restrained her hands. "Let me."

He pulled the top over her head and stripped the pants away, then stood and stared at her slim, smooth nakedness as if bewitched. "Dear God, you're magnificent."

Dropping to his knees at her feet, he buried his face in the soft flesh of her belly and hugged Gayle to him as if she were a rare treasure. His hands slid up to cup the fullness of her breasts and he raised his eyes to her. "This is what I wanted to do this morning. To see you naked, to touch you with my hands and taste you with my mouth, to smell you on fire for me. I want to hear you moan my name and feel you hot and wet beneath me. It haunts my dreams. Sometimes I think I'm going crazy.''

His words were like shock waves; their power buckled her knees and she inhaled sharply, whimpering his name. Ben stood and lifted her onto the bed. Quickly shedding his clothes, he climbed in beside her. His hands caressed her softness, his mouth worked magic until she was writhing under his touch.

"Now, Ben. Please, now," Gayle begged, opening to him.

He tried to hold off, and sweat beaded his brow as he struggled to regain his control.

"Please, love, now," Gayle whimpered, tugging at his buttocks.

Ben was lost.

His eyes feverish with desire, he moved over her and took her with a powerful surge, driving deeply, sheathing himself in the velvet wonder of her flesh. He thrust once, twice. Riptides of pleasure sucked at her, pulling her under, and she arched and cried out as a final tremor of ecstasy thundered through them both at the same instant.

With trembling forearms, Ben held his weight off Gayle. His head drooped as he tried to catch his breath. "Angel, I'm sorry. Did I hurt you? I didn't mean for it to be like that. I swear I meant to go slow and easy.''

Gayle laughed softly and smoothed his damp hair from his forehead. "No, you didn't hurt me. It was wonderful.''

In the aftermath of their passion, Ben rolled to lie alongside her and hold her close, this woman he loved more than his own life. He stroked her glistening body and nestled her in his arms as her breathing slowed to the contented purr of sleep. He kissed the palm of her hand and whispered, "Princess, you hold me right here."

When Gayle awoke, she found the place beside her empty. Then hearing the distant noise of the chain saw, she realized that Ben must be working on the tree.

Ben. She smiled and hugged herself with the memory of their lovemaking. Never had she encountered anything quite like it, and Gayle was surprised at her own behavior. She had been as wild and hungry as he. It was overwhelming.

In the midst of her romantic reverie, her stomach rumbled. Gayle chuckled. "Looks like I can't live on love alone," she said aloud. "I'm starving."

After she freshened up and pulled on the baggy sweatsuit once more, Gayle went looking for something to eat. In the refrigerator, she found packaged biscuits to go with a couple of cans of beef stew from the pantry. While the oven was heating, she gathered up Ben's and her wet clothes and, after cleaning out the pockets of their things, dumped them in the small washing machine set in one corner of the kitchen.

Her bare feet were getting chilly on the linoleum floor, so while the biscuits baked and the stew simmered, Gayle went to Ben's bedroom to get some socks. She had seen a bunch there earlier when she was looking for clothes to wear.

The socks, along with papers, fishing lures, and a strange assortment of odds and ends, were a jumbled mess in the dresser drawer. Not a single sock was with its mate. How did he ever find two to match? Her basic sense of order was offended. Gayle took out the drawer, dumped the contents on the bed, and set about sorting.

When she finally found a pair of white tube socks without holes in the toe, she pulled them on and finished her task. She'd found mates for all but three. Neatly rearranging the things back in the drawer, she noticed a Cayman Airways ticket folder. Why she picked it up and looked inside, she'd never know. But she did.

And what she found made the blood drain from her face. There, in bold red letters, was the date of his arrival in Houston from Grand Cayman. October fourteenth. She closed her eyes and wished the date away, but when she opened them, it still screamed from the page. Arrival in Houston 10/14, 3:42 P.M.

October fourteenth. The day before Calvin McDonough died.

Her hands shook. A spasm gripped her heart like a cold fist. She felt sick at her stomach. He had lied.

Why?

"Gayle!" Ben's voice bellowed from the kitchen. "Something's burning!"

Gayle managed to shove the drawer back in place and start to the door before Ben intercepted her.

"Babe, what's wrong? You're white as a ghost."

"I'm fine," she said, trying to push past him, trying to shake off the grip he had on her shoulders. "I've got to check the food."

"Forget the damned food! I'm taking you to the hospital right now."

Nothing she could say would convince him otherwise. And to be honest, she'd just as soon be at the hospital as to be here alone with Ben now. She barely had time to turn off the stove and grab her wallet and keys while he pulled on a shirt. He didn't wait to button it before he picked her up and charged toward the station wagon.

Ben drove like a madman while Gayle sat huddled against the door, hands clenched together, trying to calm herself, trying to make some sense of the damning evidence she had found. Why had he lied to everyone?

Maybe he hadn't. Maybe the airline had made a mistake. Yes, of course. Airlines sometimes make mistakes. That was it. She would ask him. He would explain everything. *Confront him, Gayle. Now.*

But when she opened her mouth, nothing came out. She was afraid to ask. Afraid of what the answer might be.

One part of her trusted him, knew that there must be a reasonable explanation for the ticket date, knew that Ben was an honorable, caring man. Another part was still wary, suspicious, anxious to believe him dangerous, ruthless. Knew that he had lied and would lie again to get what he wanted: McDonough Bearings.

And if Ben had been in Houston the day before Calvin's death, that meant he might . . . No! She refused to think about the possibility.

It had to be a mistake. How could she find out without asking Ben directly? For her own sanity she had to know.

The station wagon!

It was rented. The proof of his honesty was only inches away from her knee. He would have rented the car at the airport, and the papers would be in the glove compartment. The date would be on them.

They screeched to a stop at the door of the emergency room, and Ben dashed around the car to help her out.

An hour later they were on their way back to Houston. The doctor had pronounced her healthy, but had prescribed a day or two of rest and had given them both antibiotics to counteract any effects of swallowing lake water.

Gayle tried to feign sleep to avoid conversation with Ben, but she couldn't keep her eyes off the glove compartment. She had to know. Now.

"Gayle, are you sure you're okay? You're awfully quiet and jumpy. I don't know if I trust that doctor. He didn't look a day over sixteen."

"I'm okay, Ben. I'm just tired. And thirsty. Would you stop somewhere and get a Coke for me?" That would get him out of the car. Then she could look at the rental papers.

"Whatever you want, princess." He took the exit ramp and pulled into a service station.

Damn! He stopped not three feet from the drink machine and was out and back before she could get the glove compartment open. He handed the Coke to her and she smiled a feeble thanks.

"Ben?"

"Yes, sweetheart?"

"Do you know what I'm hungry for? A Twinkie."

"A *Twinkie?*"

Gayle nodded. "There's a convenience store right across the street. Would you mind getting one for me?"

"I'll get you anything you want, love."

His voice was so gentle, so solicitous, Gayle felt like a dirty dog for being deceitful. But the minute he was out

177

of sight, she opened the car pocket, pulled out the rental papers, and looked for the date.

October fourteenth.

A wave of despair washed over Gayle and she felt as if something had died within her. Hope had been jerked away. Her head drooped dejectedly. There was no mistake. Ben had lied. She didn't even want to think about why.

Gayle couldn't eat a bite of the Twinkie. And she sat curled up in the corner, eyes closed and stomach tied in a thousand knots, all the way home.

When they were finally at the door, Gayle sighed with relief. The tension coupled with her earlier frightening experience had exhausted her. She wanted to be alone, wanted some time to make sense of what she'd discovered.

Ben refused to cooperate. Instead, he unlocked the door with his keys, turned off the alarm system, and followed her inside. It had never occurred to her before that he had keys to the main house; came and went as he pleased.

Mrs. Jenkins was still with her sister; Hector was nowhere about. She was alone with Ben in this big house.

Ben, who had lied about being in town when Calvin died; Ben, who had eavesdropped on her conversations and dogged her every move; Ben, who had reeked of gasoline the night of the fire; Ben, who was determined to have McDonough Bearings; Ben, who may have wheedled or blackmailed a lonely old man out of a fortune. Gayle had seen his violent streak when he had turned on the drunken cowboy two nights ago.

Gayle's heart began to beat faster as fear crawled over her. Maybe he was some kind of sociopath. She had

178

dealt with a few cases in her career. Often hard to distinguish, they were invariably likable, charming people who would lie or cheat without a twinge of guilt, who could smile as they stole your life savings or cut your throat.

A hand clamped on her shoulder and she sucked in a strangled gasp.

"Gayle? Sweetheart, what's wrong?"

Calm. She had to remain calm, act perfectly normal. "Why, nothing is wrong. I'm just tired." She managed a pitiful excuse for a smile and said, "I'm going right to bed. Good night, Ben." She opened the door for him to leave, but he didn't budge.

"Since Mrs. Jenkins is gone, I'm spending the night here. I'll sleep across the hall in one of the guest rooms if that's what you prefer, but I'm not leaving you alone. You go on up and get into bed. I'll rustle up some food and bring you a tray in a few minutes."

She might as well have tried to reason with a post. No argument she could muster could dissuade him. While she undressed for bed, she tried to convince herself that there was no real basis for being afraid of Ben. He had pulled her from the water when he could have easily let her drown.

No matter what the evidence, no matter what the suspicions, Gayle couldn't believe that Ben would hurt her. Nor did she really believe he was some sort of crazy man without a conscience who could bilk Calvin McDonough out of his company, who could commit murder and arson. She'd let her imagination get out of control.

Come to think of it, Ben had never said when he arrived in Houston. It had been Ariel and Mrs. Jenkins who told her. Of course Ben hadn't corrected her misconception, but there must be some perfectly logical reason. He deserved a chance to explain.

Her body trembling with exhaustion, Gayle climbed into bed and sank back into the pillows. He could explain. She was sure of it. She couldn't have fallen in love with a warped person. Her judgment wasn't that clouded. With that thought, she relaxed and snuggled between the covers. She'd confront him and he'd tell her the truth. And it would be perfectly logical.

When Gayle awoke, sunlight filtered between a crack in the drawn draperies. She rolled over and looked at the clock. It was almost noon. Had she slept so long? Her first thought was of Ben. She needed to talk to him right away.

Rolling out of bed, she winced with every movement of her stiff, sore muscles. A hot shower helped to relieve the aches, and by the time she had dressed in comfortable jeans and velour top, she was feeling much better.

Downstairs she found Mrs. Jenkins in the kitchen cutting up vegetables for a pot roast. The older woman looked up and smiled as Gayle entered.

"Good morning, I expect you'll want your coffee," the housekeeper said, wiping her hands and reaching for the pot.

"Yes, thanks," Gayle said, accepting the mug and sipping its contents.

"Mr. Ben was mighty worried about you. Said to let you sleep as long as you wanted."

"Where is Ben?"

Mrs. Jenkins reached for an envelope on the windowsill and handed it to Gayle. "He had to go out of town for a few days. Very important business, he said. Didn't want to go at all, but I convinced him that I'd look out for you."

Disappointed to have missed him, Gayle took the letter and sat down at the kitchen table to open it.

Gayle:

Sorry I couldn't wait for you to open those beautiful blue eyes. I have important business or horses couldn't drag me away. Mrs. Jenkins has promised to take care of you for me. I'll be back as soon as possible—no later than the end of the week. Dream of me.

All my love,
Ben

Gayle looked up from the note and asked, "When did he leave?"

"Not more than an hour ago. About wore a hole in my kitchen floor, but said he couldn't wait any longer or he'd miss his plane. He sure seemed put out that he had to go off. I think Mr. Ben has taken a real shine to you."

When Gayle felt herself flush, the housekeeper laughed and said, "I think you've taken a shine to him, too. He's a fine figure of a man. Reminds me a lot of my Leon when I see Mr. Ben watching you. Real hungry-looking."

"Leon?"

"Leon was my husband. Killed in Korea in '51. We hadn't been married but two years, and I was a widow by the time I was twenty-three."

"Did you have any children?"

She shook her head and turned back to gather ingredients for an omelet.

"And you never married again?"

"Never found a man to equal my Leon. After I lost him, I moved in with my mama and looked after my baby sister, Maggie. Then I came here."

"You've worked for Mr. McDonough for a long time, haven't you?"

"Twenty-four years next July. Right after Mama died. She worked for him till she took sick. Mr. Calvin saw to it we never wanted for a thing."

While Gayle ate the brunch the housekeeper prepared, she was able to confirm that Ben hadn't shown up at the house until the day after Calvin died. She also listened to long dissertations about the fine character of Ben Lyons. Everybody, it seemed, including Mr. Cal, was just crazy about that wonderful young man.

Ben should hire Grace Jenkins as his press agent, Gayle thought as she thanked her for the meal and walked outside to the patio. With fingers stuck in her back pockets, she wandered down the stone steps to stand at the edge of the lazy bayou and watch the ducks quack and paddle on its muddy surface.

Maybe it was a good thing that Ben would be away for a few days. His presence complicated things; made Gayle forget her priorities. Now she could concentrate on her work, on her commitment to Ariel.

She sat down on the steps and ran her fingers over the rough surface. It had been on this very spot that Calvin McDonough had died. Rather than give her a creepy feeling, sitting there somehow drew her closer to the old man. She could almost feel his vitality.

"I'm going to save your business if I can," she said to

the breeze playing through the willow trees. "And before this is over I'm going to know all about everybody connected with McDonough Bearings. If the person behind all this maliciousness is with the company, I'll find him. I promise."

A few minutes later, Gayle retrieved one set of keys from the pot-bellied stove. Deciding her hiding place was as safe as, and certainly more convenient than, the bank, she left the spare set there and spent the rest of the afternoon in the study.

A search through the remaining file drawers turned up nothing out of the ordinary. Ariel called about the time she had finished the last of the papers in the metal cabinets.

"How are the pieces coming?" Gayle asked her friend.

"So-so, I guess. I can't concentrate as I ought because I'm worrying about what's going on down there. Have you found out anything yet? Did the Summers Profile find any suspicious characters?"

"Ariel, it's only been three days since you left. It's going to take some time. I haven't even started testing."

"Well, why in heaven's name not?"

Gayle sighed. Of course Ariel was impatient, but she had no idea of the mess things were in at the plant. She didn't understand the importance of things like records and credit and payrolls and equipment. Trying to explain would be an exercise in futility.

"I had to do some other things first. I'm going to begin tomorrow, but remember, it will take several days just to complete the testing. Interpreting them will take even longer."

"Have you checked out Hector's story with the Blue Line Express office?"

"Not yet. I plan to stop by on my way to the office tomorrow morning. I also intend to check with the arson investigator to see if he's turned up anything. Martin Brewer said Mr. Sands was nosing around the plant Thursday and Friday, but I didn't run into him."

"Is Ben Lyons still bugging you about selling out to him?"

"I think we've reached an understanding for the time being." Gayle kept silent about her growing involvement with Ben. It wouldn't do to give Ariel something else to worry about. Gayle had worries enough for both of them.

The two friends chatted for a few minutes more before ending their conversation with Gayle's promise to call if she discovered anything new.

When she climbed the stairs after dinner, it dawned on Gayle that she had never looked through Calvin's bedroom. Now was as good a time as any. She walked to the closed door at the end of the upstairs hall and paused before it. Her hand reached for the knob and hesitated. Going through the study was bad enough. Bedrooms were very personal places.

"Sorry, Cal, but it's got to be done," she muttered. Drawing a deep breath, Gayle opened the door and flipped on the light.

It was a large, masculine room done with deep forest-green carpet the same shade as the velvet draperies on the far wall and the bedspread covering the large cherry four-poster. Other heavy cherrywood pieces stood against the walls, which were papered in a muted pattern of deep greens, burgundy, and beige. A fireplace, cold and empty, stood across from the foot of the bed.

Gayle's gaze traveled to the painting over the mantel and froze. A laughing woman in a flowing white dress sat among a field of golden wildflowers. In the hazy background were blue sky and rolling green hills. The oil portrait had almost an ethereal feel, and its delicacy seemed out of place in the boldly masculine room.

Moving closer, Gayle snapped on the light attached to the intricately carved gold frame and studied the face of the young blond woman. Who was this lovely creature? She seemed familiar.

The woman in the watch. Gayle was almost sure of it. Deciding to get the gold watch from the safe and compare the two, Gayle went back downstairs and unlocked the study door. The house was quiet. Mrs. Jenkins must already have retired to her rooms.

After turning on the lights, Gayle crossed the study to the closet, opened the door, and moved aside the boxes. Kneeling in front of the safe, she dialed the combination and tugged on the heavy door. Inside lay the maroon velvet box. She picked it up and lifted the lid.

It was empty.

CHAPTER ELEVEN

The missing watch continued to plague her thoughts as Gayle walked out of the house the next morning. It must have been taken at the same time as the missing documents. After the theft, she remembered seeing the velvet box in the safe, and it hadn't occurred to her to look inside. Who would take a few insignificant papers and an old watch, yet leave cash and a valuable set of coins? And why?

Hector Luna was standing in the driveway beside the Corvette, giving the fiery red fender a final swipe with a chamois. He brightened into a gold-toothed smile when he saw Gayle approach.

"She's all polished and gassed up," the wiry man said, holding the door open.

"Thanks, Hector. It looks like a good job."

His chest swelled noticeably. "Mr. Ben said to make sure we took good care of you while he was gone. He's a good man, that Mr. Ben. Reminds me of Mr. Cal when I first came to work for him."

Gayle smiled. Ben had certainly established a fan club in the household. "Hector, do you ever remember seeing Mr. Cal wearing a gold pocket watch?"

Cocking his head to one side, Hector frowned as if

searching through thirty years of memories. Finally he shook his head and said, "No, Mr. Cal he always wore a wristwatch."

"Did you ever hear him mention someone named Margaret Cameron?"

"Margaret Cameron." He pondered the name carefully and shook his head.

After getting directions from Hector for locating the Blue Line Express office, Gayle headed toward Hobby Airport on the south side of town, puzzling over the gold watch as she drove. Somehow all the pieces must fit together.

Gayle had questioned Mrs. Jenkins earlier, and Hector's answers had confirmed the housekeeper's. Calvin McDonough had always worn a wristwatch. Neither of them knew anyone named Margaret Cameron, nor were they aware of any special significance of the painting in his bedroom. "Except," Mrs. Jenkins had said at breakfast, "he was awfully crazy about it. It's hung over that mantel as long as I can remember. 'Course he's always had lots of pretty paintings hanging about. Miss Sylvia said some of them's right valuable."

"Miss Sylvia?"

"Sylvia Norman, Mr. Cal's secretary."

"I thought she was Martin Brewer's secretary," Gayle had said.

"Is now. Used to be Mr. Cal's, though. Was as far back as I can remember. Took care of all sorts of things for Mr. Cal. Real close them two was. I always thought she had her cap set for him, but he stayed a bachelor. Too set in his ways, he used to say when I'd tell him he needed a wife."

Snaking along through the rush hour traffic, Gayle's

brow furrowed as she muttered, "Margaret Cameron". . . Perhaps Ariel would know who she was. Or Sylvia Norman. Secretaries knew everything.

The Blue Line Express office was another dead end. The supervisor, a plump, friendly woman whose name badge identified her as Joyce Stanley, assured Gayle that no one from their office had called Calvin McDonough.

"Our office delivers everything directly to the address on the package. We might telephone to confirm a delivery time, but we never ask anyone to pick up shipments. It's just not done. I told that to the Mexican gentleman the day he came in. Marilynn told the same thing to the man who came by a few days ago. I was on my lunch break when he was here, but she told him it's just not done. And there was never a package for a Mr. McDonough."

"A man came by a few days ago?" Who would it have been? "Was he with the police or arson investigation?"

The supervisor shook her head. "No, nobody like that or Marilynn would have reported it to me."

"Could I talk to Marilynn? Perhaps she can describe the man for me."

Another frustration, Gayle thought later as she pulled into the parking lot at McDonough Bearings. Marilynn was on a two-week vacation, but the supervisor promised to have her call Gayle when she came back to work.

Someone *had* lured Hector away deliberately. Who? And who had been to the express office before her? Instead of answers, Gayle seemed to find only more questions.

In her office a few minutes later, Gayle found another exotic flower arrangement. This one was magnificent spikes of calla lilies surrounding a gnarled piece of polished driftwood and mixed with lotus pods and greenery. The card confirmed what she already knew. Ben.

Much better than roses. She smiled, then caught herself. *Ben Lyons, you still have some explaining to do. Why were you in Houston on the sly? Do you know who Margaret Cameron is?*

It was tempting to jump to all kinds of conclusions, let her emotions overrun her objectivity. She'd already been guilty of doing that with Ben. Now years of training and experience as a consultant cautioned Gayle to wait until all the facts were gathered. When she had more information, things would begin to come together.

It was time to begin testing with the Summers Profile. Gayle had intended to start with the executives and board members, but in light of the situation, it hardly seemed feasible. Winston was out of town; George Schulze and his entire department were involved in setting up their new quarters; Martin Brewer was busy all day with appointments that took him out of the office. Then of course there was Ben, who had refused to take the test at all, even if he hadn't flown off to God knows where.

She would have to start with the people in sales, production, security, as well as secretaries and clerks, and arrange it so that there was as little disruption in work as possible. Since Martin Brewer was away, Gayle enlisted the aid of Sylvia Norman to help with the assessment scheduling. The woman was an organizational wonder. Before lunch their preliminary work was completed and testing could begin that afternoon.

"You're great," Gayle said. "I wonder why Cal didn't make you president."

The redhead gave a wry smile and adjusted her designer glasses. "These days I often wonder the same thing. Calvin McDonough was a fine man, a brilliant and dedicated man, but he was a stubborn old coot. And a bit of a male chauvinist. He would never admit it of course, but he was."

Watching the older woman carefully, Gayle said, "I suspect that you knew him better than anyone. And I suspect that you don't miss much of what goes on around here."

Laughter lit the secretary's eyes. "I suspect you're right. I came to work for Cal almost forty years ago as a green kid just out of business college. I've survived this long because I've learned to keep my mouth shut and my nose in my own business."

The two women looked one another straight in the eye, each weighing, assessing, then coming to a silent understanding of mutual respect. Gayle was aware that Sylvia Norman probably knew more about McDonough Bearings and its employees than anyone else, but she also knew that the statuesque redhead wasn't willing to share her information. Was it because of old loyalties? Or was there some other reason? Her Summers Profile would be interesting.

Gayle collected the score sheets from the last group of the day, added them to her briefcase, and turned to the young woman who had been assigned to assist her. "Thanks, Angie. I think that's all for this afternoon."

Angie offered an open, bright-eyed smile. "Thank you, Ms. Summers, for letting me help. Being a receptionist is so boring sometimes, but this is great. I'm majoring in business, you know. Organizational and behavioral management. Of course, since my dad got laid off last year, I'm having to work and finish up at night." The blonde glanced down at her watch and added, "And I'd better hurry or I'm going to be late to class. See you tomorrow."

Gayle waved as her assistant ran out the door. It had been Sylvia's idea to change Angie's assignment, and Gayle was delighted. While she might appear to be a bit bubble-headed, the girl was obviously bright. Gayle smiled. Who was she to throw stones? She'd played the airhead when it suited her purpose.

With Angie's help, the testing should be complete by the end of the week. Then Gayle could begin the difficult task of interpretation. A little trickle of apprehension crept through her defenses. Ariel was counting on Gayle to find something significant in the protocols. What if she found nothing? Or worse yet—a familiar shiver of her old fears slithered up her spine—what if she found a murderer?

Tuesday night Gayle was nursing a headache the size of Mount Rushmore when the phone rang. The noise ripped through her pounding skull like a bullet. Slamming her pencil down, she grabbed the receiver.

"Hello." Her tone was short, impatient.

"Princess, is something the matter?"

"Just a headache. Where are you?"

"Not where I'd like to be." Ben's voice was low and husky. "Are you sick? Have you been taking your antibiotics?"

"Are you kidding? Mrs. Jenkins stands over me and watches me swallow every pill."

"Then why the headache?"

Gayle closed her eyes and sighed for the hundredth time that day. "McDonough Bearings, what else? We've had another monumental disaster. George Schulze came running in today about to have apoplexy. The temporary office is ready and equipped, but when he sent someone to collect the backup records from the off-site location, they found nothing but empty boxes. Every single computer tape is gone. Vanished. Everybody is running around in a state of panic, and I have a headache."

Ben was silent for a minute, then said quietly, "I know where they might be. Try the Prestwood Warehouses on Mitchelldale. Hector should have the key and can direct you."

"How do *you* happen to know where they are? And why aren't they where they're supposed to be? Tell me that."

"Sweetheart, you're just going to have to trust me."

"Trust you? Trust you?" Gayle's voice rose an octave. "How can you expect me to trust you when I know you lied to me about when you came to Houston?" Damn! Why had she blurted that out? She'd meant to present her case rationally and give him a chance to explain. The thudding ache in her head increased.

"Gayle, I didn't lie."

After the torture she'd put herself through over his deception, his calm denial irritated her. "Ben, I saw the date on your airline ticket when I was straightening your socks. And don't tell me it was an error, because I checked the rental date on the station wagon."

"And as usual you assumed the worst about me; jumped to all the wrong conclusions." His voice was cool, tinged with barely controlled anger, or was it regret? When he spoke again, it was in slow, measured tones. "I didn't lie to you. You never asked me. You asked Ariel, Mrs. Jenkins, the paper boy for all I know. You never asked me."

"I'm asking now, Ben."

"Yes, I got into Houston on the fourteenth. But I went directly to the lakehouse to spend a couple of days getting things ready for Cal's and my fishing trip. That's why I rented a station wagon with a trailer hitch, so I could haul stuff, take the boat to Conroe for repair. I have the work order if you want to check it. And I'm sure I could round up several witnesses who saw me."

"Oh." Of course, it was perfectly logical. She had sounded like a self-righteous snoop. Shame caused a sinking feeling to settle in the pit of her stomach. She wanted to cry. Why did she continue to doubt his motives? Was it some form of self-protection? "I'm sorry, Ben. I'm truly sorry. Can you forgive me?" Gayle's voice broke as she spoke. A tear trickled down her cheek and she sniffed.

"Gayle, honey, are you crying?"

"Of course not. I rarely cry." She sniffed again.

Ben groaned. "Babe, don't do this to me. It tears me up for you to be upset. I don't blame you for thinking the worst of me. Hell, the truth is . . . Well, damn." He groaned again. "I'll be there in a few days and we'll get this straightened out."

Gayle wiped her nose with the back of her hand. "When are you coming back?"

"No later than Sunday. Sooner if I can swing it. God, I wish I were with you right now. Princess, I'm hurting to hold you, to feel your sweet body close to mine," he said, his voice husky, seductive. "I lie awake at night thinking of all the places I want to touch, to taste. I want to bury my face in your soft skin, kiss every beautiful inch of you from your cute red toenails to those luscious lips and make my way down again . . . slowly. It's driving me out of my mind.''

Gayle sucked in a shuddering breath as his words ignited a fire in her blood. ''Holy hell, Ben,'' she whispered.

''My sentiments exactly.'' His chuckle was deep, throaty. ''I've got to go now. I have to meet someone for breakfast. Dream of me tonight, princess.''

After she replaced the receiver, Gayle sat staring at the picture of Ben on the study desk. Waves of longing washed over her and she rubbed the smiling photograph with her thumb. Never had a man affected her the way he did. Even her earlobes tingled.

It wasn't until much later that it dawned on her. Gayle was in bed, arms snuggled around her pillow, thoughts replaying her conversation with Ben, vowing to trust him from now on. Then the newly patched, delicately stitched trust began to unravel.

Breakfast?

Why was Ben having a breakfast meeting at night? She sat straight up in bed. Where in the world was he? Trying to make some sense of it, Gayle did a quick calculation of time zones. He must be halfway around the globe. What would he be doing in the Orient? It was something to do with McDonough Bearings, she was sure. But what? Then she remembered the sales and warehousing operation which had been such a financial disaster for the company.

Singapore. That's where he was. She'd bet her new

computer system Ben Lyons was in Singapore. Damnation! What was that scoundrel up to now?

The backup records were exactly where Ben said they would be. How had he known about them? Why weren't they where they were supposed to be? Things were becoming more convoluted by the minute.

With the help of a warehouse worker, Hector loaded the material and delivered it to the plant. Gayle had watched every box as it was loaded and followed the truck to the plant. She personally supervised the duplication of the tapes and hired an independent delivery service to transport the extra copies to another location. No one else would know the new site or have access except Ariel or her.

It didn't take a genius to figure out that something fishy had been going on with the records. Was the fire at the plant set to cover up irregularities in the books? Was George Schulze or someone in his department responsible? Gayle reminded herself that she mustn't jump to conclusions. She needed proof. By the end of the following week, the auditing firm she hired would be scrutinizing every document with a magnifying glass. If something was wrong, Mason Butcher and Associates would find it. They were the best in the city.

On Friday afternoon, Gayle and Angie sat in the conference room waiting for Martin Brewer, Sylvia Norman, and Winston Dasher to finish their tests. They were the last of them. George Schulze and his entire department had completed theirs earlier in the day. Now Gayle would have the information she needed on everybody connected with McDonough Bearings from the night watchman to the president—except Ben Lyons. She had even persuaded Hector Luna and Grace Jenkins to fill out a questionnaire.

Gayle glanced at her watch. It was almost five o'clock. As soon as these three were done, she planned to go home, soak in a hot bath, and after dinner start the process of scoring and interpreting the protocols. She intended to hole up in the study for the weekend, or as long as it took, and delve into the secrets and personalities of over a hundred people.

Sylvia Norman finished first, and a few minutes later Martin Brewer handed his materials to Gayle and left the room. Winston closed the booklet and stood.

"That was relatively painless," he said, smiling at Gayle. "Angie, I see you moved into a new job while I was gone."

"Oh, yes. And it's wonderful," she gushed. "Did you know that Ms. Summers is an academic celebrity? I told my Organizational and Behavioral Management professor about what I was doing, and he was impressed that we're using the Summers Profile. He's read all the papers that Ms. Summers has published in the journals, and did you know—"

"Thanks, Angie," Gayle interrupted, "but I'm sure Mr. Dasher isn't interested in hearing about rather dull research." She handed the young woman a stack of material and said, "Would you drop these off on my desk?"

When Angie had left the room, Winston smiled and said, "She's a nice kid, and obviously impressed with the chance to work with you. I didn't realize we had a real live celebrity in our midst."

Gayle laughed. "I'm hardly star quality."

"I suppose that's a matter of opinion," Winston said, his blue eyes twinkling as he looked Gayle over. "You rate about five stars with me. I've had a hard time keeping my mind on business all week for thinking about tonight. What time shall I pick you up?"

Gayle looked puzzled. "Pick me up?"

"Don't tell me you've forgotten. You promised to have dinner with me tonight."

"Oh, Winston, I'm sorry. I have tons of work I need to do."

"You know what they say about all work and no play. Martin tells me that you've been working late every night. You need to relax for a few hours. Besides, I've already told Mrs. Jenkins that I've made reservations for Tony's and she could have the night off."

Not really wanting to go out, Gayle hesitated. She wanted to get started on the profiles, but Winston looked so imploring, and she *had* promised. And it was business, she told herself. This would be a good opportunity to question the company attorney about personnel. "Okay," she finally said.

Winston flashed a grin. "Great. Is seven thirty all right?"

The two of them chatted as he walked Gayle back to her office. When they reached her door, Winston brought her hand to his lips and brushed it with a kiss. "Until tonight," he said.

Gayle sank into the big executive chair in the empty office and kicked off her shoes. She massaged her feet, but her fingers lacked the expertise of Ben's. Ben. She looked at the arrangement of flowers that had come yesterday. In a low oriental-style container, this one was a tall, graceful study in white Fiji mums, cascading orchids, and a swirl of Scotch broom. Much better than red roses.

197

Gathering the material she would need into her brief-case, Gayle slipped into her shoes and left the office. In the parking lot she waved to Angie and Winston, who stood talking beside Angie's little compact, and climbed into the Corvette. She dreaded the trip home in the rush-hour traffic, and she dreaded spending the evening with Winston. Not that he wasn't a perfectly nice man, thoughtful and handsome, but compared with Ben, Winston seemed downright . . . dull. Of course Winston was polite, charming—and if the goo-goo eyes Angie had been making over him were any indication—very attractive to most women. She couldn't imagine seething with fury about something Winston said or did. But neither could she imagine her earlobes tingling with passion for him.

It took an hour of stop-and-go driving before she pulled into the garage. She was surprised to find the lights on in the house and Mrs. Jenkins in the kitchen.

"I thought you might have gone to your sister's to-night instead of waiting until tomorrow," Gayle said.

"No, I telephoned her after Mr. Dasher called, but she already had plans for the evening, so I thought I'd fix myself a sandwich and watch a movie on television."

Gayle bade her good night and went upstairs. At least she'd have time for a long hot bath. As she went through her wardrobe later, trying to find something appropriate for a posh restaurant, Gayle wished she could wear jeans and eat another chicken-fried steak. She giggled as she pulled a black silk dress over her head. Somehow Winston didn't seem the chicken-fried steak and beer type.

He wasn't, she discovered as the waiter stood beside the candlelit table and took their orders. Winston preferred veal and very expensive wine, rather three very expensive wines. One with appetizers, a second with the entrée, and a third with dessert. It was after nine o'clock, and Gayle reminded herself to sip her cocktail slowly or she'd be sloshed by the time dinner was over. They'd already spent an hour or more over drinks at the Remington, which must be the current "in" place for the elite of the city to gather. Winston had seemed to know most of the crowd and had introduced Gayle to several people, but the names meant nothing to her.

"How is your work coming along?" Winston asked.

"Slowly, I'm afraid. I suppose you heard about our difficulty locating the off-site records. It gave us a fright for a few hours."

Winston nodded. "I talked to George for a few minutes this afternoon."

"Poor man. He was so upset that I was afraid he was going to have a heart attack."

"That's George. He gets very distressed if everything isn't just so. But he's a good man. George has been with McDonough Bearings for as long as I can remember. I was surprised that Cal didn't name him president when he decided to retire. I think George was surprised, too. He seemed to be the logical choice. I don't think the company would have gotten into the state it's in if he'd been in charge."

Gayle raised her eyebrows. "You think Martin Brewer is to blame for the problems?"

Winston raised his hand in denial. "No, Martin is a fine fellow, but his mind isn't on the company these days. I imagine you know about his wife."

Shaking her head, Gayle said, "No, tell me."

"Lydia has been very ill for about five years. She has

to have constant care and frequent dialysis treatments. It's been a serious drain on Martin both emotionally and financially."

Their conversation was interrupted when the waiter brought the appetizer. When they were alone again, Winston smiled and said, "I want to hear more about your test, the Summers Profile. Can it really do the things Angie says?"

"Exactly what has she been telling you?"

Winston laughed. "You know Angie. From what she says it can do everything except wash your socks. She mentioned something about some prison studies."

Gayle waved a dismissing hand. If Angie were here right now, she could cheerfully strangle that girl for talking so much. It had never occurred to Gayle that someone from the plant would know about her research with criminals. People in business rarely read academic journals. "Angie exaggerates. I did some work with the Colorado prison system, mostly aimed at vocational education and rehabilitation with inmates." She laughed and tried to pass it off lightly. "You know, try to find something they might be good at besides stealing cars and holding up liquor stores."

"That's all the test is for?"

"It was designed as a tool in personnel selection," Gayle said, carefully evading his question. "Who knows?" she added, leaning forward and cocking her head playfully, "I may discover that you're better suited to be a break dancer than an attorney."

Winston laughed and reached across the small table to capture her hand and bring it to his lips. "Have I told you how very lovely you are tonight?" His eyes were all but devouring her.

"Thank you," she said, easing her hand away and reaching for the wine. He was making her uncomfortable. She could never think of Winston as more than a friend. To escape his gaze, she took a sip from her glass, a bite of her appetizer, and nervously scanned the room. Her glance froze on a figure at a table across the room and she choked on the escargot.

Even with the dim lighting, she couldn't mistake the broad shoulders in the dark suit. Or the mane of gold-streaked hair. It was Ben Lyons.

A surge of conflicting emotions raced through her rattled brain as their eyes met. Surprise, elation, anger, curiosity, anxiety. Guilt. A king-sized case of guilt that Ben had seen Winston kissing her hand. No, she reminded herself. There was no reason for her to feel guilty. Her dinner with Winston was perfectly innocent. And just exactly what business did Ben Lyons have sitting there spying on her? How dare he traipse off to God knows where, then waltz back in and expect her to be waiting for him!

Just because one of his sexy smiles could have her breathing hard or a single touch could ignite a flame that would blister her nail polish was no reason to overlook his other behavior. She was sick to death of his strange comings and goings, his secrets and deceptions. This time he had some explaining to do. And in the meantime, he could sit there and brood like some Gothic hero. See if she cared.

Knowing Ben was watching her every move, Gayle turned to Winston and bestowed one of her best molasses-dripping smiles. She took another sip of wine and glanced toward Ben with a smug lift of her chin.

Ben's posture was rigid and there were cold, sharp

daggers in his predator's glint. He stood, tossed back the rest of his drink, and started toward their table with a purposeful stride.

Gayle realized at once that she had made a severe tactical error. She recognized that look. *Dear Lord, he's going to make a scene.* Gayle grabbed her purse and said, "Excuse me for a moment, please."

Cursing her spike-heeled evening sandals every step of the way, Gayle practically ran to the ladies' room. She almost made it through the door before a strong hand clamped around her arm.

"What are you doing here?" His voice was gruff, terse. The muted illumination of the hallway didn't disguise the dark shadows under his eyes or the droop of his lids. Weariness etched furrows across his forehead and alongside his mouth.

Gayle would have been concerned about his exhausted appearance if she hadn't been so caught up in her other emotions. She twisted from his grip and glared up at him. "I'm about to go to the bathroom, if you don't mind."

"You know what I mean. Why are you here with that prissy-assed lawyer?"

"We're having a pleasant dinner, obviously." Gayle faltered when she saw Ben's expression. She wasn't afraid for herself, but she'd seen Ben's jealousy surface once before. She didn't want Winston subjected to Ben's tirade. "And discussing business."

"If you're discussing business, why does he keep leering at your bosom?"

"*You're* the only person I know who leers at my bosom. What are you doing here, anyway? I thought you were tending to your *banana business.*" She drawled the

202

last two words and searched his face for a reaction. Was he going to lie again?

Ben frowned and raked his fingers through his hair. "I have been tending to business and I've had one hell of a week. I busted my butt to get back to you, and what do I find? Mrs. Jenkins tells me you're out to dinner at Tony's with fancy-pants. Do you have any idea what it did to me to sit there and watch the two of you? Watch that slick sonofabitch practically drool over you?" Ben clenched his jaw. "I've a good mind to break his god-damned neck."

Gayle was furious with Ben's evasion of the truth and with his jealousy, so angry that she had to bite back the blistering words burning her tongue. But before she lost her temper completely and made a spectacle of herself, she whirled to go into the ladies' room.

Ben grabbed her firmly by the arm and turned her back to face him. One hand cupped her chin and his voice softened as he said, "Sweetheart, I told you I didn't want you going out with other men. Why are you with Dasher? I want the truth."

"The truth?" Gayle hissed. "The truth? You wouldn't know the truth if it jumped up and bit you on the be-hind. Take your hands off me, you devious possessive jackass." Ben immediately let her go and stepped back. "I've told you before and this is the last time I intend to repeat it. I'll go where I choose, when I choose, and with whom I choose. And if you say one cross word to that poor man, I'll never speak to you again. Is that clear?"

A tiny smile lifted one corner of Ben's mouth, then spread to a lazy grin. "You're one hell of a woman when you're mad."

How dare he laugh at her! The nerve of that throwback to a Neanderthal! She grasped for words to cut him off at the knees. Then a devilish thought formed a wry smile and she chucked his chin. "Don't wait up for us, big fella. Winston and I have a *long* night planned." She turned toward the entrance to the powder room, then with one hand on the door, she glanced back over her shoulder. "By the way, did they buy many bananas in Singapore?"

Inside, Gayle sank into a chair and dropped her head into her hands. How did she get herself into such a mess? How could she have fallen in love with such a crazy, complicated man? Why couldn't she be attracted to someone like Winston Dasher?

Gayle sighed. Hormones did strange things.

Well, her hormones were going to have to control themselves and learn to live with frustration. Ben Lyons was simply too taxing to her emotional well-being. She was tempted to call Ariel and tell her to sell McDonough Bearings to him. Then she could go back to Denver, build her business there, and be rid of this whole nerve-wracking mishmash. To hell with Ben Lyons. She didn't need the bother.

Gayle fixed her makeup, washed her hands, and stalled for time until she was sure Ben must have left the restaurant. She was halfway to the table when she saw him. He was sitting beside Winston, laughing and talking to the attorney as if they were old Army buddies, and scarfing down the rest of her escargot.

Both men rose when she approached. Winston looked uncomfortable, but Ben grinned and held her chair. "I knew you wouldn't mind if I invited myself to

204

join you and Winston. Why eat alone when you can enjoy a meal with friends, I always say."

Gayle smiled and took great pains to step directly on Ben's toe with her spike heel. Ben kept the grin plastered on his face and never even winced.

Usurping the role of jovial host, Ben was charm itself during the entire meal. He directed the conversation, saw to it that wineglasses were kept filled, and was so generally solicitous, Gayle was surprised that he didn't cut her meat for her. Winston, of course, was too well bred to be anything but polite. Gayle managed to eat, but the delicately prepared veal medallions sat like boulders in her stomach as she considered all manner of revenge.

Ben didn't even allow Winston to pay the check. But the last straw came when he said, "Winston, old boy, there's no need for you to go out of your way to drive Gayle home. Since we're living at the same place, I'll be glad to take her."

Gayle smiled at Ben and delivered a swift kick to his shin. He winced this time, but only slightly. "Winston will take me home," she said firmly.

Ben assumed a look of wide-eyed innocence. "Why of course, sweetheart, if that's what you want. I was just trying to be helpful."

"And pigs can fly," Gayle muttered as she marched out of the restaurant with Winston trailing along behind.

As she and Winston pulled out of the parking lot, a big silver Lincoln Town Car pulled out behind them and followed on their bumper all the way home.

When they turned into the drive, every room in the house was brightly lit, and a police car, blue and red lights flashing, sat in front. Ben jumped out of his Lincoln and was in the house ahead of them.

"Oh, Mr. Ben," Mrs. Jenkins said, wringing her hands. "I'm so glad you're home. Somebody broke in the house. They've wrecked Miss Gayle's room and tried to break down the door of Mr. Cal's study."

CHAPTER TWELVE

Gayle keyed in the last of the Summers Profile protocols, rubbed the back of her neck, and shrugged her tired shoulders. Her fancy new portable scanner had worked like a charm at first, then refused to take the last thirty answer sheets. Calling it names hadn't helped. Reduced to entering the remainder of the data on the computer by hand, a tedious, time-consuming process, she only hoped the rest of the equipment worked as it was supposed to. Having hard copy of the information would be more convenient than being tied to the computer screen, and the local representative had assured her that the printer she had rented would interface with her system.

After giving the appropriate commands, Gayle closed one eye, crossed her fingers, and waited.

The printer came to life and began spitting words across the page. It worked! Thank heavens, she thought as she watched the printouts roll from the machine.

Knowing it would take several hours for all the data to print, Gayle stood and stretched, then headed toward the kitchen for a soft drink. On her way she picked up a piece of candy from the basket Mrs. Jenkins had left on the hall table and glanced at her watch. It was after five o'clock and the trick or treaters would be coming soon.

Before she left this morning, Mrs. Jenkins had reminded Gayle that tonight was Halloween and the kids would be disturbing her work. The housekeeper had hesitated to leave her alone, especially after the scare last night, but Gayle had insisted that the older woman not cancel her plans. Hector and Ben would be close by, not that she was feeling kindly disposed to Ben Lyons.

In fact, after his abominable performance at the restaurant the night before, she had been decidedly cool with him. In his typical cavalier fashion, Ben had ignored her frosty behavior, asking her out to dinner as if nothing unusual had transpired between them. As if he hadn't acted like a total and absolute boor. Gayle had informed him in her haughtiest tone that she planned to work the entire weekend, and he could take a flying leap into the bayou for all she cared. Ben had only grinned and winked and proceeded to change all the locks in the house, whistling "Hard Hearted Hannah" the whole time. The tune had nearly driven her crazy until she remembered the name of it.

No reason was offered for his mysterious trip to Singapore, if indeed that was where he'd been. When she had brought up the subject, he'd neatly sidestepped the issue. Ben still had a lot of explaining to do.

"Hard Hearted Hannah," indeed!

Gayle selected a can of soda from the refrigerator, popped the top, and took a sip. As she had done scores of times since last night, she tried to figure out who had broken into the house. At least she knew it wasn't Ben or Winston. But whoever it was had scared poor Mrs. Jenkins out of her wits.

The telephone rang, startling Gayle from her reverie.

When she answered the kitchen extension, Ariel said, "What's going on? Have you found anything yet?"

"I'm working on it," Gayle said. "We've had some more excitement around here though."

"Excitement? What happened?"

"Winston and I went out to dinner last night and when we got home we found the household in an uproar. Mrs. Jenkins had heard a noise and when she went to investigate, she glimpsed a man in dark clothes and a ski mask trying to jimmy the lock on the study door. She tripped the alarm and barricaded herself in her room until the police came. By that time, of course, the culprit had vanished."

"What was he after?" Ariel asked. "Is anything missing?"

"Nothing. And only my room was ransacked. But it was a disaster. Every drawer was emptied onto the floor, my clothes were thrown around, even my makeup was dumped. It looked as though every corner of the room had been searched, but nothing was missing. It made me sick to think that someone had been through my personal belongings, violated my privacy. After the police left, it took Mrs. Jenkins and me over an hour to clean up the mess. I suspect that whatever he wanted was in the study, but it was locked and the keys hidden. And Mrs. Jenkins heard him before he could break the lock."

"Did the police find any fingerprints?"

"They dusted everything," Gayle said, "but Mrs. Jenkins thinks he was wearing black gloves. I doubt if they'll find any. I can't imagine what he was after. Obviously it was something in the study. The only thing important in there is my data. I've finished all the testing and the protocols were in the study. But I can't imagine why anyone would want to steal those. They're useless to anyone but me."

"Maybe someone doesn't want you knowing their deep, dark secrets."

"Possible, I suppose, but who would know the capabilities of the Profile? I think it was something else they were after, but what? And there was another thing that's a little scary. To have gotten inside, the intruder had to have had a key and known how to turn off the burglar alarm. That means it was someone familiar with the house. Probably someone with McDonough Bearings, someone we know."

"It's all connected, isn't it? The financial problems with the company, the fire, Uncle Cal's death. Gayle, whoever murdered him is doing all this. I don't want you in danger. Maybe we should call off the whole thing. Sell out to Ben Lyons and forget it."

Gayle couldn't believe what she said next. "No, Ariel, I'm determined to get to the bottom of this mess. I think we're getting close. I'm not in danger, at least I don't think so. The police have promised to have a patrol car make frequent rounds for the next few nights. Hector and Ben are both nearby most of the time, and Ben changed the locks today."

"Ben? *He* changed the locks? Isn't that like letting the fox guard the henhouse? Maybe it was Ben Lyons who did it. There's something very suspicious about that man."

"You're telling me," Gayle said. "But Ben couldn't have done it. He was having dinner with Winston and me last night."

Ariel chuckled. "I'll bet that was an interesting dinner."

"I'd just as soon forget it. Ariel, do you know of any reason why your Uncle Cal would move the backup records of the company to another site?" Gayle explained the problem with the missing records.

"I don't have a clue. It sounds as if he was protecting them from tampering—or maybe checking them over, looking for irregularities."

"That's what I think. Maybe he found something and . . ."

"And somebody killed him," Ariel finished.

"It's possible. If the company had folded, the problem would be swept under the rug. But you refused to allow it, and the records division was set afire. That much makes sense. What I can't figure out is the significance of those items stolen from the safe. But it's got to be connected."

"Gayle," Ariel said quietly. "Who do you think might have done it?"

"I don't really know. The most obvious candidate is George Schulze. As comptroller he had the best opportunity and, from what I understand, he was bitter about not being made president when your uncle retired. But we don't have enough information yet. I'll know more after I get a look at his Profile. I'd hate to accuse the poor man unjustly."

"I'll bet he did it," Ariel chimed in. "I never did like the wimpy little twit."

"Being a twit doesn't make him guilty. Let's hold off until we have some proof. Mason Butcher and Associates will go over the records next week, and if there are any irregularities, they'll find them." Gayle remembered the painting in Calvin McDonough's bedroom and asked Ariel about it.

"All I know about the painting is that Uncle Cal loved it. Once when I asked about it, he said it reminded him of Scotland and all he'd sacrificed to go awandering. 'The folly of youth,' I believe he said. What does that have to do with anything?"

"I'm not sure."

When the doorbell chimed with the unmistakable impatience of excited young fingers, Gayle ended the conversation and went to the door. Standing on the porch, clutching orange plastic pumpkins and large grocery bags, were three junior-sized goblins and a plump little honeybee with blond curls and rouged cheeks.

"Trick or treat!" they shouted in unison.

Gayle gasped in mock horror and pretended to be frightened as she gave candies to all the giggling little ones.

Children came in a steady stream until after nine o'clock. With all the interruptions it was impossible to do any work. After her first few efforts to concentrate on the information already transmitted by modem from the Denver mainframe, she gave up and enjoyed the kids. There were so many that the candy and gum ran out along with all the fruit and cookies she could find in the kitchen. She was reduced to digging in the bottom of her purse for coins to give the goblins.

By a quarter of ten, things seemed quiet and Gayle was in the kitchen munching on a sandwich she'd finally had time to make. Her stomach had been protesting its emptiness for the past two hours. She'd only taken a couple of bites when the doorbell rang again. Looking longingly at the roast beef masterpiece she'd just built,

Gayle sighed, got up, and trekked to the front door. Only three pennies and a nickel lay in the bottom of the basket.

She opened the door to a black-caped figure in a grotesque rubber mask with bulging green eyes and red fangs dripping painted blood. Gayle's eyes widened as she looked up at the monster looming in the doorway, towering over her.

This was no child!

Before she had time to slam the door, Dracula grabbed her wrists and shoved her backward. Gayle screamed and began to struggle, kicking and trying to wrest her arms from the painful grip. She fought the enshrouded figure with a frenzied desperation born of mad terror. They slammed against the hall table and a brass lamp crashed to the marble floor. The treat basket skittered from the table, flinging the coins across the polished surface as Gayle twisted and thrashed about.

Managing to jerk one arm free, Gayle shrieked and beat against her assailant, lashed out with her feet, but to no avail. Her strength was a pitiful match for his, and despite the rush of adrenaline, she was tiring quickly.

With a brutal surge of power, Gayle was flung to the floor, facedown, her arms yanked almost out of their sockets as they were twisted behind her back. She emitted a terrified squawk as the menacing figure straddled her and held both of her wrists in one leather-gloved hand.

"Be still," he hissed, his voice raspy and muffled by the mask. "And I won't hurt you."

Gayle's breath came in strangled gasps as her cheek lay against the cold, hard marble. Her heart thudded as if it would burst. Survival instinct compelled her to struggle against her captor.

The monster jerked her arms and grabbed a handful of hair in a punishing fist. "Be still, I said." The words were a muffled, guttural growl.

Dazed, exhausted, Gayle managed to nod her head. She felt his weight shift, then heard a ripping sound. Her wrists were bound behind her, her ankles taped together, and a wide strip slapped across her mouth. She heard the front door close and cherished a fleeting hope that he had gone. But the squeak of his rubber-soled shoes brought the bitter taste of fear and bile to her mouth. She swallowed it down, having the sense to know that her own nausea could kill her as quickly as this menacing monster.

He dragged her to the hall closet, shoved her inside, and closed the door. Gayle had never known claustrophobia until now. The darkness, the confinement, the cramped position of her bound body closed in on her, began to overwhelm her. It felt like a coffin. Fear slithered up her spine and choked her.

She was going to die. Like Greg, she would be another victim of the Summers Profile and the madmen it threatened.

No! She was not going to die, or if she was, at least she refused to die like a helpless coward. Using every ounce of courage she possessed, Gayle forced herself to breathe deeply, to relax. Calm, she reminded herself. She must remain calm.

When Hector had come running in shouting an incomprehensible mixture of English and Spanish, Ben jumped up from his desk, knowing immediately that

214

Gayle was in danger. Since dark they had been taking turns walking the grounds, watching the main house.

Ben grabbed Hector's shoulders and shook him. "What's wrong? Is it Gayle?"

"Sí," he managed to gasp. "A big monster in black. He went in the front door. Miss Gayle, she scream."

"Call the police," Ben shouted over his shoulder as he took off in a dead run, cursing every step of the way, fear dogging his heels, pouring fire into his blood.

The front door was closed and locked. Swearing and yelling Gayle's name, his finger stabbed at the bell and his fist pounded the door. When there was no answer, Ben broke out in a sweat and his hands shook as he fumbled for the keys in his pocket. After what seemed an eternity in hell, he managed to unlock the door and fling it open.

Charging inside, Ben shouted for Gayle. He could hear noises coming from the study and ran toward it. As he rushed through the doorway a black-clad figure in a rubber Halloween mask dashed past him, and Ben made a grab for the fleeing form. All he got was a handful of cape. Flinging it aside, Ben whirled to pursue the intruder, then froze mid-stride, ears attuned to a strange sound. A muffled banging came from the hall closet.

He yanked the door open and nearly died when he saw Gayle crammed on the floor, bound, a strip of tape across the mouth of her pale, tear-streaked face. Her eyes were wide and pleading.

He dropped to his knees beside her. "Oh, my God, babe. Oh, my God." His fingers were trembling as he pulled the tape from her lips.

"Ben," she whimpered as she slumped against him.

After stripping the bindings from her wrists and ankles, Ben lifted her gently and carried her into the living room. Holding her close, he sat down in one of the plush couches and cradled her in his arms, rocking her like a child, whispering soothing words, silently damning the black devil who'd done this to her. *I'll kill him if I ever find him. I'll break him like a matchstick.*

Gayle clung to him like a lifeline, wrapped her arms around him, and nestled her head against the strength of his shoulder. "Ben," she whispered. "Ben."

She was safe.

By the time the police left and the house was quiet, it was almost midnight. Ben had not ventured from Gayle's side. Despite his urging, she had refused to let him call a doctor or take her to the emergency room. Physically she was fine; emotionally she was a disaster area. She trembled inside; felt as if her nerves were held together with chewing gum.

Ben had plied her with cognac, watched her carefully, held her hand, or kept his arm around her as if he needed constant reassurance that she was all right. Gayle didn't complain. Though at other times she might have upbraided him for hovering, tonight his presence was a warm comfort.

At Gayle's insistence, every light in the house was on. They sat side by side on a plush couch in the living room sipping their third—or was it their fourth?—cognac.

"You need to go to bed and get some rest," Ben said.

Gayle didn't answer. Instead she stared into the snifter she held cupped in her hands, swirled the amber liquor and watched its motion. "Did I ever tell you about how I became a widow?" she said suddenly.

216

"No, I don't believe you did." Ben's tone was gentle.

Still staring into the glass, she said, "A man, a crazy violent man, stormed into our office one day. He had a gun. He knocked me out of the way, pointed it directly at Greg, and pulled the trigger. It wasn't even Greg's fault. It was mine."

"How could it have been your fault?"

Gayle set the snifter on the coffee table and clasped her arms across her chest as if she were cold. "Because I'm so good with the Summers Profile."

"I don't understand," Ben said, frowning.

"It doesn't matter. For a long time I felt guilty for living. I wanted to die." Gayle looked up at Ben, her blue eyes bright with a shimmering film of tears. "Tonight I faced the same kind of violence. And, Ben . . . I'm so glad I'm alive."

Fiercely, Ben hugged her to him, pulled her into his lap, and held her close. He buried his face in her hair and breathed her sweet scent. "I'm glad, too, sweetheart. I'm glad, too." After a moment, he scooped her into his arms and stood. "You need to go to bed."

Gayle clung to his neck and laid her head against his shoulder. "I don't want to be alone," she whispered.

"I'm not leaving you alone."

Ben carried her upstairs and, with one foot, pushed her door open wide. He strode past the peach-colored bed and into the bathroom. Gently, he sat her on a velvet vanity bench and knelt beside the tub.

"What are you doing?" Gayle asked as she watched him turn on the faucets and adjust the temperature.

"I'm drawing you a bath." Ben picked up a bottle, unscrewed the top, and sniffed the contents. He looked at the label and said, "Giorgio. I'll have to remember

the name. It's the potent stuff that haunts my dreams."
He poured a liberal measure into the water and grinned
up at Gayle. "Or rather the lady who wears it."

He scooted over and slipped off her moccasins and
socks, then stood, pulled Gayle to her feet, and reached
for the bottom of her sweater.

"Ben," she said, stilling his hands with hers. "What
are you doing?"

"I'm going to give you a nice warm bath with lots of
sweet-smelling bubbles. But first we have to take your
clothes off. It works better that way."

"But, Ben—"

"Shh," he said. "It's okay. There's not a single delicious inch of you I haven't seen and isn't indelibly
stamped in my brain."

"Ben, I'm perfectly capable of bathing myself."

"I know you are, princess. But let me take care of you
tonight. Tomorrow you can be Ms. Independent Executive again."

Gayle looked into Ben's gold-cast eyes. There was no
hint of the predator's gleam. Instead they shone with
some other emotion. Warm, intoxicating, hypnotic.
Trust me, they said.

And she did.

With their eyes still locked, Ben reached for the snap
on her jeans, popped it, then slid the zipper down. He
pushed the denim over her hips, knelt, and with Gayle
holding his shoulders for balance, freed one leg, then
the other. Tossing the jeans aside, he stood and peeled
off the blue sweater. It went into the opposite corner.

Gayle could see the muscles in his jaw twitch as he
reached around to unclasp the back of her lacy bra.
When it was dispatched, Ben's gaze traveled over her

218

and stopped at the full breasts bared to him. He sucked in a deep breath and unconsciously licked his lips. In answer, her nipples sprang to hard peaks and warmth flooded through her.

Ben sucked in another breath and blew it out slowly.

Gayle gave a soft, playful laugh and arched her back slightly, teasing, offering.

"Holy hell, honey," he groaned. "Keep that up and you won't get a bath until next July." He stripped off her bikini and turned quickly to shut off the faucets. Keeping his back to her, he tested the temperature of the water and said, almost gruffly, "Get in."

"You don't have to be such a bear." Gayle stepped into the tub and slid her body into the mountain of frothy bubbles.

"I'm sorry, princess. This isn't as easy as I thought it would be."

Gayle fought back a chuckle and looked up at Ben, who stood, hands on his hips, staring down at her. Her gaze wandered down the length of him and back up again before it settled on the straining evidence of his arousal. She looked back up, lifted her eyebrows, and gave a playful smile.

He grinned and shrugged. "What can I say? When I'm around you, it's a permanent condition. Don't worry about it." He watched her lean back in the tub, his eyes darkening and his breath quickening. "Will you be okay for a minute? I'll run down to Cal's room and take a quick shower."

"There's plenty of room for two in the tub if you want to join me."

A pained expression twisted his features and he groaned. "Don't do this to me, babe. I'm trying to take care of you tonight. If I climbed in that tub with you, you wouldn't last thirty seconds. I'd be all over you like feathers on a duck."

Cocking an eyebrow, Gayle said, "So?"

Ben gave an exasperated growl. "I'll make it a cold shower," he said, and strode from the room.

Gayle leaned back in the warm, scented water and closed her eyes. Dear Lord, she loved that man. If she'd had any doubts before, tonight had dispelled every one. Perhaps there were things he was keeping from her, but surely he had sound motives. Motives Gayle didn't understand. She'd have to trust him.

She did trust him. She loved him. Beyond all reason, she loved Ben Lyons—outrageous behavior, gentle caring, broad grin, and all.

Out of some misguided sense of chivalry, Ben was determined to play Sir Galahad tonight and treat her like a fragile flower. She didn't want to be treated delicately. What she felt was a wild, primitive need, a desperate urgency to reaffirm life at its most basic level.

For some reason she couldn't begin to understand, Ben brought out the wanton in her. It was a totally new experience. Though she still felt a bit of glow from the drinks she'd had, Gayle couldn't blame her earlier seductiveness on the liquor. She'd wanted him. And she wanted him now. Wanted to feel his bronzed skin beneath her fingers, his tongue on—

"Gayle?" he called softly. "What are you thinking?"

He stood in the doorway, leaning with one forearm propped against the frame. The other hand rested on his hip at the band of navy silk pajama bottoms slung low below his navel. Lamplight from behind cast a golden aura around him, outlining his bare muscular torso, shooting sparks off the pale streaks in his tawny hair.

Gayle's breath caught and her hunger quickened. Desire came in rippling waves and gathered low in her body. She moistened her lips. "About you."

Rising from the foamy bath, she stepped out and stood unashamed before him. "About how much I want you."

Fists clenched at his sides, Ben was before her in two strides. He didn't touch her, but his eyes devoured her. Finally, one hand lifted slowly and gently flicked away a cluster of bubbles that clung to the tip of her left breast.

Gayle shivered at his touch.

Pulling a peach-colored towel from the rack beside him, he quickly dried her and grabbed another to swathe her body. "I'll get you a gown," he said, turning.

"Ben," she whispered, breathy sensuality teasing the space between them. "I don't need a gown." She smiled and let the covering slither to her feet as he watched.

Shock waves of desire shot between them, electrified the air like chain lightning, hissed and sparked and glowed white-hot. Ben's pupils dilated and his chest swelled. Gayle's lips parted and her smile changed subtly. There was no mistaking her intent as the atmosphere pulsated with simmering sexual current.

"Princess," Ben said as his gaze caressed every silken swell and curve, "you've shot my good intentions all to hell." Desire for her blazed openly and hungrily in his expression and he stepped toward her. "I'm going to make love to you all night and into next week."

Her laughter danced across the air and she held out her arms.

Ben yanked her to him, molded her body to his, and groaned as he took her lips with a savage hunger. It was like drinking fire.

His tongue thrust and retreated, hot and probing, as his mouth devoured hers in a flaming assault. Gayle was vibrant with passion, lost in the exquisite power of his possessive urging. She clung to him, her nails digging into his broad back, her tongue matching each hot thrust, her lips as ravenous as Ben's as she filled her mouth with the taste of him.

Sliding his hands to her hips, Ben clutched her to him and ground his body against hers. He tore his lips away from the violent fusion, threw back his head, and groaned. "My God, my love, you're burning me alive."

They were both breathing hard and trembling with need stretched taut, with sexual anticipation magnified to volcanic rumbling. Gayle slipped her hands along the corded body that promised untold pleasure and she knew that their lovemaking would be beyond ecstasy. She ached with longing.

"Wait, babe," Ben said, stilling her sensuous strokes. "Don't touch me. Hold off a minute or I swear to God, I'll lose control and take you right here on the floor." He swept her into his arms, strode to the bed, and laid her on the velvet spread. "I want to savor every sweet inch of you."

Starting with her toes, Ben's fingers roamed her body masterfully, and his lips and tongue followed in a fiery trail. Nuzzling, nibbling, touching, teasing, he explored every intriguing curve and crevice, murmuring love words and driving Gayle into a writhing mass of sensuality, evoking responses she never knew were possible. With his mouth he covered every inch of her body—her back, her throat, the sensitive undersides of her breasts, the soles of her feet.

He kissed and touched her everywhere and she wanted to touch him, taste him in the same way, but when she tried, Ben stilled her movements. "Not yet, sweetheart, not yet. I couldn't bear it."

The tip of his tongue circled the nipple of one throbbing, swollen breast before his lips closed around the hard pebble of flesh and he tasted her tenderly. He rubbed his cheek against the creamy swell and moved to its mate, uttering a guttural sound and cupping the tingling fullness, straining to consume it all.

Gayle almost burst into flames and she writhed and moaned, clutching at his back, feeling the ripple of tensed muscles and the slick sheen of perspiration along its smooth surface. Her hands went to his hips, tugging, begging to ease the ache building inside her. "Ben, please," she entreated. "I'm dying!"

Ben chuckled deep in his throat and left the breast, wet with his suckling, to slide his tongue down her diaphragm, circle her navel, then thrust its probing tip into the recess. Praising the silken perfection of her body, one hand kneaded the fullness of her breast while the other stroked the delicate softness of her inner thighs and cupped the moist core of her desire.

Flames ran rampant through Gayle's blood and she moved wantonly against his hand, straining, seeking. Gayle moaned and opened to him, desperately craving release.

Ben rose up to look into her face. "You're on fire for me." His voice was thick with passion and his breathing shallow as he watched the sorcery his two hands made as they stroked and caressed the sweet, writhing flesh.

Suddenly he withdrew and shucked the pajama bottoms. He returned to kneel between the waiting juncture of her long legs and watch her face as he scooped up her hips in the palms of his hands.

Gayle's eyes blazed blue fire and her nostrils flared as she saw the proud evidence of his desire straining toward her. She gasped his name and he smiled.

"It's all yours, love," he said. "Come to me."

She arched and flung herself forward as he thrust into her with a fervent lunge. A primeval cry erupted from his throat and he thrust again, deeper, harder. Gayle met each move with a frenzied undulation, clinging to him, riding the whirlwind until she quivered with the violence of her need.

A volcano of passion rumbled and roared and shook Gayle with its mounting force. Their joining was hotter, deeper, faster, until the heat spilled over, flowed like a river of fire, then exploded into a cascade of rapture as Ben erupted into her. Gayle arched and screamed as ecstasy burst forth in shock waves of golden fulfillment.

Breathing rapidly, they clung together, bodies slick with sweat and glowing with the wild abandon of their lovemaking.

"Oh, my love, my sweet, sweet love. My heart, my soul," Ben murmured, his breath ragged. "You're beyond my wildest dreams."

Gayle was stunned by the onslaught of power generated between them. This time had been even more overwhelming than their first. Breathing out a shuddering sigh, she managed to whisper, "Holy hell, Ben Lyons. Holy hell."

CHAPTER THIRTEEN

Gayle's eyes fluttered open, then closed again to savor the delicious fantasy of her dreams before the daylight chased them away. But the heavy, solid form dipping the bed behind her was no dream. He was very real. And the strong, tanned fingers cupping her breast were no illusion.

After their first violent joining, they had fallen into an exhausted slumber, Ben holding her close as they slept. Near dawn they had awakened and come together again. And the second time, though it seemed impossible, had been more potent than the first. Gayle thrilled anew with the memory of it. Never before had she experienced such sexual excitement as she had with Ben. Never had she imagined that passion of such intensity was possible. This was the stuff of erotic literature or French movies with fuzzy subtitles, not something in the life of a management consultant.

Ben was an inventive lover, considerate, thorough, but it was the sheer undisguised hunger evident in his every move that drove Gayle into a frenzy of mindless passion, shattered her boundaries, wrenched away reason. He had roused a wildness in her and it had burst forth with an alarming power. He had uncovered a part

225

of Gayle Summers that she didn't know, alien uncharted territory, and it frightened her. Loving this sensual, demanding man frightened her.

The hand on her breast moved and panic began to form and grow inside her until she tensed with the building anxiety. She wanted to run, find refuge in old familiar patterns of her life.

"Gayle, what's wrong, honey?"

"I thought you were still asleep."

Ben nuzzled the back of her neck. "No, I've been awake a long time. Watching you. Did you know that you have the most intriguing little mole right here?" He teased the top of her shoulder blade with the tip of his tongue.

Gayle flinched and jerked from his touch. When she tried to get out of bed, Ben held her fast. "What's wrong?"

"Nothing's wrong," she said, straining to loose herself from his arms. "I have to go to the bathroom. Do you mind?" Her voice was tinged with a sharp sarcasm born of survival instinct.

"Whoa," he said, pulling her back as she strained again. "No, I wouldn't mind if I thought it was the truth. But you went less than an hour ago. Princess, what's wrong?" he asked gently. "Look at me. Tell me."

Rolling her toward him, Ben propped his head in one hand and stroked her cheek with the back of his forefinger. His eyes were filled with tender concern and Gayle felt herself begin to melt.

"I'm scared, Ben," she whispered. Gathering her into his arms, Ben held her close and said, "There's no reason to be afraid. I won't let anyone hurt you again. I promise that you'll be safe if I have to move an entire army bivouac in the front yard."

"That's not what I'm afraid of."

"Then what?" He frowned and drew away to search her troubled face.

"Of you . . . of us . . . of myself mostly."

"I don't understand."

"It's difficult to explain," Gayle said, having a hard time holding her gaze steady with his, trying to ignore the callused palm that unconsciously stroked her thigh from hip to knee. "I . . . I . . . ." Heat from the monster Ben had awakened began to stir and gather in her lower body. She closed her eyes, drew in a shuddering breath, and stilled his hand with hers. "I can't think when you touch me."

"Is this some kind of morning-after guilt trip you've conjured up? If it is, I won't have it. What we've found is something special. My God, Gayle, what happens between us generates more power than a nuclear reactor."

"I know," she said. "That's what scares me."

Ben was quiet for a minute, dread crawling over him like a spider. He had to play this just right or she would dart away like a spooked fish. He halfway understood what she meant. The voltage they generated shook him to his toenails and blew his mind. He'd never known anything like it before, but he sure as hell wasn't about to let her get away. Call it fate or call it luck, whatever it was, he'd found the perfect woman for him. Sure the sex between them was nothing less than fantastic, but everything about Gayle was fantastic. She was *his* and he'd fight for her—even if it was Gayle he had to fight.

"This sounds like something we need to talk about," he said lightly. "And I don't know about you, but I could use a cup of coffee." He gave her a playful swat on the rump and added, "I'll run grab a shower in Cal's room and meet you in the kitchen."

Wanting nothing more than to spend the day making slow sweet love with the woman who set fire to his soul, but wise enough to know the time for a tactical retreat, Ben left Gayle's room and headed down the hall. In the master bedroom, Ben looked up at the painting over the mantel and grinned. "You were right. Boy, were you right."

Gayle lingered in the shower as long as she could without turning into a prune, dawdled as she dressed in tan slacks and a loose yellow jersey, stalled for time as she brushed her hair and did her face. Finally, when she had run out of excuses to delay going downstairs, she stared into the mirror and cocked an eyebrow.

"You've got a tiger by the tail," she said to her reflection. With a wry grin she corrected herself. "No, make that a Lyon. The question is, What are you going to do about it?"

Time, she needed time.

Tantalizing aromas of coffee and frying bacon wafted through the house and up the stairs, cutting into her musing and reminding Gayle that she was hungry. She could always think better on a full stomach. Surely she could sit across the breakfast table from Ben and have an ordinary meal without wanting to jump him.

When she walked into the kitchen, Ben was sitting at the table sipping from a cup, reading the newspaper. He looked up as she entered and grinned. "Good morning, sunshine. Coffee's ready." While Gayle poured herself a steaming mug, Ben got up and shoved a pan under the broiler. "I hope you like cheese toast." He kept up a steady stream of light banter as they ate.

After the meal was finished and they were having a second cup of coffee, Gayle looked at Ben and said, "We have to talk."

"It sounds serious."

"It is serious." Gayle groped for the right words to say. She felt awkward, silly now sitting in the sunlit kitchen trying to discuss her sex life and innermost feelings over dirty breakfast dishes. Her vocabulary failed her. Maybe the timing was wrong; maybe the place was wrong. Maybe she was chicken.

Ben reached across the table and took her hand in a comforting gesture. "Princess, it seems to me that you're a little overwhelmed by what's happening between us. Hell, it's knocked the props out from under me, too."

Gayle took a deep breath and plunged in. "It terrifies me, Ben. I've never experienced anything like this, and I don't know if I can handle it."

"I never figured you for a coward."

The challenge stiffened her spine. "I'm not a coward."

A tiny, self-satisfied smile lifted one corner of Ben's mouth. He fought the urge to take her into his arms and kiss her until her knees turned weak, tell her in a thousand ways how much he loved her. Slow and easy, he reminded himself. "Let's take it one day at a time and see where things go. We'll back off and take it slow and easy."

Gayle gave a little chuckling cough. "Isn't that a bit like telling a tidal wave to back off?"

"Maybe," Ben said, breaking into a grin. "How

about we spend the day at the Renaissance Festival? I hear it's lots of fun."

Gayle shook her head and got up to load the dishwasher. "It sounds tempting, but I have tons of work to do interpreting all the Profiles." Gayle turned around, leaned back against the counter, and crossed her arms. "This is the perfect time for you to take the test. Everyone else has."

"It's too beautiful outside to stay cooped up with a bunch of psychological mumbo-jumbo. You work too much. Come on," he insisted, tugging her along with him. "You'll enjoy it."

Against her better judgment, a few minutes later Gayle found herself sitting in the silver Lincoln bound for the festival. Arguing with Ben, Gayle discovered, was like fighting a gorilla with a switch. She seemed to always come out on the short end.

And he'd refused to take the test again. Why was he so stubborn?

In less than an hour, they were strolling through a festive wooded area with cavorting players in medieval costumes. It was jolly old England in a Texas clearing, alive with chattering children, tradesmen hawking their wares, and laughter. Smells of earth, grilling meat, and pungent spices mixed with the sounds of folk songs and dulcimers and bagpipes.

Ben insisted they have a garland of flowers woven for Gayle's hair, and he selected yellow blossoms to match her jersey with yellow ribbons intertwined with deep blue ones the color of her eyes.

"There," he said, placing the floral crown on her head and kissing her forehead. "Now you really look like a princess."

"I've been meaning to ask you, why do you call me princess?"

Ben cleared his throat and smiled. "That night you fell asleep in the car and I put you to bed, you reminded me of Sleeping Beauty. His smile broadened into a lopsided grin. "Except when I kissed you, you didn't wake up the way Sleeping Beauty did for the prince. You just turned over and kept snoring."

Gayle's eyes widened. "I don't snore!" She gave him a playful swat, then asked seriously, "Do I?"

"No, Princess Gayle, you don't snore." He kissed the tip of her nose.

Hand in hand, they continued their stroll through the grounds, buying Ben a jaunty cap with a feather, watching the woodcarvers and glassblowers, stopping for a puppet show, a juggler's act, and a bit of Shakespearean drama.

While Ben gnawed on a huge turkey leg, Gayle ate plump strawberries and juicy chunks of fresh pineapple and cantaloupe from a skewer. With Ben sipping beer and Gayle wine, they watched the knights joust, then wandered to the Gypsy camp to have their fortunes told.

"Much love and many children," the Gypsy girl said, barely able to keep her eyes off Ben and on Gayle's palm.

A wandering magician entertained them with bawdy stories and sleight of hand, and they watched the sword swallower do his act. Robin Hood and his band of Merry Men transformed Texas trees into Sherwood Forest. They visited the booths of the artists and craftsmen, laughing together over the caricatures they posed for. Gayle bought a fringed leather vest with intricate beadwork for Ariel, snakeskin belts for her brothers, and at

231

least a dozen other gifts. Ben's arms were piled high by the time she finished her shopping spree and they found their way out the exit and to the car.

"Don't complain," she said to Ben as he pretended to stagger under the load. "I just did all my Christmas shopping in one swoop."

"Did you have fun?"

Gayle's eyes were shining and her cheeks still flushed with excitement. "I had a delightful time. Thanks for the wonderful day."

It was dark by the time they arrived home. Ben carried her purchases into the house and greeted Mrs. Jenkins. With a promise to the housekeeper to be ready for dinner in an hour, they parted to bathe and change.

After dinner Gayle announced that she needed to do some work, but Ben, knowing her fondness for Agatha Christie, said, *"Death on the Nile* is on cable TV tonight."

"Oh, no," she said, clearly torn.

"Oh, yes." Ben grinned as she sighed and preceded him into the den.

"You're turning me into a wicked and decadent woman, Ben Lyons."

Ben wiggled his eyebrows in a bad imitation of Groucho Marx. "I certainly hope so, m'dear."

Gayle curled up on the couch, and Ben kicked off his shoes and slouched down beside her, his feet propped on the coffee table. He flipped on the remote control and pulled her over next to him, wiggling and twisting until she was settled in the crook of his arm and her head lay against his shoulder.

Snuggling into the nest he had made for her, Gayle

relaxed and watched the movie. She was yawning by the time the last credits rolled.

Ben looked down at her. "I think it's time for you to be in bed. Shall I sleep in a guestroom or with you?"

Gayle tangled her fingers in the hair that peeped over the opening of his sport shirt. Even though their day had been relaxed and playful, her desire for him had been crouched at the edge of her awareness, ready to spring with the least provocation.

"With me," she whispered.

They barely made it through the door of Gayle's room before they were tugging at one another's clothes, kissing, caressing. Their lips were greedy, their touches urgent, as if it had been months instead of merely hours since they had made love.

Ben tried to go slowly, tried to be tender, but Gayle refused to let him. She ground herself against him, clutched at his back and his buttocks with a hunger that drove Ben into a wild man. Their joining was hot, deep, hard. It sent them soaring with an explosion that surely rocked the foundations of the earth.

When they lay gasping in each other's arms, panting from the quick, fierce lovemaking, Gayle managed to say, "Ben, will it always be like this?"

"I don't know," Ben said, his breath ragged, his voice husky. "God, I hope so."

The whole thing struck Gayle as funny and her damp body began to shake with silent laughter. Then a chuckle fought its way to her throat and escaped. She felt Ben's answering chuckle shake his chest and they both burst into laughter.

"Aren't we a fine pair?" Gayle said between bouts of giggles.

"Sweetheart, we're a hell of a pair."

A few minutes later as Gayle lay curled up beside him, her fingers enjoying the feel of the smooth, bronzed skin of his belly, Ben said, "Do you like to scuba dive?"

"I don't know. I've never tried it." Gayle frowned and rose up to look at him. "What brought that up?"

"I have to go to the Caymans on business for a few days, and I want you to go with me. I thought we might go diving while we're there."

"When were you planning to go?"

"Tomorrow."

"Tomorrow?" she asked. "I can't leave here. I have work to do."

"Princess, it's very important that I go, and I'm not going to leave you here alone. Come with me."

"No."

"Please, babe. You'll like scuba diving. Next to making love to you, it's the nearest I've ever been to heaven."

"No."

Ben threw his suitcase in the backseat and turned to Gayle. "Are you sure you won't change your mind?"

"Positive. You know I have too many things to do here."

Ben frowned and stood with his hands on his hips. "Babe, I don't want to leave you. But since you won't come, I've hired a security firm to watch after you and the house. Someone will be around twenty-four hours a day. At night two men with dogs will patrol the grounds. Nobody can get near the house without identification and permission. Lock yourself in and don't go out at night for any reason. If you need them, yell. They're for your safety."

"Like bodyguards?"

Ben nodded. "Unless I'm with you, where you go, one of them goes."

"Oh, for gosh sakes, Ben. I don't need bodyguards. You changed all the locks."

"Humor me, sweetheart." He pulled her to him and held her close. "I don't want anything to happen to you. This security firm is supposed to be the best."

She kissed him good-bye and waved until he drove past a nondescript sedan parked beside the winding drive. A man sat inside. The bodyguard. Truthfully, her protest had been half-hearted. With Ben gone, she felt relieved about the extra protection.

Glancing at her watch, Gayle groaned. The morning was almost gone, and she hadn't looked at a single profile. With a determined stride, Gayle marched into the study and closed the door.

Separating out the summary sheets, which would give a thumbnail sketch of each person, Gayle quickly scanned security and production employees. Her eye fell on the name of Roosevelt Weems, the night watchman who had reported the fire. Nothing wrong there. The profile of an honest, dependable man.

She noted a few names to go over in more detail later, but other than typical personnel placement problems, nothing was out of the ordinary. The same was true for the sales force. Flipping through the rest of the sheets, Gayle frowned when she saw some unusual configurations. She pulled five complete protocols from among the remainder of the printouts and placed them to one side. These required careful study.

There was a knock at the door.

"Come in," Gayle called.

The housekeeper came in carrying a vacuum cleaner. "It's after one o'clock. I fixed you a nice lunch and left it on the table. I figured while you ate I'd run the vacuum in here."

Gayle was surprised to discover that she'd been working as long as she had. "Thanks, Mrs. Jenkins," she said, "but I'm not hungry, and I need to finish something I'm working on. You can skip cleaning in here today."

The older woman folded her arms and stood her ground. "It's past regular time for lunch, and before Mr. Ben left, he made me and Hector promise to look out for you. You're to eat and rest proper and not go anywhere without one of them men skulking around outside going with you. He'll have my hide if I don't do my part." Mrs. Jenkins smiled. "Like I said, Mr. Ben's right taken with you. Now, you wouldn't want me to get in trouble, would you?"

Gayle laughed. "Okay, I know when I'm licked," she said, rising and stretching. "Don't move any of these papers, please."

"Won't move a thing. I'll just vacuum and tidy up the bathroom a bit."

The day looked so lovely that Gayle took the salad plate and iced tea out onto the patio to eat. When she had finished she walked down the steps to the bayou and watched the ducks for a moment. Already she missed Ben. Funny how he had become such an integral part of her life in such a short time.

Picking up a pebble, she tossed it into the water and watched the circular ripples on the surface. Certainly theirs was no casual relationship, but what would the future bring? What would it be like to be married to Ben? Exciting? Definitely. Volatile? Probably. Dull? Never.

She turned and walked back up to the patio and paused. This was where she had first seen him, glimpsed the golden gleam in his predator's eye. The sparks had been there even then. Remembering, she smiled and trailed her hand along the chaise.

It was time to get back to work. She went inside and walked to the study, hoping Mrs. Jenkins was through with her chores by now. Gayle was stunned by what she saw when she got to the door. Martin Brewer and Sylvia Norman were searching the desk.

Martin looked up and smiled. "I hope we didn't disturb your meal. Mrs. Jenkins said you were having lunch. We have some papers from the bank that need your signature."

Gayle looked from the desk to the pair beside it. "Were you looking for something in particular?" she asked, a hard edge to her voice.

"As a matter of fact, we were trying to find a telephone directory. I wanted to call the garage to see if my car has been repaired, so Sylvia could drop me off and quit having to play chauffeur today."

Gayle located the phone directory, and the secretary made the call while Gayle signed the papers Martin pulled from his briefcase.

"If you don't mind my asking," the president said, "who's the fellow standing guard outside? He wouldn't let us in until he checked our identification and had Hector vouch for us."

"Just some extra precautions," Gayle said lightly.

"There's been some trouble in the neighborhood. Are things running smoothly at the plant?"

"Fairly well," Mr. Brewer said. "George Schulze is out today, but he'll be back by tomorrow. He had a pretty bad asthma attack Saturday morning and his doctor admitted him to the hospital for a couple of days. He was released this morning."

"Is he going to be okay?" Gayle asked.

"Yes, he'll be fine. He has a flare-up now and then. I suspect it's related to all the stress we've been under."

Gayle casually checked through the papers on her desk. Nothing seemed to be missing. They discussed a few items of business and the pair left. Gayle watched from the bay window as the guard stopped them and spoke briefly.

The phone rang. It was Winston Dasher.

"I called the plant but Angie said you were working at home. I thought you might like to have dinner with me tonight," he said.

"I'm sorry, Winston, I'd love to go with you, but I have so much work that I'm drowning in it," she said, trying to keep her tone light.

"Tomorrow night, perhaps?" His voice was gentle, hopeful. "There's a very chic little French restaurant I know you would enjoy."

"I'm sorry, it's not possible. I'll be tied up." Gayle tried to make her excuses sound sincere. "Why don't I give you a call when I get things under control and have some time."

"I'll be waiting to hear from you."

When she hung up the phone, Gayle picked up the five summary sheets she had set aside and searched through the stack of printouts for the complete data for each.

The first was Angela Bennett's. Angie, the cute blond receptionist who'd helped Gayle administer the test, who was majoring in Organizational and Behavioral Management. Gayle laughed as she looked over the information. With a few minor differences, she could have been looking at her own protocol. Knowing herself, Gayle knew Angie. If Gayle had needed an assistant in her business, she'd hire the young woman in a minute. Angie was a bit too open and trusting, but with time and training, she'd learn.

Sylvia Norman's was next. Gayle had been right in her original assessment of the red-haired secretary. According to her Summers Profile, Cal should have made her president of McDonough Bearings. The company would have been in capable hands. Her talents were wasted as a secretary.

Gayle picked up the next profile and shook her head. Martin Brewer. He had about as much business being president as Gayle had being a trapeze artist with the circus. Worse than unsuitable, he was totally incompetent. No wonder he was unhappy and wanted to retire. Why hadn't Cal let him? Calvin McDonough must have known that the position was beyond his capabilities. Brewer must feel trapped and miserable.

George Schulze was the fourth. Gayle tapped her front tooth with her fingernail as she studied the scores of the various components, scrutinized every sentence of every page. When she was done she fell back into the chair and blew out a big breath. Bad news.

Though she was already sure, Gayle decided to double check. She turned on the computer and linked up, by modem, to the mainframe in Denver. It only took a few minutes to verify her conclusions. George Schulze had the classic profile of an embezzler. And it was the records in his department which were destroyed.

Gayle frowned as she studied the information on the screen and compared it to the printout she held in her hand. An embezzler, yes, but George Schulze lacked the cunning and the courage for a large-scale operation, and nothing indicated that he could murder anyone. Of course, any person might be capable of murder if the circumstances were desperate enough.

She picked up Martin Brewer's profile again and looked at it. His wife was ill; he hated being president; he was under tremendous emotional and financial strain. Desperate. And desperate men did desperate things.

The last protocol belonged to Winston Dasher. Gayle felt the blood drain from her face as she read the scores. *Oh, dear God.* And she'd never even suspected. But there it was printed boldly on the page of his complete report. SEVERE SOCIOPATHIC PERSONALITY.

Gayle dropped her face in her hands and let the sickening reality of it wash over her. Winston Dasher was capable of anything. He was totally egocentric, impulsive, without conscience. He could lie, cheat, steal—even commit murder if it served his purpose—and all without so much as a twinge of guilt. And he was cunning, ruthless, and charming.

Gayle shuddered with the thought that she'd had dinner with him, talked with him, and never even suspected. Yet she knew that sociopaths were consummate actors, con men who could dupe the Pope himself.

But, she remembered, Winston had been at a party

240

the night of the fire. Or, at least, he claimed to have been. And he was with her when someone tried to break in the study Friday night. Unless he had hired someone to do the jobs or . . .

She picked up the profiles of Martin Brewer and George Schulze and flipped through the pages.

Or, she thought, unless he had a partner. Or two. Maybe all three of them were involved in something. One of them had set the fire and broken in Friday night while Winston had an alibi. Was it Brewer or Schulze? George Schulze had been in the hospital with an asthma attack, so, while he might have been the one Mrs. Jenkins scared off Friday night, he couldn't have been the masked intruder from Halloween. Besides, the monster was taller than the short comptroller. More the size of Martin Brewer or Winston Dasher.

What were they after in the study? The Summers Profiles? Or something else? Was Brewer really looking for a telephone directory earlier? But Sylvia was with him, and the secretary was definitely not a suspect. Her protocol showed her to be scrupulously honest.

Gayle picked up the president's profile and examined it carefully. If she had to sum him up in one word, it would be loyalty. "Incompetent as he was, he was loyal, wasn't he?" Gayle asked Calvin's portrait. "You knew that he was loyal to you and you trusted him. That's why you made him president. That's why Sylvia is his secretary. To keep him out of trouble."

No, she didn't think Martin Brewer was a part of it, though she still puzzled over Cal's reasons for retiring. But Winston Dasher and George Schulze were as guilty as sin of something.

But what?

McDonough Bearings was almost bankrupt because of the loss of government contracts and the huge drain of the disastrous venture in Singapore. Was it industrial espionage? Large-scale embezzlement? Blackmail? Fraud? Had Calvin McDonough discovered some scheme and been murdered before he could turn them in?

Gayle wished that Ben were here. Ben knew more than he was telling her. She'd bet her reputation on it. He never had explained what he was doing in Singapore.

Needing a break, Gayle went to the kitchen to get a Coke, and on her way back to the study, picked up the mail from the hall table. Seated once more behind the big desk, she sorted through the envelopes and came upon a bank statement. A feeling of unease began to gather at the edges of her consciousness as she ripped open the envelope and quickly sorted through the canceled checks. Her hand froze as she came to a large one to Allied Investigations, marked *final payment*.

Calvin McDonough had hired a detective. Gayle grabbed the yellow pages and thumbed through until she found an ad for Allied Investigations which offered experience in undercover work, internal theft, and embezzlement. Dialing the number listed, Gayle's heart was pounding as she listened to the ring. A nasal recording switched on. "The number you have reached is no longer in service; if—"

Gayle slammed down the receiver in frustration and searched her memory. She had looked through every record in the house and she couldn't recall seeing a single current bank statement. Nor had there been a detective's report. If Cal had hired a detective, there must be reports.

The safe.

She ran to the closet, shoved aside the carton of continuous forms, and dialed the combination. She went through every piece of paper in the document folder. Nothing. If the reports had been there the thief had beaten her to them. Closing the safe, she slid the heavy box of computer paper back in position.

Computer paper? Why hadn't it dawned on her before? Why would Cal have computer supplies if he didn't have a computer?

Gayle found Grace Jenkins rolling out pie dough in the kitchen. "Mrs. Jenkins, did Mr. McDonough have a computer?"

"Oh, sure he did. A big fancy one."

"Then where is it?"

"Mr. Ben took it with him down to the guest house when he got the other things."

"What *things?*" Gayle could feel a ball of anxiety forming in the pit of her stomach.

"I don't know exactly. Some papers he said he needed."

Fury flashed over Gayle and she felt as if she could spit thunderbolts. Calm, she reminded herself. Stay calm. "May I have the key to the guesthouse? I need to check some of the papers," she said casually.

Mrs. Jenkins didn't have a key, nor did Hector. Gayle didn't intend to let a little thing like a lock stop her. She grabbed a hammer from the garage and strode toward the guest house with Hector following after her, wringing his hands and muttering in Spanish.

Given the power of her anger, smashing the lock and

243

getting inside was simple. The computer, a top-of-the-line model, sat on a big desk in the living area. A tall stack of printouts beside it were records from McDonough Bearings. Why had he secreted these things away? Her fury with Ben grew until she was shaking. How dare he keep information from her!

Yanking open a drawer of the desk, she found a stack of bank statements and a quick check revealed that Ariel's Uncle Cal had been paying the detective agency for months. A further search of the drawers turned up a thick folder with Allied Investigations printed on the tab.

The detective reports. Ben had them all the time. Damn his black heart to hell! Gayle tried to push her anger aside long enough to read the file. Her eyes grew wide as the reports told of industrial espionage, with McDonough Bearings' bids being sold to competitors, and profits from the Singapore installation being funneled to a corporation in the Caymans.

The Caymans! Dear God, Ben was in the Caymans on business. Was he investigating or . . . Gayle closed her eyes and anguish twisted her face. Surely, please God, he was not part of this. Please, God. She'd come to trust him. She loved him.

Dread rode her shoulder as she opened another drawer. Grave-cold horror swept over her.

There lay the gold pocket watch.

CHAPTER FOURTEEN

It was mid-afternoon when Gayle collected her bag and hailed a taxi outside Owen Roberts International Airport on Grand Cayman. Eyes gritty from lack of sleep and body humming with exhaustion, she was too tired to enjoy the scenery of the tropical island.

Thoughts of Ben's betrayal clung to her like a leech as she alternated between anger and despair. What a fool she'd been to trust him. She'd known from the first he was dangerous, but she'd let her heart and her hormones get in the way. Although she wasn't exactly sure how it was all connected, Ben was in this whole scam up to his neck. She might have been able to explain away the things he'd taken from Cal's study before she arrived, but the watch . . . the watch had been stolen from the safe. The missing birth record was in his desk as well. Gayle still didn't have a clue as to who Margaret Cameron was.

After she'd found the damning evidence in the guest house, after she'd gained some semblance of control over her emotions, Gayle's first impulse was to call the police. But if a huge sum of McDonough Bearings' money was in the Caymans concealed in an account of a dummy corporation, and she had no proof that it was, the local police were powerless. The Cayman Islands were part of another country, and, like Switzerland, a great portion of their economy depended on the banks and their reputation for protection of clients' privacy. While the United States was making progress in many cases and was sometimes able to obtain evidence of secret bank accounts in drug trafficking and illegal money laundering schemes, the Cayman Island banks were still a haven for many who didn't want their business to come under close scrutiny.

Carefully examining her options, Gayle had decided that there was nothing to do but to go to the Caymans and investigate the situation herself. She hadn't the foggiest notion what she expected to find or where to look, but she had to start somewhere. By midnight she'd filled Ariel in on the latest developments and made a few phone calls to old friends who might have a connection in the Caymans. One of them had given her the name of a local attorney, Eli Chase, and a promise to phone ahead so that he would be expecting her.

It had taken forever to find a connecting flight, one that would get her there before next Christmas, and make hotel reservations. She'd tried to get a few hours' sleep, but after doing nothing but toss and turn and endure her mind's replay of the whole ugly situation in living color and stereophonic sound, she finally gave it up and spent the remainder of the night pacing the floor.

Just after dawn, Gayle had dressed, packed a bag with a few essentials, and retrieved the three thousand dollars from the safe. She'd stuck the complete profiles of Brewer, Dasher, and Schulze in her leather portfolio and, along with the cash, detective's reports, a few other papers she might need, locked them in her briefcase. Both sets of study keys went in her purse.

Carrying her briefcase and a small overnighter, she'd planned to sneak away before anyone was awake, but she hadn't counted on the housekeeper's keen ears. Or on the bodyguard Ben had hired. Gayle was rather pleased with the story she concocted for Mrs. Jenkins (who was sure to repeat it to anyone nosing around).

"My mother is seriously ill, and I have to fly to Jackson for a few days," Gayle had told her. She didn't tell the bodyguard anything. She simply roared past in the red Corvette and, in a series of maneuvers that would have done A. J. Foyt proud, lost him on the way to the airport.

Nine hours and a long layover in Miami later, she was headed for the Holiday Inn Grand Cayman and the white sands of Seven Mile Beach. As soon as she was settled in her room, Gayle shed her jacket, kicked off her shoes, and called Eli Chase's office.

"I'm sorry, but Mr. Chase is engaged for the remainder of the day," his secretary said. "Though he was expecting your call and asked if he might meet you at your hotel for lunch tomorrow."

Disappointed with the delay, Gayle sighed. "Yes, of course. I'm at the Holiday Inn."

After she hung up, Gayle walked out onto her balcony and looked with longing at the pool below, surrounded by thatched umbrellas, palm trees, and cascades of fuchsia bougainvillea, and at the beach and ocean beyond. Never had she seen sand so white or water so blue. The sparkling waters of the Caribbean, shading from pale aqua at the shoreline to deep lapis in the distance, beckoned her with a peaceful promise to soothe her body and her soul.

And she didn't even have a bathing suit.

Remembering that there was a boutique in the hotel, Gayle slipped on her shoes and went shopping. She found a flaming red bikini, sure to lift her spirits, and added a coverup, sandals, shorts, and an adorable yellow cotton sundress she couldn't resist.

By the time she'd donned the bikini and was wading in the gentle blue waters of the ocean, Gayle had almost forgotten her reason for being here. She splashed and swam; walked the beach looking for shells and enjoying the feeling of warm sand between her toes. She watched the sails of small catamarans and the larger vessels, drank a delightful rum concoction, and dozed beneath a thatched umbrella.

It wasn't until she sat, spellbound, as the sun slipped below the horizon in the most breathtaking sunset she'd even seen, that memories of Ben came out of hiding. For a moment she'd wished he had been there to share it with her.

Then she remembered, and with the reality came the pain. It clutched at her heart, clogged her throat, stung her eyes. A tear spilled over and rolled down her cheek. Gayle dashed it away, rose, and went back to her room.

After showering and washing her hair, Gayle dressed and went down to the restaurant for dinner. Strolling through the lobby on her way back to her room, Gayle glanced toward the desk and went rigid. There, talking to the clerk, stood Ben Lyons.

Gayle ducked behind a potted palm and caught her breath, trying to still her racing heart. Was he looking for her? Of course not, she tried to tell herself. Nobody knew where she was except Ariel—and she wouldn't tell.

Was he staying at the hotel? No, that didn't make any sense; he owned a condo on Grand Cayman. It was simply a coincidence that he happened to show up here, now. Not willing to take any chances, Gayle kept her back to the desk as she slunk along the wall and out of sight. All she could think of was to get to the safety of her room and barricade herself inside.

Racing to her room, her fingers shook and her palms were sweaty as she fumbled the key in the lock. Finally she managed to get the door open, but before she could step inside, a hand clamped on her shoulder.

"Your mother must have made a miraculous recovery," a deep voice behind her said.

The blood froze in Gayle's veins as she stood dead still, not daring to turn around. Now that she knew about his connection to all the crimes, what would he do to her? Would he hurt her? She knew he was capable of violence when he was pushed. The Ben she thought she knew, the Ben she'd learned to trust, wouldn't harm her, but that Ben was a lie. The lobster she'd had for dinner begin to churn in her stomach and she swallowed.

"I . . . I don't know what you mean."

"Don't give me that," Ben said, pushing her into the room and slamming the door behind him. "Get your things together. You're coming with me."

"I'm not going anywhere with you. Get out of my room."

"You're coming with me. You can come quietly or you can come kicking and screaming, but you're coming." Ben grabbed her suitcase and began throwing things into it. When he was finished, he snapped it shut and hoisted in one hand both her briefcase and the overnighter with half of her new red bikini hanging out the side. "Let's go."

"No," she said, clutching her shoulder bag and making a break for the door.

Ben was there two strides ahead of her, and in one fluid motion he swept her up and over his shoulder like a stalk of bananas.

"Put me down!" Gayle shrieked and beat on his back as he strode down the hall to the stairs and out through the hotel.

"New bride jitters," Ben explained to a group of gaping tourists in the lobby.

"You cretin, you Neanderthal!" she screamed as he tossed her cases in the backseat of a Datsun, deposited her in the front seat, and climbed in next to her. "This is kidnapping. I'll have you thrown in jail!"

Ben didn't say a word. He simply started the car and drove to a condominium complex a few blocks away. Grabbing her bags from the back, he said, "Do you want to walk or shall I carry you?"

"I'm not going anywhere with you of my own accord," Gayle said.

"Fine," Ben said, his voice totally devoid of emotion. He dragged her out of the car, tossed her over his shoulder again, and strode to the door of his condo. When they were inside, he dropped the bags and gently set Gayle on a large couch in the sunken living room. He wasn't even breathing hard. But his eyes were shooting topaz sparks.

"What do you mean by telling Mrs. Jenkins your mother was sick and roaring off like a bat out of hell?

250

That stunt took about ten years off my life. I spent the afternoon calling every Stone in Jackson trying to find you. Then I remembered that your mother was a CPA, and I started calling every accounting firm in the city. Imagine how I felt to find your mother perfectly healthy and you nowhere to be found. I've been scared half out of my mind. I've imagined all sorts of things. You ought to have your butt paddled. Explain yourself. Right now!"

Gayle jumped to her feet with eyes blazing a fire to match his, anger thrusting aside her earlier apprehension. "How dare you! How dare you make accusations against me, you snake. If you talked to Mrs. Jenkins, then you know that I broke into the guest house. I found your cache of pilfered loot, and you knew I'd be on your tail. You've lied and stolen and God knows what else." She planted her hands on her hips and stared him down. "You're the one who needs to explain himself."

Ben sucked in a breath of air and raked his fingers through his hair. "Gayle, I've never lied to you, not really. I've skirted the truth a bit, but it was for your protection and Ariel's and for . . ." He clenched his jaw. "I didn't steal anything."

"Then how do you explain the gold pocket watch and the papers you took from the safe?"

"Princess, you're just going to have to have a little faith in me."

"*A little faith?* Right now I couldn't muster up an ounce of faith in you if you had the President's seal of approval stamped on your rump! You seem to have conveniently forgotten that Ariel inherited everything Calvin McDonough owned, and she has given me complete power of attorney. *I* am in charge and *I* am responsible. I want straight answers and I want them now."

"Cal meant for me to have the watch," Ben said quietly. "He told me that it was to be mine."

Gayle thought for a moment. Other than sentimental, the old watch really had no great value. His explanation seemed plausible. Maybe she could let it pass.

"And you weren't involved in any way with the other break-ins?" she asked, searching his face for any evidence of guile.

"No."

"With the fire at the plant?"

"No."

"With any kind of blackmail or embezzlement or selling of information about McDonough Bearings?"

"For God's sake, Gayle," Ben said, his tawny eyes reflecting pain at her line of questioning.

"I have to ask, Ben, and for once you have to tell me the truth. Were you?"

"No, of course not. I loved that old man. I was trying to do everything in my power to help him. Princess, I swear to God that I'm telling you the truth. Don't you know how much I care about you? Don't you know how it tears my guts out to know that you don't believe in me?" Stepping close, he reached out to caress the side of her neck and cupped her chin in his hand. His eyes were pleading. "Gayle, I'd lay down my life for you. Can't you believe in me?"

Ben's words sliced her in two. Once and for all, she had to decide. Did she trust him? She loved him, and even now his touch, his nearness, brought a warm glow, but did she trust him? She didn't have his Summers Profile to provide any answers. She had only her instincts and her heart to guide her. This was the ultimate test.

There was only one answer.

"Ben," she said finally, "I trust you." Laying her hand along his cheek and touching his lips with her thumb, she added, "I'll believe whatever you tell me. I know that you're an honorable man. I suppose deep down I've known it all along."

Ben hugged her to him, buried his face in the slope of her shoulder. He moved to kiss her, but Gayle gently pushed him away.

"You know very well I can't think when you touch me," she said. "And we need to talk. You've had a lot to say about my trusting you, but the time has come for you to trust me as well. There are things you need to explain."

"Fair enough. I'll tell you anything I can, sweetheart. What do you want to know?"

"So many things that I don't know where to begin." Gayle sank down on the couch and leaned her head back on the plump cushion. "Let's start with the reason you took the company records, Cal's bank statements, and the detective reports and kept the information from me."

Ben sighed and walked over to the sliding glass door. With his hands crammed into his pockets, he stared out at the moonlit water beyond. "Cal suspected that something was going on—embezzlement of some kind. He had the backup records copied and moved to a safe location. He'd hired some genius from Rice University to go over the books." Ben turned and looked at Gayle. "I don't know who the man was or what he found. Cal died before he told me. I've been trying to go over the records, but so far I haven't come up with anything. I took the detective reports and the bank statements because I was trying to protect Ariel—and you, when you became involved."

"Protect me? From what?"

"The final report from Allied Investigations is missing. I tried to find the detective, but I discovered he'd had an 'accident' the day after Cal died. It was a hit and run."

"And you don't think it was an accident?"

Ben shook his head. "That's why I wanted to keep you and Ariel out of it."

Gayle shivered. Ariel's hunch had been right. They were dealing with a murderer. "Can't we get access to the agency's files?"

"That was the first thing I tried. But it was a one-man operation, and his wife told me that, for security purposes, he never kept copies of anything." Ben rubbed his forehead with the heel of his hand and let out an exasperated sound. "Knowing that stubborn, hotheaded Scot as I did, I imagine Cal lit into someone with the information he had."

"And that someone lured Hector away from the house, and when Cal waved the evidence under his nose, killed Cal and took the final report," Gayle finished.

"Yes, and then he made sure that the detective wasn't able to talk. I don't think he knew about the other reports, and I didn't want you or Ariel to discover them and become a threat to the killer. Knowing the two of you, I figured you'd go charging in like the Light Brigade and buy yourselves a mess of trouble."

"I see." Gayle was hurt that Ben hadn't trusted her

enough to confide in her, but she kept silent. "What do you think he was after in the study?"

"I don't know, but he must think something's there and now you're in danger. That's what scared the hell out of me when I found out you'd gone. I thought he'd lured you away." Ben started toward Gayle, but her warning look stopped him.

"Why did you go to Singapore?"

"After I read the detective's file, I wanted to check out the warehouse and sales installation for myself."

"I don't understand," Gayle said.

"Didn't you read the reports from Allied Investigations?"

"Yes, but I only glanced over them. I haven't had time to study them carefully."

"I had lots of time to study them. And lots of time to feel guilty as hell. I felt even worse when I got to Singapore. I encouraged Cal to expand his market in the Orient. Everybody on the board did. On paper it looked like a sweet deal."

"What did you find in Singapore?"

Ben walked to the bar, poured a glass of wine for Gayle, and splashed a generous shot of bourbon for himself. He handed Gayle the wine and collapsed into the deep couch beside her. "Nothing."

Gayle frowned. "Nothing? But I thought—"

"That was the problem. There was nothing there. No million-dollar warehouse and sales office, no employees, no four million dollars' worth of unsold inventory. Nothing. The entire operation was a hoax. Money and goods went to Singapore all right, but McDonough Bearings got no benefit from it. The man in charge rented a rundown warehouse just long enough to sell everything, funnel the proceeds into a dummy corporation account here on the islands, and skip out." Ben tossed back the drink and got up for a refill.

"But how could he pull off something like that? Unless . . ."

"Unless he was working with somebody in Houston, somebody trusted in the company? Probably the same person selling bid information to our competitor? He couldn't. I don't even think the guy in Singapore was the brains behind the whole deal. But I don't know for sure who was."

Gayle grinned. "I do." She got up, sauntered over to her briefcase, and picked it up. "I've got some answers right here," she said, patting the side.

"What have you got in there, a Ouija board?"

"Better than that. Summers Profiles of the leading candidates."

Ben groaned. "A Ouija board would've been better."

Gayle looked at him sharply, irritated with his attitude about something as important to her as the test she'd invested so much of her energy into developing. "While we're playing truth games, would you tell me what you have against the Summers Profile? If your motives are so lily-white, why wouldn't you take it?"

Ben looked uncomfortable. "I took a test like that in high school once and it almost ruined my life."

"Ruined your life?" Gayle laughed. "I find that hard to believe. How?"

"The test results suggested that I should be a surgeon, and I spent three years in pre-med before I discovered that I couldn't stand the sight of blood. I switched to business management and vowed then that I'd never take another one of those things."

Gayle grinned. "You probably took an interest test, which only suggests that your personality and interests are similar to people in certain fields, not that you have the aptitudes needed. The Summers Profile is entirely different. It's much more comprehensive. And it's good. Better than Ouija boards, crystal balls, or tarot cards. You'll see."

While Ben poured them another drink, Gayle removed the leather portfolio from her briefcase and sat back down on the brightly patterned couch. When she slipped the printouts from the pocket an envelope fell out. Ben picked it up and tossed it facedown on the low teak coffee table.

He handed her a full glass of wine and said, "Okay, Madame G., let's see your magic act."

Although it was hard, because she was tired and testy from lack of sleep and the emotional strain she'd been under, Gayle ignored his jibe, took a swallow of wine, and set her glass atop the envelope on the coffee table.

"I've checked the profile of every person employed by McDonough Bearings or Cal, including Grace Jenkins and Hector Luna. Three of the protocols have significance." She handed the first one to Ben. "This one is Martin Brewer's. He's loyal and basically honest, but he's totally incompetent. It's no wonder that all this mess went on right under his nose without his being any the wiser. He needs to be retired immediately."

Ben raised his eyebrows. "I agree. But how can you tell that from all these numbers and the rest of this gibberish?" he asked squinting at the pages he held in his hand.

Gayle yawned and took another swallow of wine. "Trust me. I can." She showed him the report on

George Schulze and then the shocking analysis of Winston Dasher. "I think the two of them were in cahoots. George had access to the records and Winston had the cold-blooded cunning."

"I'm not surprised about fancy pants. No wonder Crystal left him. He's no better than his old man."

"What are you talking about? I thought Winston's father was a old friend of Cal's."

"Oh, he was. They'd been partners from the beginning, but Edward Dasher drank too much and gambled way beyond his means trying to support a Virginia society wife in a lavish life-style. Cal loved him like a younger brother. From what Cal told me, he was always pulling him out of one scrape or another. But about the time Winston was in college, Ed tangled with the big boys and amassed a monumental gambling debt. He came to Cal, crying and begging, afraid for his life. Cal, of course, came to his rescue. He bought out most of Ed's share.

"After he paid off his debt, Ed was left with nothing from the sale. His fancy wife left him and went back to Virginia, and Cal secretly paid for Winston's education. They put out the story, and I think Winston believes it to this day, that Ed wanted to devote more time to his practice. But the truth was, Ed was a lousy lawyer, and if Cal hadn't paid him a hefty retainer as the company attorney, he wouldn't have had two nickels to rub together or a dollar to buy the booze that finally killed him. It was Winston who built the practice when he got out of law school."

Ben tossed off the rest of his drink and scowled. "Cal was Winston's godfather and as proud of him as if he were his own son. He trusted him. God, it galls me to think that bastard may be behind all this."

"Now all we have to do is find the proof."

"And how do you propose to do that?"

"I don't know yet," Gayle said, blinking against the drowsiness that was overtaking her. "I have an appointment with an attorney here tomorrow. Maybe he can help us find out if Winston and George have a bank account here."

"Princess, we don't even know the name of the company the money went to, and this island is as tight as a jug when it comes to secret bank accounts. Did you know that you can get thrown in jail for even trying to get information?"

Gayle took another sip of wine and put the glass back down on the envelope. A vague impression tugged on the coattails of her memory. It was important, but she couldn't reach it through the fog that was fast overtaking her. She curled up and put her head on Ben's shoulder. "We'll think of something," she said snuggling against him.

Gathering her close, Ben nuzzled his face in the sweet scent of her silky hair. "We'll think of something tomorrow," he said. "Right now all I can think about is you. Do you have any idea how much I love you? How much I want you?"

She didn't respond.

"Gayle?"

Twisting his head down to look at her, Ben chuckled. Sleeping Beauty was out like a light.

Gayle's eyes popped wide open.

"The envelope!"

Flinging aside the arm wrapped around her, Gayle jumped out of bed.

Ben bolted upright like a shot. "What's the matter?"

Noting that it was daylight and she was dressed in only a lacy bikini, Gayle frowned and looked around the lavish bedroom. "Where are we?"

"In my bedroom." Ben chuckled and lay back on his side, propping his head in one hand. "You fell asleep on me last night. God, I thought you'd never wake up." His voice was husky as he patted the sheets next to him. "Come back to bed, princess, and let me kiss you good morning."

"I've got to find the envelope. Where is it?"

"What envelope?"

Gayle didn't wait to explain. Racing out the door, she quickly searched out the living room and went to the coffee table. Her empty wineglass was still sitting on the envelope. Fingers trembling, she said a silent prayer as she ripped it open and examined the contents.

"Hot damn!" she shrieked. "Pay dirt!"

Struggling with the zipper on a ragged pair of cut-offs, Ben charged in. "What the hell's going on?"

Laughing, Gayle flung her arms around Ben and leaped up to lock her legs around his waist. She planted a loud, smacking kiss on his mouth and laughed again. "I found it!"

Ben grinned as his arms went around her, crushing her breasts against his chest and holding her firmly anchored to him. "I don't know what you've found, but if it makes you react like this, I hope you find some more." He began nibbling on the side of her neck.

Gayle giggled. "Put me down and I'll show you."

"Do I have to?" Ben asked, continuing his nibbling.

"Yes."

Ben gave an exaggerated sigh and set her on her feet.

"Look," she said, waving the contents of the envelope in his face.

"What is it?"

"Several days ago—a couple of days after the fire, I think—Winston gave Angie an envelope to give to George Schulze. But Angie was busy at the switchboard, and since I was going to see George anyway, she gave it to me to give to him. I stuck it in the pocket of my portfolio and forgot all about it." Gayle waved the contents again. "Look!"

She fanned out ten one-thousand-dollar money orders, made out to George Schulze, and dangled a note, handwritten on Winston Dasher's letterhead.

Phase one complete. Will begin transfer 10/26 remainder your share Crystal Resources stock from HIB&T to Bmt.

Wrinkling his brow, Ben read the note. "What does this mean?"

"I'm not sure about all of it yet, but we'll figure it out. I'll bet anything this is part of the money they stole and that Crystal Resources in the name of the dummy company here. Is there some way we can find out?"

Ben tossed the note aside and reached for Gayle. "Mm-hmm," he said, dropping a kiss on each eyelid. "But the government administration offices . . ." He outlined the shape of her lips with his tongue. "Won't be open for another two hours."

Her laughter was low and throaty. "Any ideas about how we can kill the time?"

"A couple." Ben grinned. "But we have on too many clothes for what I have in mind."

Amused, Gayle looked down at the bit of blue lace she wore and the abbreviated cutoffs hanging low on his hips. "That's easily solved." With an impish grin she reached for his fly. Looking up at Ben all the while, she slowly eased the zipper down its track, the back of her fingers nudging his growing hardness. His belly contracted sharply and she laughed again.

Gripping her waist with his long fingers, Ben's nostrils flared and his pupils widened. "Woman, you're asking for big trouble."

Her lips parted in a seductive smile and one blue eye gave a huge wink. "I think I can handle it."

Ben groaned as Gayle's hands slipped beneath the waistband of his jeans, kneading the tight muscles of his derriere as she peeled off his shorts.

"Very nice gluteus maximus," she commented, pinching his bottom playfully.

"What?"

She flashed a pert smile. "I like your buns."

"Why, Ms. Summers," he drawled in mock horror, "you shock me." Gayle laughed and Ben cocked a brow as devilment danced in his eyes. He rubbed against her hands and said, "Shock me some more."

Leaning closer, she teased his chest with a light brush of her nipples until Ben made an impatient sound deep in his throat. With one fluid movement the scrap of fabric covering her became a tiny blue puddle at her feet. He kicked his cutoffs aside and slanted his mouth across hers with a low growl. His tongue slid between her lips and Gayle met it with her own, then retreated, inviting a deeper entry.

Her breasts swelled and ached for his touch. As if he'd read her thoughts, Ben wrapped his arms under her bottom and hoisted Gayle off the floor until he could reach the fullness that tingled for his mouth's warm caress. With her fingers tangled in his thick, tawny hair, she guided him first to one breast, then the other, reveling in sensation as his moist tongue laved the creamy flesh; tasted the sensitive undersides. When he drew one tight peak into his mouth and sucked gently, Gayle gasped with pleasure and arched toward its source.

Gayle could feel Ben's chuckle vibrate against her skin. "You like that?"

"Mm-hmm," she sighed.

He reached up to capture her lips once more with hard, fierce possession. Very slowly he let her body slide down his long, taut length in an erotic motion that overloaded her senses, sucking the breath from her lungs. She was acutely aware of the solid strength of him, as his aroused male power pressed against her like a burning brand. Desire gathered and throbbed in her hot moist core.

Gayle sank to the soft cushions of the couch and pulled Ben down beside her. With hands and mouths they explored, discovering the tastes and textures of one another's bodies, seeking out sensitive areas with curious tongues and sedulous fingers. No vulnerable spot went unfound, untouched, untasted.

Ben kissed a trail up her spine and teased the curve of her ear with the moist tip of his tongue. Murmuring love words, he branded her with a flurry of fervent kisses that drove her beyond any sense of conscious control.

He lay back and pulled her astride his body. His hands slipped up her thighs and, guiding her hips, he slowly lowered her onto him. Pierced with a bolt of exquisite pleasure, Gayle threw back her head and gave a sharp cry. She was filled with him, alive with pulsing sensation as she sat high and free.

As Ben's hands moved to stroke the fullness of her breasts, Gayle closed her eyes and settled herself more deeply. She basked in the feel of the fluid friction, contracting and relaxing, undulating in a primitive, instinctual rhythm.

"Look at me, love," Ben said, his voice husky, hypnotic. "I want to watch your face."

Liquid with renewed longing, Gayle uttered a responsive moan and obeyed. Their eyes met and held as she rocked against the source of her pleasure. Leaning forward, she rubbed her breasts across his mouth and silently begged for his touch.

"Tell me what you want," Ben demanded.

"Kiss them," she pleaded. "Make them wet with your tongue."

When he drew one hardened nipple into his mouth as if to devour its sweetness, Gayle became a frenzy of movement, moaning, whimpering, calling his name. Moving harder and faster as her passion grew, the knot of longing inside her burgeoned, exploding with a series of rippling spasms that ignited Ben's fierce desire.

Ben cried out as his back arched and he convulsed beneath her. Exhausted, marvelously sated, Gayle collapsed against him. Resting on his broad chest, her cheek rose and fell with his ragged breath.

"I may die," Ben gasped, "but, God, what a way to go."

Gayle laughed and they lay together, still joined, for a long time; she, content in the silent closeness of the man she loved, he, thanking fate for the precious treasure he held in his arms.

Finally, Gayle spoke. "We'd better get dressed if we're going to the government administration office."

Not moving, Ben agreed. "I guess we should."

When Gayle started to push away to get up, Ben refused to release his hold. She could feel him begin to stir inside her. Her eyes widened and she slowly lifted her head to look at him.

"Ben!"

A lazy grin broke over his face. "What can I say? I've told you it's a permanent condition when you're around. I want you again, love."

CHAPTER FIFTEEN

One thing had led to another, then another. And it was closer to three hours later than two when Gayle and Ben stood in front of the government administration building in Georgetown. Called the "Glass House" by local residents, the main executive building was an ultra-contemporary four-storied structure flanked by precisely clipped hedges and flagpoles.

Ben, who obviously knew his way around, greeted several people as he steered them to the Registrar of Companies' office. Once there, he casually asked a woman he seemed to know, "Do you have the local address of Crystal Resources?"

In no time the woman handed him a piece of paper. "There you go, Mr. Lyons."

Ben smiled and thanked her and hustled Gayle out the door before he turned and grinned. "Bingo."

Gayle answered his grin and felt an adrenaline surge as Ben unfolded the note. Then her face fell. "It's only a local post office box."

"I didn't expect more," Ben said. "But at least we know for sure that Crystal Resources Limited is incorporated in the Caymans, which means the company has a bank account here. The question is which bank?"

266

Gayle pulled Winston's letterhead from her purse. "HIB&T. Something, something, Bank and Trust, don't you think? Surely there can't be that many banks on this little island."

"Oh, no? Try about five hundred."

"Five hundred? You've got to be kidding."

Ben shook his head. "And about that many insurance companies. It's a tax haven and financial paradise." Taking Gayle's elbow, Ben said, "Come on, let's go shopping."

Gayle dug in her heels. "Shopping? I can't believe you said that. Ben, we have more important things to do than go shopping."

"Name one."

"We have to figure out the name of the bank, and I have to meet Eli Chase for lunch. That's two."

"It's a couple of hours until lunch. Trust me."

A few minutes later they were wandering through duty-free shops in Georgetown. While Gayle was admiring the lovely black coral, Ben said, "Stay here. I'll be right back."

Gayle was holding up a necklace when he returned with a package under his arm. "Like that?" he asked.

"It's lovely, but I can't decide which piece I like best. They're all so unusual. I've never seen black coral before."

"Let's look some more," he said, steering her out of the building and across the street to an exclusive little shop where pieces of the polished ebony material were set in breathtaking gold designs.

Before she could stop him, Ben selected a ring, a necklace, earrings, and two bracelets. "I can't let you buy all this."

He looked crestfallen. "But I thought you liked it," he said, holding up an exquisite collar of black coral and hammered gold.

"It's magnificent, but—"

"We'll take it," he said to the clerk. When it was packaged and paid for, Ben added it to the bag he carried.

"What else did you buy?" Gayle asked.

Ben lifted one corner of his mouth in a slow grin. "About a quart of Giorgio . . . and a *Cayman Islands Yearbook and Business Directory.* It has a list of all the banks on the islands."

Ben was being secretive again and she hated it. As soon as they'd come in from dinner, he'd kissed her cheek and excused himself to make a phone call. She could hear the low rumble of his voice from the bedroom. It was tempting to pick up the extension or go stand outside his door with a glass to her ear just for spite.

Gayle kicked off her high-heeled sandals, padded across the living room to the sliding glass doors, and slipped outside to the darkened patio. Wind blowing through the trees made a beguiling sound as the ocean lapped gently on the sand. There was just enough pale moonlight to sprinkle the water with glistening sparks and outline the palms scattered along the shore.

The day had been both a disappointment and a delight. By process of elimination, they had decided that the bank in Winston's note must be Hudson International Bank and Trust, but there they hit a dead end. And Eli Chase, the attorney she'd met for lunch, had been absolutely no help whatsoever. A charming man with a British accent slurred and softened by the island, he very politely informed her that there was nothing he could do to help. It was impossible to secure the information she needed—confidentiality, you know.

By the time Ben picked her up after lunch, she'd wanted to scream with frustration, but he'd teased her out of it. "Relax, enjoy," he'd said. "I have a friend working on an angle." He wouldn't say any more.

Together they'd had a marvelous afternoon, shopping for batiks, snorkeling, lazing in the sun. For dinner, they'd dressed and gone to a casually elegant little restaurant with a thatched roof. Afterward, they'd danced for a while, enjoying the feel of each other's body as they moved to the rhythm of the Caribbean music. When the current between them had grown to overwhelming proportions, they'd silently agreed to slip away.

Only now Ben was on the telephone. And she was out here in the dark, literally and figuratively. Strange how he wanted her trust, yet was so unwilling to reciprocate. Now that she had time to reflect on it, her trusting him had never been the real problem. It was his lack of confidence in her, his secretiveness and overprotectiveness, that was the basis for their difficulties.

Sadness swept over her.

"Enjoying the moonlight?" Wrapping his arms around her waist, Ben pulled her back against his chest and nuzzled the soft, bare skin of her shoulder.

"Ben?"

"Hmm?" His tongue was making a slow journey along the side of her neck.

"Who were you talking to on the phone?"

"Don't worry about it," he said, nipping the lobe of her ear and sliding his hands up to cup her breasts.

269

Gayle stilled his hands and turned her head away. "I hate it when you keep things from me. You're always talking about trust, but can't you have some faith in me? Share with me?"

Ben was quiet for a moment. "I was talking to a contact, trying to get some information about the Crystal Resources account."

"And?"

"It looks like I *may* be able to get the information."

"Oh, Ben!" Her laughter caught in the breeze and danced across the tropical night as Gayle spun and threw her arms around his neck. "When?"

"*If* I can get it, tomorrow morning. But don't get your hopes up too much, princess. It may fall through. That's why I didn't want to tell you until I was sure."

"I understand," she said, giving him a quick kiss. "Thanks for sharing with me."

Gayle could see the flash of his white teeth as he smiled. "Ever been skinny-dipping in the Caribbean?"

"Ben! We can't go swimming naked. What if somebody should come along?"

"This part of the beach is private, and there's not a soul around at this time of night." His tone was playful as he added, "I won't let the fish nibble on your . . . toes." Shucking his shoes and socks and reaching for the collar of his white knit shirt, he said, "Come on, I'll race you."

By the time Gayle had laid her coral jewelry on the patio table and shed her new yellow sundress, Ben was standing before her gloriously nude. She reached for the band of her panties and hesitated.

Ben laughed and grabbed her hand, "Come on, chicken. You can leave them on."

They ran down the steps, across the pale sand, and into the water glistening with prisms of moonbeams. They splashed and played and floated on the tide gentled by a ring of protective reefs.

Ben ducked under the water, stripped off the bit of nylon and lace riding low on her hips, and flung it at the moon. The ocean slipped over her skin like silken fingers, teased every unrestrained curve and crevice with an undulating caress.

Standing chest deep, Ben reached for Gayle's waist and pulled her to him. He held her so that the silvery water caressed the undersides of her breasts and lapped gently at the coral-hard peaks, then bent and added his mouth to the sweet, warm, pulling tide.

Gayle arched her back at the first deft touch of his tongue and sucked in her breath at the wildly erotic sensation of man and ocean and breeze. He lifted her higher and his mouth went lower, shooting a spear of longing deep in her body.

With one of her long sleek legs on either side of him, Ben laid her back to float on the soft buoyancy of the salt water. Her dark hair fanned out and rippled over the silvery surface as his lips and teeth and tongue worked magic. She moaned and sighed, lost in exquisite delight under a canopy of stars and a bed of endless sea. Every inch of her body was alive and vibrating with sensation as Ben and the current caressed her.

The sweet agony grew until she was overwhelmed with frantic yearning, an urgency to be filled. Aching to touch him, kiss him, cling to him, Gayle breathed his name over and over. "Oh Ben, I need you. I want you."

"Where do you want me, love?" Ben murmured.

"Inside me. Deep inside me."

Slipping his hands from her buttocks to her shoulder blades, his muscular forearms supported her back as he lifted her to him. Gayle reached for him, clung to him, covered his parted lips with hers in a devouring kiss. Reveled in the wet, salty taste of him.

Ben's tongue slid into her mouth and, as he lowered her on to his waiting hardness, Gayle gasped and wrapped her legs around him. The water slowed his thrusts to delicious torture, yet compensated with a million molecules of sensual delight.

"You surround me like warm velvet," Ben whispered. "Oh, princess, I love you so."

His words caught her like a whirlwind and ripped away control. She ground against him with an fierce undulation, writhing, rocking, locked in fervid passion. A surge of desire was building within her with a power that trembled and roared as it gathered force. On and on it came, swelling and growing like a tidal wave heaving and lifting the sea.

As it billowed and broke over her, Gayle stiffened and cried out, clutched at Ben as the same wave crested through him. They were swept away, flung among the stars.

As they floated back to reality, they clung together, wrapped in gentle moonlit sea, and basked in the warm afterglow of their lovemaking.

"I love you, Ben Lyons," Gayle whispered. "I love you beyond reason."

It was late morning when Gayle awakened. She smiled and stretched and reached for Ben. Startled to find the place beside her empty, she sat up and looked around.

The tantalizing aroma of coffee brewing told her where he was.

Grabbing a red silk night shirt, Gayle slipped it on and buttoned it as she padded barefoot toward the kitchen in search of Ben. As she remembered her night with him, love for him swelled up and spilled over, warming her, making her smile.

When she rounded the corner, Gayle stopped and leaned against the door jamb, letting her eyes play over Ben's bronzed length. Clad only in a brief pair of purple satin running shorts, he stood with his back to her talking on the phone. She savored the muscular thickness of his long, tanned legs; the cute buns, trim and sleek, under the satin shorts; the broad expanse of his back; thick waves of his gorgeous hair.

"No, Clay *Graves*. He's an Assistant D.A. Yes, he knows me. We've talked several times," Ben said, running his fingers through his hair in a familiar gesture of frustration. "Ben Lyons. I'm calling long distance from the Caymans."

Gayle stood dead still, the smile fading from her face as she listened to Ben's end of the conversation with Clay Graves. Ben was filling him in on the information they'd uncovered about George Schulze and Winston Dasher. He hadn't awakened her with the news she was anxious to hear. She had to overhear him telling someone else that he'd learned most of the money had already been transferred to an account in a Dallas bank, and the rest was being moved to a second bank in Beaumont.

Ben listened for a few moments, then said, "Our flight gets in about three this afternoon. . . . Seven o'clock is fine." When Ben hung up the phone, he noticed Gayle standing there. His face broke into a broad grin. "Good morning, sleepyhead. Ready for some coffee?"

Sadness sat on Gayle's shoulders, making them slump, weighing her down. "Who were you talking to?" When Ben hesitated, Gayle said, "Don't evade the truth anymore. I heard the whole thing. Have you been in contact with the District Attorney's office the entire time?"

Ben stuck his fingers into the waistband of his shorts and looked up. Then he sighed and looked at Gayle. "Yes, sweetheart, I have."

"The authorities have suspected all along that Cal's death, the detective's death, the fire at the plant . . . all of it . . . all of it is connected. Haven't they?"

"Yes, princess, they have."

"And you didn't tell me?"

"Honey, I've explained . . ." He held out his hands in an appeal for understanding. "I wanted to keep you safe."

Gayle felt a foreboding, a terrible premonition that there was worse to come. Her mind swam with all the ugly possibilities, and the question she had to ask floated closer and closer to the surface until it came out. "What else haven't you told me, Ben?"

Pain wrinkled Ben's brow as he looked into Gayle's eyes. "I meant it when I said I'd tell you anything you want to know."

"Ah, yes," Gayle said, sarcasm dripping off each word, "but we have to play a little game. I have to ask just the right questions and drag it out of you bit by bit like a magician's box of scarves. Let's see," she said, looking pensive and stroking her chin in a deliberately theatrical gesture. "What questions haven't I asked?"

Raising one finger in the air, she said, "I know. Here's a puzzler: Who is Margaret Cameron?"

Shifting his weight, Ben looked down at the floor. "My mother."

"What?"

Ben looked at Gayle and repeated quietly, "She was my mother."

Gayle looked perplexed. "Why would your mother's birth record be in Calvin McDonough's safe? And why did you take it?"

"Leave it alone, Gayle. Please?"

"The truth. All of it. Now."

Masking his emotions behind a sober façade, Ben walked to the sliding glass doors and stared out at the sea. Only a slight twitch of his jaw betrayed his tension. "When my grandmother was dying, she made me promise to take it to Cal. It was Gram's last request. She said when Cal saw it he'd understand and explain. She'd saved an old newspaper clipping, written when Ariel's parents were killed, that mentioned Cal's company and the fact that he lived in Houston."

Ben walked to the coffeepot and filled two mugs. "Let's sit outside and I'll tell you the rest."

When they were seated at the table, Ben took a sip and leaned back in the patio chair. "It was the picture of my grandmother, Catherine McKeen she was then, that Cal carried in the gold pocket watch she gave him when he left Scotland. They were both only eighteen, but very much in love. Gram's family was wealthy and had better things in mind for her than marriage to someone as poor as Cal. So he left to make his fortune to offer for her hand."

Gayle remembered the watch's inscription, rubbed

faint by a loving thumb. *For all time* it said. "But the time was wrong for making fortunes," Gayle said.

Ben nodded. "Though Gram's family probably disposed of the letters, Cal said he wrote to her while he was gone, but for several years he and his brother traveled the country looking for work, trying to survive the Depression. It was seven years before he made it back to Scotland."

"And your grandmother had married someone else."

"Six months after Cal left, her parents forced her to marry a distant cousin, and they were packed off with her large dowry to make their way in Florida. After years of abusing my grandmother, Michael Cameron deserted her when my mother was about eight. Gram managed to find a job in a dress shop to support them."

"Why did she want you to take your mother's . . ." Gayle's words trailed off as the reason dawned on her. Tears sprang to her eyes.

"My mother was born nine months to the day after Calvin McDonough left Scotland. He was my grandfather." Ben took another swallow from his mug. "The day I handed that paper to Cal, he broke down and wept like a baby. He'd loved her for more than fifty years."

Tears trickled down Gayle's cheeks as she thought of the lonely existence each of them had lived apart. Now she understood the painting hanging above the mantel in Cal's bedroom. It was Catherine McKeen, the love of his youth, the love of his life.

Gayle wiped her eyes with the back of her hand. "You were the only part of Catherine left. How he must have loved you. No wonder he wanted you to have his company."

"I never wanted it. With a loan from him, I built up

276

my own businesses, but he was a stubborn old coot. Every year, on my birthday and at Christmas, he gave me interest in McDonough Bearings. He was determined by hook or crook to rope me in. I imagine that's why he pulled that stunt about retiring with a weak heart."

"Ben, why didn't you simply tell Ariel and me about this before? Why all the secrecy?"

"Cal wanted to protect my grandmother's honor. You have to remember that they were from a generation when an unwed mother was the worst kind of disgrace. Her family had married her off and sent her away to hide their shame, and Cal was the cause of it. It ate at him till the day he died. In his mind he couldn't acknowledge me without branding his own child as a bastard and Gram, a fallen woman. It tore him in two. He and I both loved Gram and we didn't want anything to bring shame to her name. So we kept our relationship secret. He made me promise not to tell anyone unless there was no other way I could gain interest in the company. He hadn't planned on dying before the transaction of shares was complete."

"And that's the whole story?"

"That's the whole story." Ben glanced at his watch and stood. Dropping a kiss on the tip of Gayle's nose and giving her shoulder a squeeze, he said, "We'd better get a move on. By the time we eat and pack, it'll be time to leave for the airport. Clay Graves, the Assistant D.A. I was talking to earlier, will be by tonight to pick up the note and the money orders. His office is bringing some of the federal agencies into this thing, and they're checking out the Dallas and Beaumont bank accounts today. By this time tomorrow, Dasher and Schulze will be in jail."

"I'm glad it's almost over." Gayle captured his hand and kissed his palm. Holding it alongside her cheek, she stared wistfully out over the white sands and azure sea. "It's so beautiful and peaceful here I hate to leave."

Ben smiled as he pulled her up and into his arms. "We'll come back as often as you like, princess, and go skinny-dipping in the Caribbean."

When Ben wheeled the red Corvette into the winding drive and pulled to a stop in front of the garage, Gayle asked, "Where is the bodyguard? I didn't see him."

Ben grinned and said, "When the body left, I canceled the guard for letting you get away—right after I made several very loud remarks about the size of his brain."

"Poor man," Gayle said, climbing out of the Corvette. "Mrs. Jenkins must be out. I don't see her car."

"It's her day off," Ben said, wiggling his eyebrows and giving an exaggerated leer. "We have the house all to ourselves." Hoisting Gayle's bags in one hand and his in the other, he followed Gayle up the steps to the side entrance.

Gayle started to unlock the door, then stopped when she noticed that it was slightly ajar. Pushing it open, she peered inside and strangled a gasp. Hector lay on the floor in the breakfast room, his wrists and ankles bound and a wide piece of tape across his mouth.

When he saw her, Hector shook his head violently. Gayle's heart was in her throat as she knelt beside him and stripped away the gag. Ben had dropped the luggage and was removing the bonds.

"Two men with masks. I think they're still in there," Hector whispered, motioning with his head to the rest of the house. "I'm sorry, Mr. Ben. They made me unlock the house."

"You two get out of here and call the police," Ben said softly. "I'll check the house." He pulled off his shoes and crept away as Hector and Gayle slipped out the side door.

When Hector muttered something about a *pistola* as they ran for the garage, Gayle stopped in her tracks and a sudden chill shot up her back. "A *pistola?* Hector, did the men have a gun?"

"Sí, the big one, he had a gun."

"Quick, go call the police." For a moment Gayle was paralyzed with fear. Memories of another man with a gun screamed through her mind. Sights and sounds and smells assailed her as she relived the acrid spit of gunfire and the blood spreading across Greg's chest.

No! she silently wailed. *Not again. Not Ben!* She couldn't let it happen again. She had to warn him. Gayle whirled and ran back to the house. Trying to be quiet as possible, she made her way to the study, but she was sure anyone listening could hear the deafening heartbeats pounding against her chest.

The hallway was empty. Creeping forward, she froze when she heard a male voice from the study growl, "Get over here."

Oh, God, she was too late. Gayle slunk forward and peeked around the study door. Papers were scattered everywhere. Two men in ski masks stood with their backs to her. The taller one held a gun on Ben, who looked ready to split rocks with his bare hands.

Terror beyond any she'd ever known shot adrenaline

into Gayle, and she reached for the first heavy object she could find. Grabbing a small metal sculpture of Ariel's, made from lead pipes and gears put together to vaguely resemble a flower arrangement, Gayle charged in, wailing like a banshee, and whacked the one with the gun across the back.

Ben leaped forward, yanked the weapon from the dazed man's hand, and flung him on the floor. Holding the revolver on the two men, he ripped off the masks of Winston Dasher and George Schulze. True to form, Winston tried to charm and lie his way out of the situation, but George, who was scared out of his wits, was a bubbling fountain of information.

"He made me do it," the comptroller whined, wringing his hands. "It was all his idea. He's a crazy man. I never wanted to do any of it, but he blackmailed me."

"Shut up, you fool," Winston barked. "They can't prove anything."

But George wouldn't shut up. The whole scheme tumbled out of him in a torrent. Feeling unappreciated, Schulze had been dipping into the till for years. The amounts were small, but Winston discovered it and blackmailed him into participating in the larger plot for millions. The attorney had always been bitter because his father had forfeited Winston's potential inheritance, valuable McDonough Bearings shares, to cover foolish debts. And when Crystal, the wife he adored, deserted him for a wealthier man, Winston was determined to amass a fortune to lure her back. If he could bankrupt the company he'd come to hate and cover his tracks at the same time, so much the better.

George was still babbling when the police came and took the two away. He confessed to helping pass along bid information, setting the fire, and the first break-in attempt to find the letter Angie was supposed to deliver. But it was Winston Dasher, he said, who masterminded everything, who killed Cal and arranged an accident for the detective, who broke in on Halloween night.

"He's a crazy man," the comptroller said as the officer handcuffed him.

The next morning Gayle stood on the steps at the edge of the bayou tossing food to the ducks. "Well, we got it all straightened out, Cal. Winston and George are in jail and Ben thinks most of the money will be recovered. I hope you don't mind, but we told Ariel that Ben's your grandson. She was thrilled to have a cousin. She promised not to tell anybody, and she's going to sign all her shares in McDonough Bearings over to him. He'll take good care of it for you."

Gayle stared into the murky depths and watched the weeping willows sway and dip their branches into the water. Her job was finished. She sighed. It was time to go back to Denver and get on with her life, try to establish her business there. She had faith in herself and the Summers Profile once again.

Ben's face formed in her mind, laughing, cocking his eyebrow in that sexy way of his. She loved him so much. It would be hard to leave him, but he'd never indicated that he wanted more from her than the sizzling love affair they'd had.

And it had sizzled. But passion of such intensity was bound to burn itself out one of these days, and what would be left between them? He had no respect for the Summers Profile; he was secretive, possessive, and overprotective. Why, after she'd saved his hide with Ariel's sculpture, he'd practically torn a strip off her, threatened to blister her butt if she ever pulled a stunt like that again.

And she still didn't know what he grew on that plantation in Colombia besides bananas.

Tossing the last of the food to the ducks, Gayle dusted her hands on the seat of her red jumpsuit. After a last wistful look at the bayou, she turned and slowly walked back toward the house.

That's when she saw him.

Dressed in a khaki safari suit and scuffed boots, he was lying on his side, head propped on one hand, watching her with a languorous predator's eye. His topaz squint glinted, mesmerized, pierced her, melted her bones.

This was how she'd first seen him. She'd wanted him then; she wanted him now.

He laughed and said, "Yes, I know exactly how ol' Adam felt."

Gayle smiled as she walked closer. "I see you remember, too."

"I remember every word that's ever passed between us." He reached over and picked up a huge bundle of fragrant tuberoses and handed them to her. "Congratulations," he said, flashing his lopsided grin.

"What for?"

"Haven't you seen the paper?"

When she shook her head, he handed her a copy of the morning *Chronicle*. "You're a celebrity."

Gayle was startled by the headline. PERSONALITY TEST HELPS SOLVE CRIME. The article detailed the use of the Summers Profile in discovering the culprits al-

leged to have stolen several million dollars from Mc-
Donough Bearings.

"It looks as if you're really going to be in demand as a
consultant after this publicity. Especially around here.
Ever consider moving your business to Houston?"

Gayle shrugged.

Ben swung his legs around and sat up. Taking Gayle's
hand, he pulled her into his lap. A lazy grin lifted the
corner of his mouth as he picked up her left hand and
looked at it. "You're not married?"

"No."

"Engaged?"

"No."

"Do you have a lover?"

Gayle laughed. "Yes, indeed."

"Wanna get engaged and marry your lover?"

Gayle sobered. "What are you saying?"

Ben's finger traced the curve of her lower lip. "I'm
saying, princess, that I love you." Cupping her face in
his hand, his mouth touched hers in a kiss of exquisite
tenderness. "I'm saying that I want us to get married
and spend our lives together. Will you marry me?"

Gayle was so stunned that she said the first thing that
popped into her mind. "But, Ben, I don't even know
what you import and export besides bananas."

Ben hooted. "What did you think I grew and hauled?
Dope?"

Gayle looked pained.

"If I tell you, will you promise not to laugh?"

"I promise."

Taking a deep breath, Ben winced slightly and said,
"Flowers. All the ones I've sent you, I grew. I have a
huge flower plantation just outside Bogotá."

Gayle threw her arms around him and squealed, "Oh, Ben, I love it! Flowers!"

"If you'll marry me, I can get all you want wholesale. Holy hell, princess, if you'll marry me, I'll even take that personality test. I trust you."

"Do you, Ben? Do you really trust me?"

"With all my heart." Gayle twined her arms around Ben's neck and drew him to her. Love swelled inside her as she kissed him, held him close.

Drawing back, she looked deeply into the golden gaze that mirrored her own longing and her hand caressed his bronze cheek. Ben captured it in his and nuzzled his lips in her palm.

"No more secrets?" she asked, running her fingers through his tawny mane of sun-streaked hair and bending to kiss the lips that could work such magic on her body.

Ben closed his eyes and wrinkled his forehead. One lid opened to a narrow squint. "There's one more thing I guess I ought to tell you. You haven't asked, but sooner or later you'd think of it." When Gayle stiffened, he tightened his hold. "The will I took from the safe . . ."

"The will," Gayle said, remembering. "Why in the world did you take a copy of Cal's will? It was already in probate."

"Well," Ben said, wincing in anticipation of Gayle's reaction. "The one I took was a more recent one. In it Cal acknowledged me as his grandson and left everything to me."

Gayle was dumbfounded. Her eyes widened, then narrowed, shooting blue fire as her nostrils flared. Nose to nose, she glared at Ben. "Do you mean to tell me,

Ben Lyons, that all the time McDonough Bearings was legally yours? You snake! You cretin! Do you mean that I went through all this mess for nothing?"

"Oh, I wouldn't call it nothing," Ben said, grinning outrageously and planting a smacking kiss on the lush lips now drawn into a grim line. "You got me."